BLOOD RED SAND

Damien Larkin

DANCING LEMUR PRESS, L.L.C.
Pikeville, North Carolina
www.dancinglemurpress.com

ISBN 9781939844781

Cover design by C.R.W.

Library of Congress Cataloging-in-Publication Data:
Names: Larkin, Damien, author.
Title: Blood red sand / Damien Larkin.
Description: Pikeville, North Carolina : Dancing Lemur Press, L.L.C.,
   [2021] | Summary: "Mars will run red with Nazi blood... After World War
   Two, Sergeant McCabe knew the British army could send him anywhere. He
   never imagined facing down another Nazi threat on Mars. In New Berlin
   colony, rivalry between Generalfeldmarschall Seidel's Wehrmacht and
   Reichsführer Wagner's SS threatens bloodshed. The Reichsführer will
   sacrifice everything to initiate the secretive Hollow Programme and
   realise his nightmarish future for humanity. McCabe, Private Jenkins,
   and the Mars Expeditionary Force must overcome bullet, bomb, and bayonet
   to destroy the Third Reich. While Jenkins fights to stay alive, McCabe
   forms an uneasy alliance with MAJESTIC-12 operatives known as the Black
   Visors. Will this be the final battle of World War Two or the first
   confrontation in an interstellar war?"-- Provided by publisher.
Identifiers: LCCN 2020054750 (print) | LCCN 2020054751 (ebook) | ISBN
   9781939844781 (paperback) | ISBN 9781939844798 (ebook)
Subjects: LCSH: Nazis--Fiction. | Mars (Planet)--Fiction. | GSAFD:
   Alternative histories (Fiction). | War stories. | Science fiction.
Classification: LCC PR6112.A746 B58 2021 (print) | LCC PR6112.A746
   (ebook) | DDC 823/.92--dc23
LC record available at https://lccn.loc.gov/2020054750
LC ebook record available at https://lccn.loc.gov/2020054751

Dedicated to Commandant Pat Quinlan, and all the men of 'A' Company, 35thInfantry Battalion, Óglaigh na hÉireann (Irish Defence Forces) for their heroic actions during the siege of Jadotville. Thank you for your service. You will never be forgotten again. Further dedicated to the twenty-six Irish soldiers who gave their lives in the service of peace with Opération des Nations Unies au Congo (ONUC) 1960 – 1964.

PART 1

TERRA'S BURDEN

THE WHITE HOUSE, WASHINGTON DC
26TH JULY 1952
21.33 EST

The blazing streak of light ripped across the Washington sky, coming to a momentary halt over the White House. What could easily have been mistaken as a meteor now looked like a fiery star as a vessel hovered within General Hoyt Vandenberg's eyeline. Tapping his finger on the window in the Oval Office, he glanced at President Truman. His commander-in-chief's hand curled into a fist. Returning his attention to the spectacle outside, Vandenberg wondered how many eyes glared at them from within that blinding light, mocking everything the American people stood for. As quickly as that thought appeared, the vessel zipped off across the night sky again, turning and twisting in impossible zigzag patterns, showcasing its manoeuvrability.

"Same as last week, Mr. President," Captain Ruppelt said, while leafing through the dossier in front of him.

"It's the damned nerve of these Germans, Ed," Truman snapped as he stepped away from the window. "It's like slapping a man square in the face and then running away before he can hit you back. Damn cowardly."

Vandenberg picked up his glass of scotch. "We can hit them anytime you like, Mr. President."

Taking his seat behind the Resolute Desk, Truman nodded. Reaching for his own glass of bourbon, he turned about and continued to gaze at the streaks of light dancing and weaving across the Washington skyline.

"Don't tempt me, Hoyt," he said after an exasperated sigh. "I'd like nothing better than to give the order to shoot those Nazi dogs down, but we can't show our hand too early, can we? No. We'll have to let the Nazis have their damned moment. How are we on the development of our fleet?"

Vandenberg loosened the collar of his pristine uniform and paced towards the side of the desk. Searching for the right words, he walked around the Oval Office, and his gaze fell over the numerous pictures and monuments. Now, more than ever, this latest provocation by the exiled Nazi forces over the capital of the United States gave him the opportunity to take decisive action. He just had to sell it to the president.

"Construction is proceeding ahead of schedule, sir." He moved closer to the window again and peered out. "It was a tough job for Wernher von Braun and the rest of Majestic-12 to reverse engineer the downed Nazi craft we recovered from Roswell, but my MJ-12 boys have created something spectacular. Our ships won't be as fast as what the Germans have, but they'll contain a lot more firepower. More importantly, they'll have the room to ferry ground troops."

President Truman turned in his seat, grabbed his glass, and took a sip of bourbon as he looked up at Vandenberg. "This again, Hoyt? I thought we've been over it. The commies will cry bloody murder if we dispatch American soldiers to Mars, and I'll be damned if I let the Reds have the glory of fighting Earth's first interplanetary war. Imagine that, Hoyt. The Reds on the Red Planet. Think of the propaganda victory, even if they did get there using American ships. I won't sanction it. If it means putting up with Nazi shows of force like this, so be it."

Vandenberg watched from the corner of his eye as

President Truman pulled himself to his feet again and glared out the window. He knew the president well enough to understand that he simmered with anger more than he let on. Only a handful of people on the planet knew the truth about the end of World War Two and the Nazi leadership's escape to colonies on Mars.

Even fewer knew of the strange, alien technology the Nazis used to make their escape and rebuild their fighting capacity. With all the resources the American government had at their disposal, Majestic-12 still hadn't cracked the surface of the exiled Germans' newfound technological prowess. But if there could be one thing Vandenberg remained certain about, it was that they couldn't learn more until they seized control of Mars.

"We have another option, Mr. President," Vandenberg said, causing Truman to look over at him. "At your behest, I've been continuing negotiations with my Soviet counterpart, and I believe we've had a breakthrough."

He nodded at Captain Ruppelt, who rose to his feet from the couch in the centre of the room. Ruppelt selected one of the thick paper dossiers laid out in front of them, crossed the floor, and handed the files to Vandenberg.

Vandenberg took the dossier and passed it to the president. "The main argument we've been having with the Ruskies is who gets the glory. They don't want our troops up there in case the rest of the world finds out that capitalists were the first to conquer another planet. Likewise, the last thing we want is a Soviet Republic of Mars. Neither side wants to fight side by side in case we infect each other with our respective ideologies."

"Leading to what, Hoyt?" Truman asked as he leafed through the dossier.

Vandenberg approached the side of the Resolute Desk. "We use a proxy force, sir. We use a body of soldiers from countries that neither side fears as a real-world opponent to do the actual fighting. To get to the point, Mr. President, the Soviets are happy to proceed with my plan using British and French soldiers to do the dirty work."

Truman tore away from his reading and looked up at Vandenberg with wide eyes and a gaping mouth. Rubbing his hand across his chin, he shook his head in disbelief. "The British and the French? After everything they've been through in the last decade? You must be joking, Hoyt. April Fool's Day was months ago."

"If I may, Mr. President, it's all there in front of you. We utilise experienced, well-trained soldiers from countries that can't interfere with our overall strategic goals. We use American ships and personnel to ferry them there, with both sides sending along military attaches for operational experience. The Soviets have agreed to the overall mission being under nominal Air Force control, since we own the fleet, but it'll be MJ-12 and I that call the shots."

President Truman reached for his glass again and emptied it in a single swallow. He quickly refilled it and took a momentary glimpse at the streaking lights racing across the sky outside before returning his attention back to Vandenberg. "You're serious about this?"

"Yes, sir, Mr. President," Vandenberg said with an affirmative nod. "It's all there in black and white. We'll have the fleet constructed by early next year. Factoring in a ten-month travel time, our forces will arrive in early 1954. We need to keep the Germans talking till then, maybe ensure one or two of their ships disappear to keep them on their toes. It's doable, sir. My contacts within the British and French military have already signed off on it. We just need your signature."

President Truman returned his focus to the dossier in front of him and continued to leaf through the pages. He scanned the words and studied the various graphs, maps, and bullet points of the plan.

"And your mole within this New Berlin colony, you believe they're the real deal?" President Truman said.

"Yes, sir," Vandenberg said, trying to conceal the hope that built in his voice. "We don't know the mole's identity, but we believe he's a member of the Jewish resistance on Mars. Whoever he is, he's given us full access to enemy troop movements, strength, and capabilities. He's also committed to leading an uprising as soon as we land to tie the German forces down. Sir, this will be like a walk in the park."

"All right," President Truman said and picked up his pen. "If you say it can be done, do it."

Vandenberg tried to look sombre as the president added his signature to the page and handed the dossier back to him. Biting down on the inside of his cheek to mask a victorious smile, he nodded at President Truman and turned to deliver the news to the rest of Majestic-12.

Soon, the rightful masters of the Red Planet would return to reclaim what had always been theirs.

ABOARD THE USAF NORTH CAROLINA, ORBITING MARS
15TH MARCH 1954
08.23 MST (MARS STANDARD TIME)
DAY 1

The deafening shriek of the siren filled Sergeant William McCabe's ears and snapped him awake. The sickly-sweet smell that permeated his dreams receded as the fluid leaked from his capsule. Forcing his eyes open, he fought the urge to pry at the capsule door and remembered his training. He waited until his sleeping pod came fully upright and watched the last of the fluid empty through a grate at his feet. After removing the breathing mask covering his face, he paused until the light hanging over the transparent door of his pod turned green, and then he pulled down on the latch. He stumbled out of the capsule and fell onto his knees. The sounds of men shouting, roaring, and vomiting filled his ears.

"Remember your training," he gasped in between dry retches. "Breathe through it, lads."

Grunts, groans, and the splash of vomit hitting the grated floor echoed back at him in response. Willing his legs to work, he forced himself to his feet and grabbed at the capsule door for support. Trying to overcome the wave of nausea and disorientation that followed his escape from the sleeper pod, McCabe glanced around at his platoon. A quick headcount showed all looked to be alive, although every one of them worse for wear. The scientists had warned them of the effects of ten months in suspended animation, but their words did little justice to the horror of those first few moments.

"On your feet," he ordered, trying to put as much steel in his voice as he could muster. "Mars Expeditionary Force or not, you're Her Majesty's soldiers. Start acting like it. Corporals, take charge. I want everyone ready for parade in ten."

McCabe pulled open his locker beside his sleeper pod, removed his Lee-Enfield rifle, and leaned it up against the open pod door. Using a towel, he wiped his face and hair dry. After unzipping the one-piece body suit that covered him up to his neck, he dried himself and dragged on his battledress. As the seconds passed, his vision focused more, and the fog dispersed from his head.

"Jenkins," he called out and paused to place a cigarette between his lips. "Stick on a pot of tea like a good lad."

"Yes, Sergeant," Private Jenkins called back.

Striking a match, McCabe lit his cigarette and then finished tying his boots. After a few minutes, Jenkins appeared with a plastic cup of scalding hot tea before scuttling back to his pod to finish dressing. Around him, and over the shouts of the corporals, soldiers bustled back and forth, eager to get their equipment ready for inspection.

With his battledress donned and his weapon at hand, he pulled open the drawer at the foot of his locker and studied the white EVA suit that gleamed up at him. He dragged the bottom half of the EVA suit over his legs and up to his waist before connecting the upper half. With everything secured, he slipped on the helmet and took a moment to get used to the bulkiness of it. Once he secured his backpack, he hooked the sling of his Lee-Enfield No. 5 Mk 2 rifle and patted the sleek features of the so-called 'Jungle Carbine.'

"Sarge," a voice rang out from across the room. "I think there's a problem with my EVA suit."

"What is it, Jenkins?" McCabe said and tapped at the console on his left arm.

"Well," Jenkins started, "not to be smart or anything, Sergeant—"

"God forbid, Jenkins," Private Murphy chimed in to

muted laughter.

"Nah, I'm being serious," Jenkins continued, while the platoon jeered him on. "The thing is, Sergeant. This EVA thing doesn't look like the ones we trained with at the Atacama Desert base."

"It's the same," McCabe replied.

The words only left his mouth when a thought struck him. He turned to face the half-dressed private and then gazed around at the rest of the platoon. Most of his soldiers stood partially kitted out in their EVAs and only Jenkins happened to spot the issue.

"I mean," Jenkins persisted, "we're going to Mars, you know, the Red Planet. Won't wearing white make us stand out to the enemy?"

Everyone stopped what they were doing and stared at the private before checking their own equipment. Back at the Atacama Desert base, the Americans trained and drilled them using red-and-black khaki EVA suits. Here, every one of the suits were gleaming, pristine white. Set against the red and brown backdrop of the planet they were about to invade, that would make them easy targets for Nazi guns.

"Christ, he's got a point," Corporal Brown murmured when he approached McCabe. "We'll stand out like a sore thumb. Fritz will shoot us like fish in a barrel."

McCabe slid up the visor of his helmet as his mind raced for a solution to the glaring problem. "Send a runner to the CQ. See if he can rustle up any proper suits. Failing that, try to acquire red and black paint and have the lads do the best that they can."

"On it, Sarge," the corporal said with a nod and set off to grab the nearest soldier.

"Compliments of the lieutenant," a voice said.

McCabe turned towards a young soldier standing at attention with a slip of paper in his hands. He took it, read the note in Lieutenant Barnes' distinctive scrawl, and waved at the soldier to relax.

"Tell the lieutenant I'm on the way." He turned to seek out Corporal Brown again. "Jim, I've been summoned to the bridge. Get everyone ready and make sure the drop

11

ship is loaded with everything we need."

"Understood, Sarge."

Observing the flurry of activity continue around him, McCabe made for the exit. As he left, a group of American Air Force engineers entered their compartment, ready to perform final checks on the drop ship. The winding corridors outside appeared to be busy, too, with rows of Mars Expeditionary Force soldiers hurrying about while the American crewmen of the USAF North Carolina went about their tasks. He turned the first corner and saluted a Marine lieutenant when he came into view. The officer returned the gesture in the American style.

McCabe worked his way through the packed corridor until he arrived outside the entrance to the bridge. Two heavily armed Air Force Air Police soldiers scrutinised his identity badge before clicking on a comm button to announce his arrival. A few seconds passed until a green light lit up and the doors to the USAF North Carolina's bridge slid open.

McCabe took a step forward and tried his best not to marvel at the rows of intricate desk stations and strange equipment that lined the bridge. American Air Force personnel bustled in all directions, checking various computer screens or speaking loudly into their headsets, co-ordinating every facet of the Allied fleet's operations. Scanning the crowded bridge, he spotted Lieutenant Barnes speaking with a small group of MEF officers. He moved to join his superior officer and snapped his hand to his head in salute when the lieutenant turned about.

"Ah, Sergeant." Lieutenant Barnes smiled as he returned the salute and waved at McCabe to relax. "I'm glad to see you made it through our long sleep. Is the platoon all accounted for? Any fatalities?"

"Fatalities? No, sir. I wasn't aware there was a risk of fatalities in this portion of the mission."

The lieutenant gave a sombre nod as he stepped away from the group of officers and beckoned at him to follow.

"Yes, indeed," Barnes continued. "Unfortunately, we suffered several deaths while in status. System failures and all that. Thankfully, not too many but still a nasty way to go if you ask me, Sergeant. I'm afraid to say that Lieutenant Colonel Fairfax was amongst them. Once the Second Battalion is fully awakened, an announcement will be made."

"Understood, sir. May I ask who has command of Second Battalion now?"

"Major Wellesley is assuming command until further notice. You've heard of him, I trust?

"Only his reputation, sir."

A knowing smile crossed the lieutenant's face. Clearing his throat, he pointed at something towards the far end of the bridge. "I thought you'd appreciate this before we go ground side, Sergeant."

Barnes led the way through the crowds of gathering officers and crewmen and pushed his way politely towards the front of the bridge. He paused beside one of the long, rectangular reinforced windows and pointed into the bleak darkness outside. A smile crept across his face as he gestured at McCabe to follow his gaze.

"You see, Sergeant? Mars."

McCabe made a conscious decision to clench his jaws together to stop them from gaping in surprise as he drank in the sight. He had seen pictures of Mars during the mission briefings, but those images failed to do the planet justice. A swirling mass of red and brown dangled in front of him, almost within hand's reach. Fascination coursed through him at the sight of the alien image. He tried to soak up every detail and commit it to memory.

"Begging your pardon, sir," he said, while studying the scene in front of him, "but according to mission protocol, we were to be woken a week prior to entering orbit to get battle ready."

The lieutenant patted him on the shoulder and guided him away from the window, towards the entrance to the bridge.

"Yes," Barnes said with a sigh of exasperation, "that was the plan until system malfunctions prevented us. Approximately half of the task force were activated on time with the remainder being woken today. A terrible mess if you ask me, but..." He trailed off with a shrug as a crowd of crewmen separated from a small group of officers.

A tall, plain-faced officer spun around and, catching the lieutenant's eye, gave a friendly nod before his gaze fell to McCabe. As quick as he made eye contact, he turned away and buried himself in a map spread out in front of him.

"Major Wellesley," Barnes said under his breath.

McCabe observed the officer but said nothing. Tales of Major "Mad Jack" Wellesley were rife amongst the rank-and-file of the Mars Expeditionary Force. The stories ranged from Mad Jack single-handedly taking out a string of bunkers during the D-Day landings to facing a platoon of Nazi soldiers armed only with a Bren light machine gun.

The more colourful recitations varied from Mad Jack murdering captured prisoners to wiping out entire villages in retaliation for the deaths of soldiers under his command. McCabe didn't believe any of those tales. Yet, something about Major Wellesley's presence sent a chill up his spine. True or not, the officer didn't strike McCabe as someone he'd willingly cross in defiance with anything less than an armoured division behind him.

Barnes opened his mouth to speak again when a series of high-pitched wails rang out from every console on the bridge. McCabe, the officers, and soldiers of the MEF froze in position at the sound. The bridge crew of the USAF North Carolina sprang into action, furiously roaring orders into their headsets and punching commands into their workstations.

Red lights flashed in time with the blaring alarms that shrieked from unseen speakers, drowning out the panicked shouts of the North Carolina's crew. The captain of the North Carolina raced towards the helm station right when the massive view screen at the front of the bridge came to life.

McCabe watched in confusion as an image of a red and yellow inferno consumed the entire screen before fading away, leaving dots of debris hanging against the background of a twinkling night sky. It took a further moment for him to realise he had witnessed the destruction of the fleet's ships before the scope of what was happening struck home.

14

"We're under attack!" someone screamed.

The sound of the alarms finally died, although the flashes of red remained.

The captain of the North Carolina took over the helm. "Battle stations!"

A split second later, the entire bridge shook. Anyone not strapped into a workstation stumbled about while the ship rumbled from a hidden force. Consoles hissed and exploded from energy surges, knocking the bridge crew to the deck.

Without any information and with no clue what to do, McCabe gripped a nearby railing for dear life as the ship rocked and shuddered from an unseen assault. Smoke choked the bridge as crew members battled to put out sporadic blazes carving through the machinery. Over the din of strange popping noises that echoed throughout the ship's hull, the crew shouted to one another.

"Kamikaze attack."

"Venting atmosphere."

"Hull buckling."

"Main power offline."

"Engines gone."

A hundred other words blended together over the cries of the men who desperately fought to regain control of their ship, but two words spurred McCabe into action.

"Abandon ship!" the captain roared.

The faces of his platoon screaming in terror moments before they were blown into the vastness of space pushed McCabe past the stunned officers of the MEF. As the ship vibrated from what sounded like another volley of attacks, he raced out of the bridge area and ran down the corridor towards their sleeper pods. The lights flickered and dimmed, casting an eerie aura on the halls of the dying vessel. Dozens of wounded or dead crewmen slumped along the debris-filled corridor. Shattered wall panels hissed electrical sparks at him.

Like a horrendous death rattle, a drawn-out screech of twisting metal filled McCabe's ears from another thunderous round of explosions. He hit the deck and nearly lost his helmet in the process when he tumbled into a pile of corpses. He pulled himself up to the sounds of shrieks and fastened his helmet tighter before staggering through the darkening halls towards his platoon. He reached the entrance to their compartment when the final death blow landed.

The vessel shuddered upwards as if lifted into the hands of a giant before slamming back down, sending cascades of screeching throughout the hull of the ship. McCabe stumbled into the confused mass of his platoon and made right for the entrance to their dropship.

"Abandon ship!" he bellowed over the backdrop of explosions.

His platoon and anyone in the vicinity sprang into action and rushed towards the hatch of the dropship. Standing by the entrance, he urged them on, grabbing and pulling at anyone within hand's reach. Screams of pain and confusion resonated from all around the darkening room, but in the dim light, McCabe couldn't see anyone else. A series of booms lanced through the ship, picking up speed and fury as the sound roared closer to their position. With the drop ship crammed, he stepped in and banged on the airlock control panel.

Moments later, a final boom threw him to the deck when the dropship burst from its launch port on the outer hull of the USAF North Carolina. Through the tiny window port on the airlock, the once-hulking figure of their mothership disappeared in a crescendo of flame and shattered metal.

GOVERNMENT DISTRICT, NEW BERLIN COLONY, MARS
09.29 MST
DAY 1

Reichsführer Ernst Wagner repressed a smile as he studied the physique of the woman held behind the reinforced glass walls of her cage. Like a tigress, she stalked back and forth. She eyed the ring of SS guards waiting to extricate her from her prison cell. The pristine hospital robe she wore covered the contours of her body, yet the elegance of her movements was breath-taking. He

16

had known many women before and after their exodus to Mars, but none compared to Anna Bailey.

The thick glass door slid open, and two SS guards stepped in with their batons at the ready. Anna stopped her pacing and stood to face them head on. Her bruised knuckles tightened into fists at her side when four more guards entered to form a picket in front of the entrance to the cell. Wagner watched in silence as she eyed them one at a time before a slight smile cracked across her swollen face.

From what he knew about Anna's life, she grew up with a family that rubbed shoulders with the rich and the powerful. Funded by her British father's aristocratic wealth and her American mother's oil money, Anna had travelled the world, graced the highest social functions, and been the belle of every ball she ever attended. Her good humour and style lay matched by her beauty and wit. Her smile could turn even the most steadfast male to a drooling mess, while her charm could reduce him to putty in her hands. All of this and more rendered her the perfect MI6 operative. One capable of infiltrating the good graces of high-ranking Nazi party members before the war but now she paid the price for her treachery. Anna also held the key to advancing humanity's fledgling grip on the stars.

The first guard took a step forward, his baton pointed at her, while he instructed Anna to step out of the room. She stood as motionless as a statue. Her gaze darted toward the baton, then towards the door, and finally to Wagner himself. A chill crept up his spine when those cold eyes looked through him, but his cheeks burned as she softened her gaze and flashed an endearing smile at him.

As swiftly as that smile appeared, it slipped from her face when one of the guards approached. In motions almost imperceptible to the human eye, Anna launched towards the guard in a lightning strike. Her fist slammed into his gut, and the bolt-like uppercut to his jaw lifted him off his feet. By the time the other guards reacted, Anna already held the first guard's baton in her hand. In the blur of movement that followed, Wagner didn't know whether to compare her to a sword fighter or a ballerina.

She smashed her baton into the nearest guard's head, knocking him to the ground. Spinning about, she deflected an attack before ramming her knee into the groin of another SS soldier. The remaining three guards circled her and unleashed a simultaneous attack, but she swung about, slamming her elbow into the face of one while driving her foot into the chest of another with enough force to knock him halfway across the cell.

The last guard managed to react a split-second faster than Anna and caught her across the back of the head with his baton. She fell to her knees. The guards who managed to regain their composure piled on top of her in a desperate bid to subdue her. Anna bucked and shouted. Every point in her body was a trained weapon as she bit at their arms and gouged at their eyes with her fingers.

In the end, it took all six of the wounded guards to hold her down and attach handcuffs and ankle restraints. Once chained and on her knees, she ceased resistance. The guards slipped their batons into their belts, each one of them sporting bruises and cuts from her brutal attacks. Limping and wincing from pain, they lifted Anna to her feet and escorted her out of the cell.

"A fine workout today, Herr Reichsführer," Anna said in perfect German as the SS guards walked her outside.

Wagner held up a gloved hand, stopping the guards in their tracks. He reached into his pocket and slipped out a silk handkerchief. After taking a step towards his prisoner, he dabbed it against her nose gently, wiping away a small trickle of blood.

"An unforgettable performance, as always, Miss Bailey," he replied in English. "I'm glad you have your blood pumping. Today will require a lot more vigour than our usual endeavours."

Anna flicked her head, moving stray hairs from her vision to look up at him with those deep, mesmerising eyes. Wagner tried to maintain his composure at the full force of her attention. He reminded himself to see past her soft, delicate features and remember that despite her natural beauty, she was his enemy. For as long as she had

Jewish blood pumping through her veins, that was all she could ever be.

"So, today's the day?" she said, without a hint of concern in her voice. "You've finally cracked it, Herr Reichsführer?"

"Yes." With a smile, he slipped his handkerchief back into his pocket. "And you, Miss Bailey, will have the glory and honour of being our first successful test subject. You will be the first living subject of the Hollow Programme."

He nodded at his guards to proceed when a door slammed open behind him. The guards flanked their prisoner and escorted her down a narrow hallway at the same time as Wagner spun about to see the enraged face of Generalfeldmarschall Seidel. Fury etched across the face of the leader of all Wehrmacht forces in the New Berlin military district.

Seidel's eyes narrowed when they focused on him. His pounding steps echoed throughout the corridor as he marched towards Wagner. With a sweep of his hand, he opened his trench coat and unholstered his Walther P38. Grinding to a halt, he cocked the pistol and aimed it right at Wagner's head.

"You have betrayed us all!" Seidel screamed, causing spittle to form at his mouth.

At the sound of his voice, several SS guards burst out of their offices with weapons drawn. Peering down the barrel of the gun, Wagner raised his hand. Without breaking eye contact with Seidel, he waited until the sound of doors closing signalled they were alone again.

"You question my loyalty, Herr Feldmarschall?"

Seidel took a step closer, pushing the gun to point-blank range. His hand remained firm and steady while his eyes burned with all the fires of hell. Under any other set of circumstances, Wagner held no doubts the veteran officer would shoot him dead on the spot.

"British soldiers have landed on Mars," Seidel hissed.

"Yes, I read the reports, Herr Feldmarschall."

Seidel's face burned an even darker shade of red. "They would have had to travel for a year to get here. An entire year! And I heard nothing. Your SS ships engaged their ships. And I heard nothing. My entire force is hundreds of kilometres from here in the middle of a tactical training exercise. An exercise you were fully aware of! New Berlin is completely defenceless while British soldiers are landing, and still, I heard nothing. You have betrayed us all, Reichsführer Wagner. I will know why before I blow your brains out."

From the look in his eyes, Wagner had no question about the generalfeldmarschall's resolve.

"I have obeyed the Führer in all matters, this included, Herr Feldmarschall."

A sliver of doubt cut across Seidel's face at the mention of the Führer. Some of the red leaked from his cheeks, and his gaze flickered. His grip on the gun remained solid, but his finger loosened from the trigger.

"The Führer would never sanction this," Seidel persisted with a slight shake of his head. "The Führer would never allow our enemies a foothold on this world and leave New Berlin defenceless."

"It is not your place to question the will of the Führer," Wagner said, putting steel into his own voice. He raised his hand in a slow, controlled motion until it approached the weapon centimetres from his forehead. With the tip of his gloved finger, he lowered the barrel of the gun until it pointed towards the floor.

Seidel kept on glaring at him, but his face no longer contorted in unbridled rage.

"The Führer has no desire to annihilate the British outright," Wagner continued, adopting the tone of the school principal he once was. "The Führer wills them to be beaten by the force of German arms in honourable combat. Let them come to New Berlin, Herr Feldmarschall. Let them know suffering and defeat as they die on our doorstep."

"I do not have adequate forces available to defend the colony. I've issued the recall order for all forces under my command, but it will be hours until they return. The British are already within the outer defensive parameter."

"You have the garrison and my SS. If you need more, activate the Volkssturm."

Seidel turned his head and spat in contempt. "The

Volkssturm is filled with old men, invalids, and young boys. The British will cut them to pieces."

Wagner took a step closer to the Wehrmacht commander. "You will fulfil the Führer's orders, Herr Feldmarschall. If you are unable to do so, I suggest you put that gun into your mouth and pull the trigger. It would save us all a great deal of hassle. Your family included."

Seidel's face glowed red with rage once more. For a moment, his hand twitched on the gun. In the end, he did nothing. Wagner smirked, soaking up the blazing hatred in Seidel's eyes.

"Good," Wagner said with a clap of his hands to break the tension, "then it's settled. Defend New Berlin, Herr Feldmarschall. Be ruthless. I look forward to reading your reports on our latest victory."

With a smile on his face, Wagner turned away from his counterpart and made toward the long winding corridor.

"You won't be joining us on the field of battle, I take it?" Seidel called after him in a mocking tone.

"No, Herr Feldmarschall," Wagner said, without turning. "I'll remain here building our legacy."

LANDING ZONE ZULU - 200KM SOUTH-EAST OF NEW BERLIN
10.11 MST
DAY 1

Bullets snapped through the thin Martian atmosphere with savage precision. MEF soldiers screamed into their helmet mikes as they emerged from their shattered dropships and escape pods, only to be mowed down without seeing the faces of their killers. Rocket-propelled grenades from the enemy's Panzerfausts slammed into the battered remnants of the downed MEF ships, murdering the survivors fighting to free themselves from the wreckage.

With battle-hardened determination, McCabe pushed aside the anger that rushed through him and focused on the job at hand. Bounding between the twisted hulls of the downed dropships and escape pods, bullets raced past, eager to cut him down. He paused at the airlock of a smashed craft, ducking as bullet ricochets pinged the metal-strewn landscape and yanked on the release catch. The airlock slid open, but in the dull light he saw piles of limbs and broken torsos thrown over each other in a grim testament to these soldiers' final moments. With a shake of his head, he lifted himself up and scanned the rest of the battlefield.

What soldiers he could muster from the crash site had mobilised into firing positions, hastily making use of any cover they could find. Light machine guns chattered back at the enemy position ahead, but in the confusion he had yet to amass a force strong enough to go on the offensive. From the hundreds of columns of black smoke dotting the surrounding valley, it looked as though the entire battalion was scattered for kilometres in every direction. Dozens of EVA-clad soldiers ran toward McCabe's rallying call, while more contacted him via their helmet comms advising of their ETAs and locations.

"Sergeant," Corporal Brown called over the comm system, "I've confirmed our location. This isn't our landing zone. It's Landing Zone Zulu. We're closer to New Berlin then we are to Germania colony. That's the Russian Liberation Army shooting at us."

Cursing under his breath, McCabe snatched up boxes of ammunition from the debris of a smashed dropship. Not only were they a thousand kilometres from their assigned landing zone, but they had landed point-blank on top of Russian collaborators who had defected to the Nazis during the war. These men feared being handed over to the Soviet authorities. To avoid that fate, they would fight to the death.

"Any sign of the Fifth or Sixth Battalion?" he called back. "This is their zone."

"Negative, Sergeant. But there's hundreds of crashed ships out there, and there's some sort of jamming signal wreaking havoc with long range communications."

"Of course there is," McCabe said and sighed. "Hold tight, I'm coming back."

Dodging and weaving between the piles of warped metal and mangled bodies, he bolted back to the lines, laden with what ammunition he could carry. He kept his gaze towards the grey structure that lay a few hundred metres away. His mind ran through a dozen scenarios. Lost in thought, he saw the hulking figure a second too late and ran full force into him. The EVA-clad soldier barely flinched from the impact. McCabe hit the ground. Out of instinct, he lifted his Lee-Enfield, but the soldier already had his own weapon aimed at him.

"You are British, yes?" a heavily accented voice said to him.

"Yes," he replied, recognising the soldier's weapon as an AK-47.

"Good. Then we are allies."

The soldier lowered his weapon and extended a hand. Pulling him to his feet, the towering figure slapped a firm hand across McCabe's EVA suit, dusting grains of rusty sand to the ground. Bullets continued to whizz past them, but the burly soldier appeared oblivious to the danger.

"Junior Sergeant Boris Alexeev, Red Army military attaché," he said with a proud thump of his chest.

"How do I know you're not one of them?" McCabe asked wearily.

"One of who?" Sergeant Alexeev said, cocking his head.

"Them." McCabe nodded towards the sound of enemy gunfire. "The Russian Liberation Army. The collaborators."

The hulking Russian turned towards the sound of the enemy gunfire and began shouting in his native tongue. Raising his AK-47, he aimed in the direction of the enemy bunkers and bounded towards the MEF positions, blasting his weapon. McCabe followed close behind until they reached one of the forward firing positions. He threw the boxes of ammunition towards Corporal Brown and his soldiers passed the ammo clips around. Alexeev leapt towards their Bren gun emplacements and began redirecting fire towards the enemy machinegun bunkers, all the while shouting in Russian.

"Is this all we have?" McCabe said, scanning the small groups of soldiers spread out across the wreckage.

"Half the platoon is over there," Brown said with a nod of his head. "On the right flank it's a mishmash of platoons from B, C, and D Company. A couple of Frenchies, too. All-in-all, I'd say we're screwed, Sergeant. Probably best to pull back and regroup."

McCabe examined the metal-strewn red sand and rocks in front of them. Aside from a few crashed wreckages, there was nothing but open ground. Any type of advance would leave them vulnerable to be mowed down by the RLA guns but withdrawing would give the enemy time to better prepare their defences. To his surprise, two machinegun bunkers guarding the main entrance fired on them while the rest stood silent. If anything, he hoped that meant the defenders lay unprepared and caught off guard by their sudden crash landing.

"We need to take those bunkers now," McCabe said after a moment's deliberation. "Here's the plan. Corporal, I want you to take First Platoon and flank them on the left. I'll lead what's left of B and C Company and hit them on the right. We'll leave D Company with our Russian junior sergeant to lay down as much suppressive fire as possible until we knock out those guns. Understood?"

"Understood, Sergeant."

Corporal Brown relayed his orders over their comm system and waited until the surviving NCOs acknowledged it. McCabe reached into his combat belt and pulled out three smoke grenades. He threw them onto the littered terrain ahead of the platoon and readied the men to move. Smoke grenades spewed dense white smoke from up and down the line as the soldiers of the MEF prepared to charge.

With a single command from McCabe, everyone sprang into action.

The Bren light machine guns continued to chatter back in response to the Russian Liberation Army's attacks. He kept his head down as he burst towards the scattered remnants of B and C Company, making use of whatever chunks of metal he could find for cover. On the left flank, the gunfire sounded when First Platoon attempted to flank the enemy positions, and he signalled at the soldiers to move. He jumped over the torn wreckage in front of him and charged through the billowing clouds of white smoke from the grenades, throwing more as he ran.

Bullets cracked past him as he dashed through the fog. Men yelled when enemy bullets found their mark, but McCabe held his nerve while he sprinted across the smoky, alien terrain. Seeing the bunker ahead, he roared at the soldiers under his command to keep up their advance. Those who carried heavier weapons took refuge behind the scant piles of scorched metal and opened up on the Russian guns. Everyone else followed McCabe as he surged ahead, firing his Lee-Enfield at the concrete and iron bunker.

The RLA's guns sprayed unrepentant death on the advancing soldiers.

The platoons of B and C Company took to the dark red and brown sand. They crawled in waves towards their objective, and their colleagues covered them with as much fire as they could lash at the enemy bunker. Even with the dense swirls of white smoke blanketing the battlefield, men died in droves as they pressed onwards.

"Grenade!" McCabe called in warning before pulling the pin out and hurling the explosive.

He repeated the action with a second grenade and flung it at the bunker. The MEF soldiers kept their heads down until the grenades detonated. Pieces of concrete and shrapnel burst from the side of the bunker, but aside from a momentary pause, the enemy weapons showered lead on the invaders.

Cursing under his breath, McCabe inched forward again. Rusty sand and rock particles sprayed across his helmet visor as bullets raged across the ground in front of him. He pulled out another grenade, took careful aim, and threw it towards the target. This time, it landed in between the machine gun emplacements spouting from the bunker and disappeared into the darkness. The guns maintained fire until a deafening bang silenced them. The structure trembled and shook from the ammunition set off in a series of detonations. Heavy black smoke leaked from new cracks and exposures in the devasted bunker.

"Forward!" McCabe thundered and lifted himself to his feet.

He pushed ahead with the surviving members of the Second Battalion and swung around to the rear of the bunker with his Lee-Enfield at the ready. With a nod at the nearest soldier to try the entrance, he took up a firing stance.

The soldier unlatched the warped metal door to the bunker and swung it open. He tossed another grenade in for good measure before slamming the door shut. The detonation finished off anyone who could have survived the first blast, but the MEF soldiers lashed the bunker with bullets to be certain.

When McCabe swung his attention to the remaining bunker on his left flank, a series of bangs confirmed its destruction. He ordered all available units to converge on the entrance to the main enemy installation, while soldiers under his command took up an all-round cover position at the metal doors. McCabe made his way to the console hanging by the main entrance, and after studying the layout, shook his head.

"It's going to take a codebreaker to crack through that," Corporal Brown said, falling in beside him.

"Either that or some C4."

Sergeant Alexeev joined them "You British," he said in a half laugh, half sneer, "you don't need explosives. Just some Soviet ingenuity."

Shouldering past McCabe, the stocky Russian pulled a small cone-shaped object from one of his EVA suit's compartments. He took a few moments to align the point with the console screen. Without warning, he drove the cone-like object into the console, splitting the screen and causing it to spit electrical sparks.

Undeterred, he twisted his hand while pushing the object deeper into the console circuitry. Corporal Brown opened his mouth to question the brawny Russian's actions when the sound of machinery humming to life resonated from inside the blast doors. After a few seconds, the doors lifted. Confused shouts flared up from the other side.

Without prompting, the two MEF soldiers on either side of the door pulled their grenade pins and hurled them through the exposed entrance. Another series of explosions erupted, followed by the shrieks of the wounded.

"Forward!" McCabe roared and charged towards the smoke-filled entrance. "Move it! Move it! Move it!"

Bullets rained down on the MEF soldiers when they surged through the now-opened front entrance. Alarms wailed as atmosphere seeped from the massive warehouse behind the door. Grey-uniformed soldiers sprinted between various strange-looking trucks and crates, scrambling to heave on their own version of EVA suits. Above them, on walkways snaking around the perimeter of the building, EVA suit-wearing Russian soldiers poured out of unseen rooms, blasting sporadically at the MEF soldiers running to confront them.

The first wave of MEF soldiers took up firing positions on either side of the entrance. Bullets pinged down at them from every direction. Blood splattered across McCabe's visor as a round punched through the head of the soldier in front of him. The fallen warrior's body slammed hard onto the ground. Roaring in anger, McCabe braved the onslaught and raised his Lee-Enfield towards the enemy above. In careful, controlled actions, he aimed at a stream of enemy defenders. Focusing on the lead Russian soldier, he exhaled, squeezed the trigger, and watched his bullet find its mark. Before the enemy soldier had fallen, McCabe's sight fell on the next soldier in line, and he fired again.

Waves of bullets battered the MEF foothold at the entrance. Men howled as RLA weapons cut them down. Those who lived found themselves hauled back outside in a vain attempt to seal their wounds in whatever way possible. Those who died instantly were dragged out of the way so as to not hinder their colleagues' furious advances.

"Corporal Brown, take the left. Sergeant Alexeev, take the centre. I'll take the right. Move it, people!"

MEF soldiers armed with Bren light machine guns poured fire onto the upper levels, carving enemy soldiers to shreds. Bodies flailed and collapsed in their droves when the three columns of MEF soldiers moved in their respective directions. Screams of anguish filled McCabe's ears as wounded men crumpled all around him, but he pressed on. Leading his small band of followers, he cut across the length of the warehouse area, searching every nook and cranny for signs of a concealed enemy. Grenade explosions and gunfire filled the air while the invaders cleared the rows of equipment and vehicles and pressed on towards the upper levels.

"Who's leading this attack?" a voice crackled over McCabe's comm channel. "I repeat. Who is in command?"

McCabe signalled at his section to carry on so he could respond to the distorted communication. "This is Sergeant McCabe, Second Battalion, Third Brigade. Who is this?"

"Sergeant McCabe," the voice said over the roar of static and gunfire. "This is Major Wellesley. I have reinforcements. We're coming in from the north. Standby."

He clicked on his left arm console and initiated the verification protocols. It took a few seconds for his EVA suit's built-in computer to confirm the security code sent along with the comm signal. His console flashed green when it registered the sender as Major Wellesley.

"Understood, sir."

McCabe relayed the major's arrival to everyone on the comm channel and proceeded on his mission. Loading a fresh clip into his Lee-Enfield, he nodded towards a set of stairs and motioned for his motley section to advance. Privates Denny and Bingham took point, and he trailed close behind, eager to take the fight to the enemy. They had reached the top of the stairs that connected to the upper level when a series of bangs barked out at them. The soldiers in front of him tumbled backwards, nearly knocking him down the stairs. Bringing his weapon to bear, McCabe took aim at the approaching enemy and squeezed the trigger, dropping the RLA fighters.

Bullets rang out, impacting the walls beside him as the enemy fought for control of the central warehouse area below. The remnants of his section turned their guns on the enemy beneath them and returned fire, showering the Russian Liberation Army soldiers and scattering their section. On the opposite side of the room, Corporal Brown's dwindling platoon-sized force forged ahead on their path, periodically firing at hidden enemy soldiers.

Trickles of MEF reinforcements stumbled through the exposed doorway and threw themselves into the fray, keen to keep the pressure on the defending Russian defectors.

"Forward!" McCabe shouted. "Let's show these bastards how it's done!"

He drove onwards until they reached a corridor with three armoured airlock doors nearby. At the end of the hallway, a single set of stairs connected to the ground level. The sound of boots banging on the metal staircase brought his make-shift section to the ready. Four soldiers wearing MEF-style EVA suits raced to the top and paused after seeing him and his assembled force.

"Identify yourself!" McCabe demanded, his weapon pointed at them.

It took a split second for him to realise that the four soldiers wore strange black visors, unlike the MEF's semi-transparent ones. He tightened his grip on his trigger, but the new arrivals acted first.

"Up yours," the lead soldier shouted and tossed a cylinder to the floor.

McCabe moved to kick the suspected grenade away when a blast filled his ears. A deafening sound like a million belfries ringing sliced through his skull, paralysing him. His vision went blind as a searing white light filled his eyes. For a terrifying moment, McCabe thought he'd been killed in an explosion. Only the surge of pain from someone punching him in the kidneys told him he was alive.

Still blinded and deafened by whatever struck him, rough hands seized his weapon and slammed him forward. He grunted when his helmet smashed into the ground. He tried to lash out at his attackers, but they bound his hands behind his back. The ringing in his ears receded as another pair of hands dragged him along the ground into the nearby room. By the time they dumped him onto the floor, his vision had returned. He made out four silhouettes of the black visor-wearing soldiers standing over three of his unmoving soldiers. He glanced to either side and saw the blurred outlines of a distraught Private Jenkins and Murphy.

One of the Black Visors finished securing the room before returning his attention to McCabe and his two soldiers. The Black Visor took to a knee and tilted his head, studying him.

"Who are you?" McCabe demanded.

He could barely make out his reflection in the polished darkened visor of the helmet glaring at him. He could see no features of the face that lay behind the helmet, but for a chilling moment, he got the sense that whoever it was smiled at him.

"We're the good guys, asshole."

It took a moment for him to register that the harsh voice that spoke those words sounded female. "Why are you doing this?" he shouted. "Release us now!"

The Black Visor reached for a handgun fixed on her belt. She slid it out, cocked it in a swift motion, and pressed the barrel hard against his helmet.

"I don't take kindly to orders from MOF scum," she said in a menacing tone.

The female soldier continued to press the barrel of the gun into his helmet, but he refused to look away. He had stared death in the face many times in his long career. Today would not be the day he faltered.

"Knock it off, Noid," an Irish-accented soldier said from the corner of the room.

The Black Visor named Noid held her gun in place for a few seconds longer until standing up and holstering it. With a sigh, she shook her head and swung her assault rifle back into her hands.

"Prick," she mumbled.

The Black Visor leader glanced back at her but said nothing more as he returned his attention to the corner of the room. A taller, stockier soldier who stood at his side reached out a meaty, gloved hand towards what appeared to be a cowering figure. After a few seconds, McCabe registered someone wearing unusual civilian garb, but that paled in comparison to the sight of the stranger standing at full height.

McCabe had seen plenty of peculiar things in his career with the British Army but nothing resembling the man in the corner. He looked to be the tallest and thinnest human being McCabe had ever laid eyes on. The civilian's tanned skin seemed an unnatural shade of colour, unlike any skin tone he had crossed in his well-travelled career. The stranger's eyes were larger and farther apart, too. Everything about him looked like a disproportionate human being, yet he also had an alien presence in how he stood and glanced around the room with fretful eyes.

The Irish Black Visor commanded Noid to join him and muttered something to her. Without delay, she started speaking fluent German to the stranger. To McCabe's surprise, the strange-looking human responded in German, albeit with an unusual tone and inflection. McCabe watched in dumbfounded fascination as they spoke briskly to one another before the Irishman started barking orders.

"Prepare to move," he said. "Mo, stick with our guest. Smack, take point. Noid, you got the rear."

"What about them?" another female Black Visor asked, gesturing towards the captured British soldiers.

The Irishman paused and focused on McCabe, as if remembering they had taken prisoners. While the other three Black Visors prepared to escort their guest out of the room, the Black Visor leader took to a knee in front of him.

"Name."

"Sergeant William McCabe," he spat.

The Irishman looked towards his colleagues then back at him. "Sergeant McCabe. Your name isn't on my list. That means you're either going to die here or you're one of the lucky few who will escape this place. What will it be, Sergeant?"

"Kill his MOF ass," Noid cursed from the door.

"They're not MOF yet," the stockier male soldier replied. "MEF first. Then MOF."

McCabe remained silent and continued glaring into the black visor of the soldier above him. In his line of work, getting killed remained an occupational hazard. If these renegades planned to murder him, he had no plan to play along with any sick mind games beforehand.

When McCabe didn't reply, the Irish soldier chuckled to

31

himself. Reaching into his pocket, he pulled out a folded piece of paper. He slipped it open and slid it across the floor into McCabe's field of vison.

"This is a signed order authorising MJ-12 personnel to take any necessary action to ensure the success of this mission. In reality, this is a blank cheque for us to do what we want, Sergeant. If you stay out of our way, we'll stay out of yours."

McCabe glanced over the words on the document. It looked official, but whether it was authentic or a forgery lay beyond his paygrade to determine. He said nothing when the soldier stood and signalled at the other female soldier under his command. Reaching into one of her EVA suit's compartments, she pulled out a metal syringe.

She took to her knee beside Jenkins, and ignoring his curses, opened one of the valves on his breathing apparatus. She pressed her thumb down on the syringe and with a hiss, injected something into it. Within seconds, Jenkins fell unconscious.

"Don't worry," the Irishman said, supressing a laugh. "We only kill when we have to. He'll wake up as fresh as a daisy in twenty minutes or so."

McCabe struggled to shift away when the female soldier pried at his EVA suit.

The Irishman tapped on the document with his foot. He looked down at McCabe. "Give that to Mad Jack," he said and laughed again. "Tell him I'll see him soon."

McCabe opened his mouth to curse at the cocky Irishman when the world turned dark. For what felt like a lifetime, he drifted somewhere between sleep and consciousness.

Sounds came to him first. He made out the intermittent blasts of gunfire somewhere far off in the distance until voices echoed closer to home. Sudden coldness caused gaps of light to break through the blackened clouds swirling around him. A heartbeat later, McCabe found himself sitting upright, gasping from shock.

Drips of cold water continued to trickle down his helmetless face. He looked up. To his surprise, Major Wellesley stood over him. The officer's EVA helmet was tucked under his left arm while he analysed the letter in his right hand.

McCabe tried to spring to his feet, but whatever the Black Visors injected him with had turned his legs to rubber. He nearly fell face-first, but the strong hands of a half-dozen MEF soldiers raised him upright and held him steady.

Major Wellesley folded the letter and slipped it into his EVA suit's compartment. Then he extended his hand. "Well, Sergeant McCabe, it's a shame we couldn't meet under more pleasant circumstances, but I'm glad to see you're still in the land of the living."

"Yes, sir," he replied groggily and shook the officer's hand in greeting.

"This installation is ours," Major Wellesley beamed, "and in no small part thanks to you, Sergeant. It appears you have a few stories of your own to tell."

The major's left eyebrow arched, but McCabe's weary mind couldn't think of anything else to say, so he settled on a default response. "Yes, sir."

"I look forward to hearing all about it when the job is done, of course. In the meantime, rest up with your men while I assess the situation. We'll be moving shortly."

"Moving, sir?" McCabe blurted out as he swayed in the hands of his soldiers.

"Why, yes, Sergeant. Have you taken a knock to the head, old boy? We're off to take New Berlin!"

WEHRMACHT HQ, NEW BERLIN COLONY
12.40 MST
DAY 1

Generalfeldmarschall Seidel stood over the map in front of him and resisted the urge to slam his fist onto the table. Thanks to Reichsführer Wagner's ineptness, that frankly bordered on treason, the enemy was in the process of regrouping. He watched the red models continue to change and move as orderlies updated the map with the latest reports streaming in.

It was true; the SS had annihilated the orbiting Allied fleet, but too many soldiers had escaped to the surface. On any other day, it would have been as simple as marching out to confront the enemy and grinding them into the dust. With most of his forces en route from cancelled exercises, New Berlin looked exceptionally vulnerable.

"...seized control of the Russian Liberation Army's main base." General Schulz moved his hand over the now-British controlled position. "Overall, we believe they have amassed three under-strength battalions, with at least several companies' worth of soldiers scattered between there and here. This means they've cut our supply lines with Germania and New Munich colonies."

General Schulz paused and glanced resignedly at Seidel before carrying on with his overview.

"The bulk of the fighting so far seems to be taking place at New Munich colony. Enemy forces have launched a co-ordinated attack and gained a foothold within the city. General Lang has been killed in the fighting, so General Berger is assuming command of the Wehrmacht forces in the area. Reinforcements have been dispatched from Germania, but by the time they reach there, General Berger believes that the British will have occupied and entrenched themselves in half the colony. To be frank, Herr Feldmarschall, the British invading us on the same day as our planned war games has put us at a massive disadvantage."

"A *disadvantage*," Seidel murmured as he placed a cigarette between his lips and pulled out a lighter. He lit the cigarette, took a drag, and cocked his head back to exhale a plume of smoke. A thousand other words rushed through his mind, but disadvantage wasn't one of them.

"It isn't a disadvantage," he said after a few moments, "it's a betrayal. The SS have betrayed us all. Make no mistake about it, gentlemen."

The entire war room fell silent at his words. Junior officers buried themselves in reports or pulled on headsets to relay orders or receive updates. The assembled generals around the map-laden table glanced at one another in unease. Every one of them resented the SS's growing power. The Wehrmacht had borne the brunt of the fighting in the last war, yet here on Mars, the SS strutted about like conquering heroes.

"With all due respect, Herr Feldmarschall, to say such a thing could—"

"I don't care!" Seidel said and crashed his fists down hard on the table.

Models and markers on the map tipped over.

"I repeat, I do not care! The SS knew the British were coming, and they said nothing. They have left us defenceless. New Berlin will fall and all they care about is their petty little experiments. I would gladly trade every one of their secret projects in exchange for a mechanised infantry battalion. Those traitorous, morphine-addicted idiots!"

An awkward quietness reverberated throughout the room. Even as he spoke those words, he knew he was signing his own death warrant. It wouldn't take long for his outburst to reach the Reichsführer Wagner's ears, and retribution would follow close behind.

Still, saying what he genuinely thought aloud for once felt liberating. For years, since their forced exile, he had chaffed under the SS yolk. He had watched from the sidelines as they consolidated their grip on the increasingly isolated Führer and pushed their mysterious agenda forward. Now, the unthinkable had happened. Everything they built stood on the verge of annihilation, and with that knowledge came a strange recklessness. The SS could line him up against a wall and shoot him, or he could die in a hail of British bullets. Either way, the end was nigh, and he wanted to die with at least some truth on his lips.

Turning his back on the table, Seidel strode to the large windows of the war room. He glanced out at the apartments below and the giant dome above that housed the colony. A decade ago, he had set foot in New Berlin for the first time. Back then, it looked like nothing more than a dome and hastily assembled barracks and refugee centres. Now it gleamed like a sprawling metropolis, an equal to anything that could be found back in Europe or North America.

General Schulz cleared his throat. "I must take full responsibility for this. It was my suggestion that we organise battle readiness drills between all Wehrmacht forces on Mars. If I hadn't—"

"No, Herr General," Seidel said, while drinking in the sight of the colony. "The responsibility is mine and mine alone. If the SS have betrayed us, so be it. There is little more that we can do except fulfil our oaths and give our lives in defence of New Berlin. How long until the British attack?"

The room snapped to life again.

The general shuffled through papers before he answered. "The British don't seem to have any armoured vehicles of their own, but their possession of the RLA outpost gives them access to hundreds of lightly-armoured troop transports. Assuming they mobilised immediately after securing the facility, they could be here within three hours."

"And our reinforcements?"

General Schulz cleared his throat as he riffled through another stack of reports.

"Approximately four hours. They have to make a detour around certain areas due to our pact with the natives, but—"

"To hell with the pact," Seidel hissed. "Order the First and the Third Panzer Divisions to make straight for the—"

A flash of light filled his sight and stopped the next words in his throat. He watched in shocked silence as a building on the far side of New Berlin exploded in flames. A second later, the deafening noise filled his ears. He blinked again, willing it to be false, but the image of the blazing building remained.

Generals rushed to the window for a better view. Junior officers barked orders into their radios, demanding reports.

Seidel spun about and stormed over to the nearest radio operator. The terrified junior officer looked up at him. His eyes were wide in terror as Seidel glared down at him.

"Are the British here?" Seidel demanded. "How did they gain access to the colony?"

The trembling junior officer shook his head, unable to tear his gaze away. "No, Herr Feldmarschall," the radio operator said. "There are no reports of the British in or near New Berlin. This was...was something else."

"Out with it, man!"

36

The young officer pressed the headset closer to his ear. He whispered for confirmation before nodding to himself and answering the question. "It was the Jews, Herr Feldmarschall. They blew up an armoury and launched a gun attack on a police station. The Jewish labourers... They're in open rebellion."

140KM SOUTH-EAST OF NEW BERLIN
13.10 MST
DAY 1

An unshakeable sense of foreboding washed over Sergeant McCabe as he sat in the crammed troop transport. His encounter with the Black Visors left him unnerved. Not so much for their precision strike but for their hasty, undetected escape with the bizarre-looking human. He knew from the minute he received his briefing on this mission that there was nothing normal about it. But now, with the indifference of the major, it took a more sinister element. Whoever their MJ-12 paymasters truly happened to be, it remained clear they were hiding a lot from the rank-and-file.

Outwardly, McCabe tried to act like himself. He chided the soldiers around him to maintain battle readiness and observed them taking turns cleaning their weapons and equipment and eating what little food they could share between themselves. To their credit, they were taking everything in stride and acting like true professionals. Even after fleeing their downed ships, coming under immediate fire, and engaging in a firefight with pro-Nazi Russians, he could describe their mood as jovial. He knew deep down that they were scared, but, like him, they put on a brave face and turned their thoughts to the task at hand.

"How long till we reach this place, Sarge?" Private Jenkins asked as he cleaned his Lee-Enfield.

"An hour or two, Jenkins," McCabe replied.

"Think they'll have any more of those...*things* there, Sarge?"

The muted conversations in the transport died off as everyone turned to McCabe. Despite his best efforts to keep his section quiet about their encounter, word of the Black Visors and their "alien" charge had spread quickly throughout the ranks. In a few hours, the story had morphed beyond recognition, describing the Black Visors as supermen and the mysterious human as a bug-like alien with eight legs.

"Stick to the task at hand, lad," he said in a dismissive tone.

Groans murmured throughout the transport compartment at his answer. From the dozens of eyes that kept gaping at him, he realised the soldiers held no plans on giving up that easily.

"I mean, he looked like us, but not like us, know what I mean?" Jenkins continued, oblivious to McCabe's glare. "How can someone look like that? Was it a birth defect or what?"

"Shut it, Jenkins," Corporal Brown snapped from the other side of the transport. "Do as the sergeant says and drop it."

"I can't, though," Jenkins said absentmindedly, still reassembling his weapon. "I mean, it's a hard thing to forget. And the way they spoke German to him, of all things. Why not English?"

"Because the Nazis probably taught him German, dim-wit," Private Murphy shouted over a chorus of derisive laughter.

"Still," Jenkins said, ignorant to the merriment at his expense, "it's a shame I don't speak German. I'd love to know what they were talking about."

The entire compartment erupted into another round of laughter. For a moment, McCabe hoped that signalled the end of the interaction, and he experienced a rush of relief. Looking around, everyone resumed their various conversations and tasks. But then his gaze met Private Woodward's stare.

"You speak German, don't you, Sarge?" the private said, causing the laughter to die off. "You told us so. Said you picked some up in the last war. Do you know what they spoke about?"

This time, McCabe knew he couldn't deflect the

question. He could order them to mind their own business, but something about this entire situation didn't feel right. Although it went against protocol, he wanted the men under his command to know the sinking truth as much as he did. Maybe then he would be able to process the bizarre events of the last few hours.

The compartment turned quiet when he sat up in his seat. Everyone stopped their tasks. Bodies froze in mid-action, cigarettes lingered between fingertips, and sandwiches lay uneaten as all eyes fixated on him.

"They started by asking his name," McCabe said, after clearing his throat. "He replied and said something like 'Gaya' or 'Gya' or something."

Intrigued babble broke out at the revelation but died under a sea of hushes. Everyone leaned in closer.

"Then they asked where he came from and that caused a bit of confusion. The…this Gya person didn't seem to understand at first. When he did, he replied with two words."

"What were they?" Jenkins shouted, with his face lighting up in excitement.

Everyone in the compartment hushed him silent again. Some hands reached out and slapped him, causing the private to fidget from the flurry of soft blows. Fobbing them off, he returned his attention to McCabe.

"Big Red."

A chorus of mumbling cut across the compartment as the soldiers tried to decipher the meaning. Raising his hands to quiet them, McCabe waited until he had their attention again and elaborated. "I think this Gya meant Mars. That must be what his…people call Mars. Big Red."

That caused a chorus of derogatory laughter from the enlisted men.

"That's a stupid name," Murphy jeered. "Sure, the only 'Big Red' that makes sense to me is Junior Sergeant Alexeev over there."

At the far end of the compartment, the large Red Army NCO looked up from his weapon and shrugged, as if unsure of the discussion. The room reverberated with mocking laughter until another round of intrigued hushes ended it.

"Anything else, Sarge?" Jenkins asked.

McCabe fidgeted in his seat and nodded.

"Yes. Just one final thing. They asked him how long he'd been here. On Mars, I assume. All he said in answer was: 'We have always—'"

A deafening boom tore through the transport. Their vessel shook in violent spasms, throwing everyone not strapped in onto the ground. Unharnessed men slammed from side to side as the craft bucked. Equipment bounced from wall to wall. The sickening crunch of bones breaking filled the compartment until the screeching sound of metal tearing along the Martian surface drowned it out. Stunned by the abruptness of it, McCabe snatched at what equipment he could grab within hand's reach and pulled on his helmet.

"Helmets on!" he roared.

The transport slowed to a grinding halt.

Outside, booms filtered through the thick bulkheads over the groans and pleas of the wounded. It took McCabe a moment to figure out where he had heard noises like that. His eyes widened as memories of those sounds came rushing back.

"Panzer shells!" He unbuckled himself and leapt to his feet. "Everybody out now! We're being targeted!"

McCabe reached down and lifted a wounded soldier to his feet before forcing his way through the shocked mass of MEF soldiers. With a quick glance around to confirm everyone had their helmets on, he yanked on the door release and jumped out with his Lee-Enfield at the ready. His boots crunched under the red sand as he scanned the damaged transport. Then he looked towards the convoy. Wisps of smoke and torn debris showed at least a half-dozen transports had been destroyed in the surprise attack.

Dozens more lay unmoving, trapped between the smoking lead and rear transport vessel. As his soldiers poured out of the wounded transport vehicles, McCabe studied their location and found the convoy caught in a sloping valley. On top of one of the ridges above them, he counted at least thirty enemy tanks with their turrets pointed towards them. Moments later, they exploded to life again, raining death upon the MEF convoy.

"Cover!" McCabe yelled and beckoned his soldiers on.

Transport doors opened on the vessels in their proximity. Confused soldiers stumbled out, eager to seek refuge. Lines of vehicles erupted in flame and smoke as the enemy shells hit their targets. Men were thrown into the air like ragdolls. Limbs and burning flesh scattered in every direction. Soldiers screamed when shrapnel lanced their EVA suits. Their colleagues desperately tried to drag them from the smouldering wreckages, and yet, the shells came.

Amidst the chaos, McCabe roared orders at anyone who could listen. He urged them to seek shelter behind the rows of jagged, alien rocks at the foot of the valley. Soldiers streamed out of the burning transports, but dozens more crashed to the ground like dominos as the enemy fire lashed at them.

"What do we do?" Corporal Brown shouted over the private channel to McCabe.

"Gather who you can, Jim. We need to take that ridge."

"We don't have armour-piercing rounds," the corporal called back with a hint of desperation in his voice. "They'll cut us to shreds."

"They're cutting us to shreds here!" McCabe shouted. "I'll take my chances on the ridge."

Slipping a fresh clip into his weapon, he rallied what soldiers he could find in preparation for their last stand. Screams filtered through his comm system, but he pushed them aside as his mind desperately raced for a plan. They stood hundreds of kilometres from the nearest base. With low supplies of water and food, retreat wasn't an option. Gritting his teeth, he prepared to act when another call cut through over the comm chatter.

"Jesus! What the hell is that in the sky?"

McCabe turned and scanned the thin atmosphere above them. Within seconds, he spotted four aircraft speeding through the sky towards them on an attack vector. Furious streaks erupted from the approaching craft, freezing him where he knelt. He watched in silence as a dozen missiles leapt from the airborne craft, pounding towards them with furious intent.

"Incoming!" someone shouted.

McCabe didn't have time to scream before the sound of death filled the valley.

SAVAGE WARS OF PEACE

140KM SOUTH-EAST OF NEW BERLIN COLONY
13.27 MST
DAY 1

The sheer violence of the missile strikes caused the ground to tremble like an earthquake. Time slowed as men froze in horror. The comm channel remained deathly silent as Sergeant McCabe waited for their imminent destruction. It never materialised.

McCabe tumbled backwards in surprise as dozens of more missiles streaked above him. The ridge where the enemy panzers had bombarded the MEF column moments ago blazed and burned. Rows of German panzers lay in twisted wrecks, their guns forever silent. Some of the Wehrmacht soldiers leapt from their panzers to flee. They survived long enough to be gunned down by the heavy machine guns of the aerial craft that circled the German forces like vultures. From beyond his eyeline, on the other side of the ridge, McCabe noticed dozens of wisps of smoke, a tribute to the devastation wrought on the enemy.

It started with a single soldier shouting, and then it spread. McCabe and the MEF soldiers had stared into the precipice of death, but now they were saved. They cheered and whooped as the mysterious aerial craft refused to relent and continued to pound the enemy.

Forcing himself to his knees, he rested his Lee-Enfield across his lap and glanced at an equally surprised, yet jubilant Corporal Brown. The corporal shrugged and extended a shaking hand towards McCabe's shoulder, patting him on the back.

Dazed, McCabe reached for the controls on his EVA suit's left arm console and scanned all available channels to contact the aircraft. It took a moment for him to recognise an MEF signal and he tapped on his console again to open a channel.

"This is Sergeant McCabe, Second Battalion, Third Brigade. To the aircraft above us, please identify yourself."

Static interference answered him. He waited a few seconds and then reached for the button on his console again. A shrill, high-pitched roar cut over the comm channel.

"YEEEEE-HAAAWWWW!! Get some! Get some! Get some!"

Heavy machine blasts rang out from above as the attacking craft circled in on more escaping German soldiers. What few panzers remained intact attempted to escape while firing up at the aircraft, but they stood no chance. The highly manoeuvrable craft dodged and weaved between the enemy panic fire and launched its own missiles back in answer.

"Howdy," a voice finally replied, "thought you boys could use a hand."

"Who is this?" McCabe asked, recognising the drawling accent as American.

Splutters of machine gun fire raged out from the aircraft, driving the last of the German attackers from the field of battle. The MEF soldiers cheered and waved at their saviours above while medics desperately rushed to save the wounded. Signalling at Corporal Brown to lead a team to the top of the ridge to secure the position, McCabe continued to watch the ships above. They swung back and forth, chasing the retreating enemy over the rocky Martian soil.

"This is Crewman Lockhart from the USAF North

Carolina. Pleased to make your acquaintance, Sergeant."

"The North Carolina?" McCabe gasped. "That was our transport ship. I thought she was destroyed?"

"That's a negative, Sergeant," Crewman Lockhart replied. "She sure as hell got her guts torn out, and her engines are totalled, but she's just about in one piece. She ain't gonna be able to leave orbit, but we have communications, weapons, and a shit tonne of these atmospheric troop transports left. They may look ugly, but they sure as hell pack a punch."

The momentary flicker of hope at escaping Mars died with the crewman's words. Shaking his head, McCabe rose to his feet and surveyed the ambushed convoy. The uninjured organised themselves into firing positions along the flanks of the damaged vehicles, and teams worked their way through the wreckage searching for survivors.

"Say, you gotta CO down there I can talk to?" Crewman Lockhart asked.

"Yes, Major Wellesley's in overall command. I'll get him now."

"Don't bother, friend," Crewman Lockhart replied. "We've got these krauts on the run. I'm coming in."

"Understood. McCabe out."

He clicked off the comm channel, slung his Lee-Enfield, and began marching through the mass of MEF soldiers surrounding the convoy. He glanced up the ridge and spotted Corporal Brown directing his sections to sift through the debris and seize the high ground.

As he walked, McCabe nodded at the survivors and patted his fellow NCOs on the back. Reeling from the shock of the surprise attack, he reached into his pocket and pulled out a cigarette before realising he still wore his helmet.

Working his way through the destruction, he found Major Wellesley hunkered by a gutted transport, speaking into a portable long-range transmitter. The major looked up at McCabe and acknowledged his presence with a nod as he continued speaking into the handset. After a minute or two, he replaced the handset and stood.

"Sir, we're in the process of securing the ridge and

tending to the wounded. I should have a full list for you in the next few minutes. It looks like some of the Americans survived the attacks. I have a Crewman Lockhart on the way down to meet you."

The major started walking and gestured at McCabe to follow. "Yes, I heard. We still haven't been able to trace the source of the jamming, so it's making long-range communication tricky, but I've managed to get through to Major General Hamilton. It looks like a small portion of the fleet survived the initial attack. The major general has also received reports that the Jewish inhabitants of New Berlin are in open rebellion against the Nazis. It is imperative that we reach the colony soon and render what assistance we can." The major held up his hand and gazed into the sky.

One of the transports descended near the Allied convoy and made its way towards a flat piece of land under the watchful guns of the MEF defensive parameter. In silence, Major Wellesley made his way towards the craft as it began its landing procedure.

McCabe followed close behind, awestruck at the ferocious firepower and manoeuvrability of such an ungainly and hulking craft.

They paused amidst a group of soldiers, who trained their guns on the transport's airlock door. The vessel landed with a thump on the hard, Martian soil. Within seconds, its massive engines turned quiet. Without waiting, Major Wellesley took a few steps forward. McCabe fell in beside his superior officer, keeping his Lee-Enfield at the ready, but he didn't aim it at the Allied craft.

The airlock door slid open. A single figure jumped out and strolled towards them. Like the MEF soldiers, the pilot wore an EVA suit, except his was the red-and-black khaki they had trained with back at the Atacama Desert base in Chile.

Private Jenkins raised up a fuss over that fact, so McCabe lowered the sound volume on his platoon's comm channel and continued on to meet the pilot.

Crewman Lockhart strode up to them and paused a metre away. His helmeted head moved from side to side as he studied McCabe and Major Wellesley.

"Sorry," he mumbled in a high-pitched voice. "I don't have a grasp on limey rank markings. Who do I salute?"

McCabe and Major Wellesley glanced at each other before returning their attention to the young American. Even behind his EVA helmet visor, he looked too young to be an Air Force pilot. His stature made him look childlike, not to mention the tone of his voice and uncertainty on military procedure.

"This is Major Wellesley," he began, "and I'm Sergeant McCabe. You don't salute in a warzone, lad. Gives the snipers something to aim at."

"Snipers?" Crewman Lockhart gasped and hurled himself to the ground.

Again, McCabe and Major Wellesley glanced at one another before McCabe stepped forward and helped the crewman to his feet. "There's no snipers actually here, but it's better to keep the saluting to indoors. No offense, lad, but aren't you a little young to be a pilot?"

Crewman Lockhart flashed a boyish grin from behind his visor as he dusted himself off.

"Caught me," he said as he wiped grains of copper sand from his shoulders. "I'm fifteen years old. My pops brought me aboard as an engineering apprentice. He was a pilot and a damned good one at that. Taught me everything I know." The young crewman grinned from ear to ear at the mention of his father, but after a brief pause, his smile faded. "He died. In the initial attack. I found him in the hanger bay with his head damn near blown off. He was trying to evacuate everyone when a console blew. The Germans killed him."

Major Wellesley rested his hand on Lockhart's shoulder and fired his razor-like glare at the young man. "I am very sorry for your loss, Crewman Lockhart, but what is the status of the fleet? Report now."

"Yes, sir," Lockhart said, looking up at the major and fidgeting with his hand as if considering saluting. "The fleet was almost totally wiped out. Only the USAF North Carolina and the USAF Ambrose Burnside held together, but they're crippled beyond repair. We managed to maintain life support on the ships and brought as many survivors in from the escape pods and other ships as we could until we knew what to do next."

"You said you had weapons back online," he pressed. "Have you the ability to target enemy positions from orbit?"

"Yes, Sergeant," Lockhart replied with a hasty nod, "but Major General Hamilton instructed us not to unless specifically ordered by him. We have no hope of getting off this rock any time soon, so we need to take the Nazi colonies intact or we're done for."

"So, we're back to square one," McCabe said with an exasperated sigh. He faced the major. "I'll have the lads pack up and prepare to move on. At least we have air support for the trek to New Berlin."

Lockhart half snorted, half laughed, causing them to return their attention to him. He held up his hand as he chuckled to himself before straightening. "Begging your pardon, Sergeant, but you got more than air support. You got full air superiority." He raised his thumb and jabbed it over his shoulder.

It took several moments of scanning the rough Martian terrain and seeing nothing unusual until McCabe lifted his gaze higher. Behind the young Airforce engineer-come-pilot a swarm of dots filled the Martian skyline. As the seconds passed, those dots raced closer and closer until he made out the outline of hundreds of similar transport craft darting towards them.

"We got more transports then we have pilots, so it may take longer than expected, but how about we give you boys a lift to New Berlin? Save all that trouble of getting ambushed again."

A rare grin crossed Major Wellesley's face. "I think we'd like that. Make it so, young Lockhart. Take us to the gates of New Berlin."

FIELD COMMAND POST – OUTSIDE THE JEWISH GHETTO, NEW BERLIN COLONY
14.29 MST
DAY 1

Generalfeldmarschall Seidel took another drag on his cigarette as he examined the map in his hands. He shivered against the artificial cold that lingered in the air; a product of New Berlin's weather control systems designed to mimic weather back in his long-lost homeland. Hunkering down in the hastily assembled field command post, he traced his hand along the map of New Berlin. Superimposing enemy locations in his mind, he tried to work out a coherent way of obliterating the Jewish insurrectionists once and for all.

At first, he thought the attacks happened to be nothing more than random outbursts by a few deranged individuals, timed to coincide with the arrival of British forces on Mars. That alone raised his suspicions that they had contacted the Allies in advance. But as time wore on, he suspected this could be the product of a fine-tuned plan designed to inflict maximum damage on the under-strength garrison that struggled to keep a lid on the peace. Within an hour of the original incidents, ten more attacks took place across the colony, sending the already fearful German citizenry into blind panic. To make matters worse, they weren't a bunch of deranged maniacs. The entire Jewish slave population had risen in revolt.

The underground ghettos, and even the small enclave where the more trustworthy Jewish labourers lived above ground, stood ablaze. Mobs of armed Jewish gangs had erected barricades, set up sniper posts, and prepared defensive positions in anticipation of the German counterattack. In some cases, ordinary German citizens had been assaulted, which caused the unnerved German civilian population to move from panic to pure outrange. In turn, they demanded action from the government, which remained silent. The mess lay in Seidel's hands to clean up.

He stood, walked towards the tent flap, and took a step outside. Pulling his leather trench coat tight around him, he stared at the Jewish ghetto ahead and studied the German soldiers massing for an assault. Even with the full Wehrmacht garrison at his disposal, he needed far more soldiers for a counter-insurgency operation of this magnitude. And with Allied forces rapidly approaching the colony, he couldn't help the feeling that he was doing exactly what the enemy wanted him to do.

As he watched his Wehrmacht soldiers jog about, setting up light machine guns and mortars, he gritted his teeth at the mismatched uniforms of the Volkssturm. Although some of the older men held experience from the last war, the young boys that filled the Volkssturm's ranks appeared too eager for what was about to happen next. Even worse, the weapons and equipment they carried with them were woefully outdated. Seeing their substandard weapons, he had been forced to allow them to draw on the Wehrmacht's ever-decreasing stores to supply them.

"Herr Feldmarschall." General Schulz strode up beside him. "The reports you requested."

Seidel took the papers and skimmed the latest updates. He flicked his cigarette butt away and paused as he checked the reports, finding one missing. He looked up at General Schulz, ready to demand an explanation, but then General Schulz reached into his satchel and produce a single slip of paper.

"I thought you should see this last, Herr Feldmarschall."

Although he tried not to show it, Seidel's heart pounded. Hours ago, he had requested additional reinforcements from the SS, yet no black uniforms mingled with the Wehrmacht's grey or the Volkssturm's mix of grey, brown, green, and khaki. Reichsführer Wagner had promised him the full support of his SS forces to bolster the depleted Wehrmacht garrison, but they had yet to show.

As he scanned the words on the page, it took all of his reserve not to tremble from sheer rage. He read and re-read the words, willing it not to be true. He wanted to believe that stress or tiredness had damaged his ability to absorb information, but no matter how many times he examined the message, the words and their meaning remained the same. He crumbled the paper in his hands and looked up at General Schulz's face. The paleness of his skin confirmed the truth of it.

"'The SS have withdrawn their forces to New Berlin's government district,'" Seidel recited in a quiet tone. "'The SS will take no part in the defence of New Berlin and will focus on defending the Führer, party members, and their families. A protective ring has been established around the government district and Wehrmacht forces are forbidden from entering this zone without express permission, under penalty of death.'"

General Schulz cleared his throat. "It sounds like the SS are preparing to make their last stand."

"No." Seidel shook his head and placed another cigarette between his lips. "This only confirms my suspicion. The SS are planning to surrender the colony to the British. But in order to do so, they need the Wehrmacht out of the way. We have the strength to challenge them, so they need us dead. Why dirty their own hands when the British will do it for them?"

"But why?" General Schulz said in a hushed tone.

Seidel merely shrugged. He struck a match and took a few rapid puffs of his cigarette before exhaling and looking across at the grubby buildings of the Jewish ghetto. "Who can ever truly understand the motivations of vermin," he mumbled.

General Schulz started to speak, but Seidel raised his hand and silenced him. He took a few more drags on his cigarette before returning his focus to his subordinate. "Has the Volkssturm been fully mobilised?"

"No, Herr Feldmarschall. They are still in the process of—"

"As soon as they're mobilised, have all available units report to the four colony entrances to bolster the Wehrmacht defences there. Issue an immediate order demanding all men of military age to report to Wehrmacht barracks for conscription. We don't need to hold New Berlin, Herr General. We just need to hold out long enough for our forces to return from the aborted exercise."

"Yes, Herr Feldmarschall," General Schulz said with a click of his boots.

He turned to leave when Seidel extended a hand and took him by the elbow. "I want you to oversee the attack on the Jewish insurrectionists. We must remove them as a potential threat before the real fighting begins. I hereby order you to take any and all measures necessary to pacify the situation. Liquidate the entire ghetto if you must."

An unexpected sliver of fear cut across the young general's face.

Seidel glared into his eyes, searching for any signs of cowardice or betrayal.

"Herr Feldmarschall, there are women and children—"

"Liquidate the ghetto," Seidel ordered.

General Schulz turned to leave when a low rumbling emanated from around them. For a moment, Seidel thought it to be the beginning of an artillery barrage, but the noise sounded far closer and not as menacing. They glanced at one another in confusion, before looking upwards at the tinted dome that towered over the colony.

Seidel gaped in stunned amazement as a rectangular aerial craft whizzed over the dome in complex manoeuvres, appearing metres away from it at best. It took a moment for him to process what he was seeing. As he struggled to articulate it, a young messenger appeared at his side with a single envelope in his hand.

Seidel waved the young soldier away before slipping open the envelope and unfolding the paper inside. He scanned the two lines of text and then crumpled it up. Despite himself, he couldn't help but smile at the calamity of it all.

"What is it, Herr Feldmarschall?" General Schulz asked, although from the look on his face, he appeared to already have guessed the answer.

"It's the British," Seidel said after a moment of silence. "They've arrived earlier than expected. They're massing for an attack on the colony."

COMMAND AND CONTROL BUILDING, GOVERNMENT DISTRICT
15.34 MST
DAY 1

Reichsführer Wagner stood behind the protective reinforced glass of his main science lab and watched as the various scientists and technicians bustled around. It had taken most of the day to calibrate the so-called

Compression Matrix, but now, the stars were ready to align. After a thorough series of diagnostics and last-minute tune-ups, his head scientist, Doctor Josef Graf, confirmed the preparations for the Compression Matrix's first human trial as complete.

With a satisfied smile, Wagner's concentration fell onto one of the two medical trolleys in the secure room slanted upright at an angle. With her hands and legs bound to the trolley, Anna Bailey lay perfectly still, radiating a serene calmness as her gaze tracked the last two technicians in the room. A silver, metallic headband rested on her forehead, like a tiara. The other bed lay motionless, with a single sheet draped over its unmoving occupant.

"The moment of truth is almost upon us," Wagner said and pressed the intercom button on the control panel in front of him. "In mere minutes we shall prove that the technology of the ancients is adaptable to the needs of modern man. Your sacrifice will not be forgotten, Miss Bailey, I assure you."

He nodded towards one of the remaining technicians in the room and the man selected an empty syringe from one of the metal pop-up tables beside the trolley. A single blood test for analysis was all that remained until humanity's new epoch could be ushered in. Laying as frozen as a statue, Anna didn't even flinch when the syringe punctured her skin and the technician drew blood from her.

The technician had just taken his blood sample and turned to leave when he halted to do a double-take. With speed that beggared belief, Anna freed her left hand from its restraint. Bound by her other limbs, she lunged, and her lithe forearm snapped around the technician's neck. In a single motion, she swung the surprised technician backwards, causing him to lose his footing and sending the table full of instruments scattering to the floor. Choking him, she pulled his entire body on top of her. Despite his bucking and his bodyweight leaning on her, she snatched the set of keys that dangled from his waist with her restrained right hand.

"Stop this!" Wagner screamed, signalling at the SS guards. "Stop this now!"

The second technician bounded towards her, but with her prize in her right hand, she gave a violent jerk of her left arm. A sickening crack echoed throughout the room when she snapped the first technician's neck without even breaking a sweat. His lifeless body slumped to the floor, tripping his colleague. The technician stumbled and crashed into Anna. Even while her right hand methodically worked the keys to undo her restraints, she seemed to see everything three steps ahead. With her free hand, she grabbed the technician by the hair and jerked his head upwards, lifting him at an awkward angle before driving his skull into the metal railing at the side of her trolley. He struck the railing with enough force to send him slamming backwards into the second trolley nearby.

By the time the SS guards reached the door of the science lab, Anna had freed herself from her restraints. Only the metallic headband rested on her crown. Like a prize fighter eager for a bout to begin, she raised her iron fists and bounced on the balls of her feet, ready to throw herself into the action.

The door swung open and the guards, sporting the bruises and wounds from their earlier encounter, stormed in with their batons drawn. The first SS soldier growled as he charged, lifting his baton to strike, but something about Anna's normally laser-like gaze had changed. For the first time, despite all previous experiments, Wagner thought he sensed unbridled rage.

She surged into action, like a wild animal pouncing on its prey. With her left forearm, she easily deflected the blow from the baton as her right fist struck with the power of a precision-aimed missile. She punched the SS guard straight in the throat with almost enough force to take his head clean off. His lifeless carcass fell backwards and crashed into his fellow guards.

Not waiting for them to react, Anna went on the offensive. She targeted the guard on the left, driving the palm of her left hand upwards, catching the guard square on the nose. The force of the blow rammed the cartilage of the SS soldier's nose into his brain and he too fell at her feet. Without pausing, she swung about and, using her momentum, threw her elbow into the face of another guard, stunning him.

The three still-standing guards swung their batons, impatient to land a blow. Their weapons caught air as Anna danced between them, as if seeing every possible action they could make seconds before it happened. She dropped to the ground and swung her right leg about, sweeping the legs of one of the guards from under him. As he hurtled to the floor, she seized his baton and drove the hard-plastic point of it directly into the groin of another attacker. He howled as he tumbled backwards, but Anna pressed onward. She lifted her baton and brought it downwards, smashing his jawbone into pieces.

Wagner watched as the last SS guard found himself completely alone. Three of his men lay dead at the remaining guard's feet, and two lay unconscious, unable to assist him. A flash of nervousness cut across the guard's face as he eyed Anna.

Anna ignored the blood splatter that dotted her cheeks and wiped a strand of hair behind her ear. She placed a dainty foot forward, stepping over the carpet of bodies and moved into range of the last SS soldier.

He darted forward first, with his left forearm raised to deflect blows, and drew back his baton with his right hand. He swung a blow, but Anna reacted quicker. She whipped her head backwards, and the tip of the baton came within an inch from grazing her chin before she lunged at her attacker. She rammed the point of her baton into the soldier's gut. The SS soldier fell to his knees but continued to lash out at Anna. Grinning like a lioness ready to sink her jaws into her prey, she avoided his attack with ease. Then she slammed her own baton across his head, knocking him to the ground.

Anna glanced up at Wagner. She lifted the SS soldier to his knees and placed the baton under the stunned guard's chin. She gripped both ends of the weapon, and gave a savage jerk, breaking her opponent's neck. She released her hold and let the body slump to the floor before locking her hard gaze on Wagner.

"You must stop this now!" Wagner demanded while he

pounded on the reinforced glass of the lab. "We stand on the brink of glory!"

"I tried as hard as I could to stop you." She dropped her baton to the floor. "I failed in my mission. But I will not stand idly by and be forced to take part in this abomination."

Taking to a knee, Anna patted at the dead SS guard's belt. She worked her way down his legs until she found a knife concealed in his right boot. She slipped the knife out of its sheath, and stood, with the blade gripped in her right hand.

"Reinforcements are on the way," Wagner shouted, failing to mask the panic in his voice. "Their lives mean nothing to me. You are everything. You hold the key. You know that, Miss Bailey."

"I'm well aware, Herr Reichsführer," Anna said, flashing him one of her trademark smiles. "I truly believe only one life is of importance to you and your experiments, and I intend to make sure you don't have it. God save the Queen."

With a single, fluid motion, Anna lifted the knife to her throat and slid the blade across it. A waterfall of crimson ran down her neck, drenching her hospital gown. The knife slipped from her fingers and clattered to the ground. She fell to her knees, with her head held high. Wagner screamed and banged on the reinforced glass, too stunned to do anything else. Doctor Graf yanked open the science lab door and raced to place his hand over the wound. Anna tumbled into his arms as her lifeblood seeped from her. A victorious smile was plastered across her pale face as she gazed at Wagner.

Her eyelids lowered. "God save the Queen," she mouthed.

"No," Wagner said as his dreams turned to ashes.

He reached his trembling hand over to the lever in front of him. With tears in his eyes, he yanked the lever down, causing the machine in the back of the science lab to hum to life.

"No!" Doctor Graf screamed while frantically trying to stop the bleeding. "She's too weak. Herr Reichsführer, you must stop this now."

Ignoring the doctor's advice, Wagner pressed his

finger down on the red button in front of him. Sparks of electricity danced over the Compression Matrix as it powered a signal from the headband resting on Anna's forehead. SS guards and medics stormed into the room, desperate to save their prisoner's life. Anna's body writhed and twitched when a surge of energy coursed through her, pulling her consciousness from her mind like a magnet. Doctor Graf howled at him as the medics attempted to seal Anna's wound, but Wagner ignored the doctor. The light faded from his captive's eyes before he turned to face the readouts on the screens in front of him.

In the science lab, Doctor Graf and one of the medics had succeeded in sealing the wound across Anna's throat. They lifted her pale, limp body onto her trolley and continued checking her vitals.

Wagner watched her chest rise and fall in slow mechanical actions as the doctor set his fingers on her wrist to check her pulse. Even with her breathing, her eyes remained vacant and wide open.

With panic threatening to overwhelm him, Wagner rapped on the screens in front of him, waiting for the results of the experiment. His heart sank as the seconds stretched on, and his gaze moved from the instruments to the cloth-covered trolley sitting on the other side of the science lab. Placing his gloved fist into his mouth, he sank his teeth into his own fingers. His life's work sat on a funeral pyre as the future went up in flames.

A single beep from his console caused Wagner to lower his hand. After wiping the tears from his eyes, he rapped at the screen again. Another beep sent a rush of excitement through him. He stared in amazement and waited for a third beep before he sprang into action. Shoving past the SS guards who tended to their dead and wounded comrades, Wagner ran into the science lab. He nearly knocked a bewildered Doctor Graf from his feet when he pushed past the unmoving husk of Anna Bailey and made for the second trolley. The stunned doctor fell in beside him, and they waited with bated breath, hovering over the blanketed trolley.

It started with a small movement at first; a barely

perceptible twitch. Wagner and the doctor watched in amazement when the sheet rose and fell as lungs sucked in air of their own accord. A trembling hand slipped from under the covers, causing the doctor to leap forward and check for a pulse.

Too astonished to speak, Doctor Graf spun about and nodded.

Marvelling at his work, Wagner clasped his gloved hands together. With the implications dancing through his mind, he forced his mental reserves into action to stop himself from collapsing to the ground and drowning in tears of joy.

"You did it, Herr Reichsführer," Doctor Graf said and whipped the blanket from the face of the woman on the trolley. "You have successfully transferred human consciousness from a host body to a replicated one. The implications are—"

Wagner swung a lamp from over the trolley and positioned it over the face of the unconscious woman. "I need to be sure."

With a flick of a switch, a piercing white light blazed down on the vacant eyes that looked up at it. It took a moment, but those deep, mesmerising eyes blinked, slowly.

Wagner covered his mouth when the eye blinks and breathing increased. The woman's chest heaved faster and faster, sucking New Berlin's recycled air deeper and deeper into her chest. Her hands balled into fists. Her legs twitched against the restraints.

Anna screamed the moment her senses exploded to life. Still shrieking, her eyebrows arched as her gaze rested upon a body that looked like hers, with a bandage covering the neck, lying across from her.

Overwhelmed by the strange sights and sounds, Anna Bailey, the first incarnation of the Hollow Programme, collapsed into unconsciousness.

**OUTSKIRTS OF NEW BERLIN COLONY
16.42 MST
DAY 1**

Sergeant McCabe and the soldiers of the Mars

Expeditionary Force gazed with hungry eyes at the Nazi colony below them. Eight hundred metres of open ground separated them from their prize. Nestled behind a line of rocky hills that could better be described as sand dunes, an unceasing convoy of transports had airlifted the MEF soldiers into position. Unharried by anti-aircraft fire, the transport aircraft of the crippled USAF North Carolina and the USAF Ambrose Burnside swung through the air with impunity, dropping off a steady flow of exhausted soldiers before setting off to ferry more in for the coming engagement. Already, an understrength division of hastily assembled survivors stood ready to mete out punishment to the enemy.

McCabe lowered the binoculars from his helmet visor and shook his head. He handed them back to Corporal Brown, glanced at his platoon spread out to his left and right, and lowered his voice. "The brass is adamant that there's no mines out there, but I don't like it. Who builds a colony without defences? Fritz has had ten years to prepare for this. I find it hard to believe they'll let us waltz right in."

Brown slipped his binoculars back into one of his EVA suit's compartments, and swinging his Lee-Enfield back into his hands, shrugged his shoulders. "Could be the krauts want to lure us in first, then machine gun us to death."

"Maybe," McCabe said as he studied the vast dome structure in front of him.

The MEF soldiers, NCOs, and junior officers sprinted about, checking on last minute preparations for the advance. Due to the sheer volume of casualties, men and officers from other decimated brigades had been utilised in haste to plug in the gaps in the newly reorganised task force. McCabe tried not to think of the faces of half of his own platoon that hadn't made it this far. Shaking his head, he glanced at his new commanding officer, Lieutenant Pierre Durand from the French contingent of the MEF.

"Christ, I could use a cigarette," Brown grumbled, his gaze crossing the sandy terrain ahead of them.

"That makes two of us."

"Sure is an ugly looking planet, isn't it?"

McCabe opened his mouth to reply when a series of shouts rang out from up and down the line.

"Stand ready!"

He repeated the command and waved at his platoon to take up their positions at the cusp of the sand dunes. They slapped fresh magazines into their rifles, and whispered words of good luck to one another before setting their gaze on the German colony.

"Prepare to advance!"

Overhead, a dozen transports hovering in the air with their guns trained on the colony jolted into action. As per Major General Hamilton's orders, they began launching smoke cannisters onto the barren terrain between the waiting MEF soldiers and New Berlin. Plumbs of smoke burst from the cannisters, spreading a hazy white fog across the plain. The transports launched their payloads until only the top of the monstrous tinted dome stood visible. Thanks to Mad Jack's eagerness for glory, the Second Battalion readied themselves to lead the assault on the eastern entrance.

"Advance!"

"Forward!" McCabe cried and leapt from his cover. "Move it, lads! Move it!"

With roars of fury, thousands of MEF soldiers sprang into action and stormed down the red sand dunes. They charged into the clouds of white smoke towards New Berlin. Above them, transports whizzed about, preparing to counter any enemy.

McCabe kept urging his platoon on as they crossed the foggy landscape. While the cannisters continued spouting thick smoke, he could hear the dark red sand crunching beneath his feet and see the vague outline of the dome towering above them. Soldiers bumped into him as they ran, gasping apologies as they stormed onwards, intent on reaching their target in one peace. The shouts of men and NCOs echoed around him, but the German colony sat as silent as a graveyard.

With half the distance crossed, McCabe found himself in a small clearing devoid of smoke. Cannisters spewed their gasses around him, but the fog cleared enough for him to spy the eastern entrance. He turned his head to spur on his platoon and prepared to carry on when a flicker of movement caught his eye. Shifting his stance and waving off a tentacle of smoke that threatened his view, he squinted at the dome's perimeter. It took him a few seconds to make out the shape of a rectangle emerge from the dusty ground on either side of the entrance. He noted several more rectangular boxes lining the colony's parameter. His heart sank when machine gun barrels slid out from the boxes.

"Get down!" he cried out, but the simultaneous roar of heavy machine guns drowned out his words.

He threw himself to the ground when bullets tore through the fog. The sound of men's agony filled his ears as MEF soldiers ran directly into the arcs of fire from dozens of hidden machine gun nests. Transports above fired controlled bursts back at the enemy guns, but with the smoke hampering their view, McCabe guessed they wouldn't be much use. Bodies thudded to the ground like dominos as he shouted to his platoon and anyone within earshot.

Panic fire erupted around him as the MEF soldiers tried to shoot back at the automated guns. In every direction, figures stumbled and hit the ground. The wounded clawed their way across the sandy terrain, desperate to find help before they bled out or the air leaked from their damaged EVA suits.

"Sergeant," a French accent called out.

McCabe turned and spied Lieutenant Durand crawling across the ground towards him.

The French officer dragged himself up beside the British NCO and checked for anyone else in proximity. "Sergeant, we must advance on our objective now. It is imperative—"

A stray bullet smashed through the lieutenant's visor, blasting a hole in his head. Chunks of brain and bone sprayed across McCabe's visor. Gritting his teeth, McCabe hugged the ground even tighter as he crawled forward.

He shouted into his comm, "Second Battalion! Anyone who can hear this, stay low. We need to get close enough to take out those guns. Anyone who has a Bren, I want suppressive fire on those guns nearest the entrance."

As the automated enemy guns pounded the MEF advance, some of the transports laid down fire across the edge of the dome in a frantic bid to subdue the enemy defences. Shrapnel pinged the ground as the Allied advance inched towards the entrance to the colony. Light machine gun fire hammered the enemy weapons, but the automated heavy guns belched waves of lead back on the faltering assault.

When the blanket of smoke disintegrated, one of the supporting transports dipped lower to the surface in a bid to destroy the guns on opposite sides of the main entrance. The heavy guns mounted on either side of the Allied craft fired high calibre rounds at the German weapons emplacements, sending mounds of red sand into the air. As the transport attempted to gain a clearer shot, one of the enemy emplacements raised itself upwards to return fire. Bullets dented the side of the craft before punching through the reinforced glass of the cockpit. The vessel reared wildly as the pilot lost control and spun about before crashing.

Seeing a chance for shelter a hundred metres from the entrance, McCabe crawled towards the downed ship while rallying anyone who could listen to his call. Corporal Brown reached the vessel with his battered section and reported finding a young American pilot lying dead across his controls. Several formed up behind the transport, hiding behind its thick metal hull for protection while they fired back at the enemy guns in a vain attempt to eliminate them.

Some of the transports providing support overhead redoubled their efforts after seeing one of their own destroyed. They turned about and committed to strafing runs on the Nazi gun emplacements while maintaining enough distance to stay out of weapons range.

Dragging himself up behind the relative safety of the downed ship, McCabe reviewed the motley crew of MEF soldiers taking refuge behind the craft.

"That smoke is starting to clear," he shouted to Corporal

Brown over the din of machine gun fire. "We need a couple of anti-tank grenades. Fire what you have on those two positions on either side of the entrance."

"Understood, Sarge," Brown said, and then he called out to the gathered MEF soldiers and anyone else crawling across the Martian landscape.

Several soldiers either taking refuge behind the crashed transport or slithering towards their objective reported back. They began fixing the projector attachments onto their Lee-Enfield's prior to mounting the anti-tank grenades onto their weapons.

McCabe moved to the edge of the transport and took a careful view of the German guns in preparation for giving the order to fire. He opened his mouth to speak when a voice from behind interrupted him.

"Report, Sergeant," Major Wellesley said.

Masking his surprise at seeing the officer so close to the front lines, McCabe gave a quick overview of his plan. Some of the transports overhead swerved wildly. At least six of them ascended much higher into the air, while others spun about, unsure of how to react.

"Incoming!" an American pilot roared across the comm channel. "They have mortar emplacements on the dome. Repeat: they have mortar emplacements on the dome. Incoming! Repeat: we have incoming!"

McCabe's gaze rose to the heavens, searching the cloudless sky for the return trajectory of the mortar rounds. The enemy guns grew mute in anticipation of the attack. McCabe listened for the tell-tale whistles of the enemy bombs on their return course back to the surface.

"Run!" a voice shouted.

A vice-like grip grabbed his arm and shoved McCabe away from the fallen transport. He spun about and found himself starring into a jet-black visor.

The stockier Black Visor pushed McCabe away from the craft before bulldozing through the fleeing MEF soldiers. The two female Black Visors shouted and cajoled any stranglers while the Irishman made right for the major. The Irish Black Visor leader grabbed Major Wellesley by the neck and prodded him along with his gun, all the while howling at the top of his lungs.

Mortar rounds crashed into the ground around them, sending pillars of copper sand and rock spewing high into the air. The landscape beneath them shuddered like a hellish earthquake under the sheer force of the explosive bombs. MEF soldiers caught in the storm of blasts were torn to shreds, and those outside of the blast zones were tossed into the air or their bodies were punctured by shards of lethal shrapnel.

McCabe heard the downed transport vessel behind them explode from a direct hit. A second later, he was thrown into the air. He landed on his left shoulder and groaned as pain lanced up and down his arm. Several more reverberations ensued as the last of the rounds landed. In the seconds that followed, a deathly silence enveloped the battlefield. For a long, strange minute, guns on both sides fell mute. The moans and pleas of the wounded carried across the comm channels. Those voices were far fewer than minutes beforehand, though.

"British soldiers," a heavily accented voice called out from about the dome in clear English. "My name is Generalfeldmarschall Seidel, commanding officer of Wehrmacht forces in the New Berlin military district. Your fleet has been annihilated, you have no hope of resupply or escape. Your offensives in Germania and New Munich colonies have been contained and will soon end in German victories. You have experienced death and destruction without having even faced a German soldier in hand-to-hand combat. You will all die here today. I give you this one chance to surrender. Lay down your arms and I assure you, you will not be harmed. You have five minutes to comply."

Ignoring the pain in his left shoulder, McCabe sat up and looked around. He snapped at his gun the moment he saw a Black Visor sprawled a metre away from him, but the renegade soldier reacted first. He aimed his own weapon at McCabe, only to lower it a second later as he collapsed onto the Martian soil.

"Christ, that hurt," the Irishman groaned as he forced himself to sit back up again.

"What do you want?" McCabe growled. He kept his barrel lowered, but his finger rested on the trigger.

"That Nazi prick is right." The Irishman waved at his three other Black Visor colleagues. "You'll all die here if you keep assaulting the main entrance. That's reinforced flexi-metal. Nothing short of a direct hit with a particle weapon will put a dent in that and, last time I checked, you boys haven't built those yet."

"A particle weapon?" McCabe asked, searching his memory for information on such a term.

"Forget it," the Irish Black Visor said and hauled himself to his knees. "My point is, you're not going to knock down their front door. You need to open it from the inside."

McCabe leaned closer to the Black Visor leader. "What do you mean?"

"There's a hidden ventilating shaft used for venting fumes out of the underground refinery. If we destroy the fans in the shaft, it should be big enough to get people down there. The room it connects to opens out onto the main entrance complex. If we can get a team down there, we can take the control room for the main entrance."

McCabe gazed around at the surviving MEF units that had thrown themselves into firing positions spread across the littered battlefield. Even armed with anti-tank grenades, he didn't relish leading them straight into the jaws of those gun emplacements again.

"If it can be done, then why don't you do it?" he asked.

The Irishman signalled at his colleagues to join him and waited until they surrounded him. "This is all I have," the Irishman said, nodding at his colleagues. "I need more firepower to take the control room."

McCabe looked across at his stunned superior officer.

Major Wellesley gave him a single affirmative nod in answer.

"The last time we crossed paths, you took my men prisoner and then knocked us all unconscious. Why in the hell should I trust you now?" McCabe demanded.

"Because the second time we crossed paths, I saved your life and the lives of your men," the Irish Black Visor said, while gesturing towards the scraps of metal that once made up the downed transport. "If I wanted you dead, Sergeant McCabe, you'd be dead. It's your choice. You can throw yourselves against the gates of New Berlin and watch your men get cut to pieces. Or you can help me unlock the front door. What's it gonna be?"

McCabe examined the worn and exhausted faces of the MEF soldiers around him. In a short space of time, they had witnessed such bloodshed and death. They would only see more of the same if they remained locked out of the German colony. "Very well," he said, with a reluctant sigh. "I'll take personal charge of a support team. But mark my words, if you put my men in danger, I'll gut you like a fish. Clear?"

Noid reached for her sidearm, but the Irishman raised his hand to stop her.

"Crystal clear, Sergeant."

McCabe ordered the twenty or so MEF soldiers surrounding him to follow the Black Visors. They covered each other when they peeled away from their positions, moving quickly lest they draw the wrath of the inactive Nazi guns. Those who had them threw smoke grenades to mask their withdrawal as they followed the Black Visor team away from the body-littered battlefield.

Falling in beside but slightly behind the Black Visor leader, McCabe followed when he led them towards a small hill several hundred metres from their staging area.

"If you knew about this way in, why didn't you tell anyone?" McCabe demanded.

The Black Visor glanced at him for a moment as he continued to jog towards the hill.

"I wasn't sure how you planned to get into New Berlin," he said. "Frankly, I didn't think anyone would be stupid enough to launch a head-on attack. It's like you're all deliberately trying to get yourselves killed."

Before McCabe could reply, the Black Visor leader came to a halt when they were about to round the base of the small hill. He waited until his fellow Black Visors and their MEF cohorts joined him. With everyone gathered, he began jabbing at the ground with the butt of his Lee-Enfield. It took a moment, but as soon as the Black Visor found a dull thud, he slung his weapon and cleared a loose scattering of rocks off what appeared to be a concealed metal grate.

The Irishman gestured at the stockier Black Visor to join him and stooped low. The two men lifted the grate in unison and peered down into the darkened shaft below. The taller female Black Visor hammered a peg into the ground and attached a thick rope to it from her backpack. Noid pulled two grenades from her belt, yanked out the pins, and dropped them into the shaft.

The Irishman faced McCabe. "Tell me something. Has Mad Jack made his speech yet? The famous one at the gates of New Berlin?"

McCabe glared at the renegade soldier, refusing to give his ridiculous question an answer. The ground shook when the two grenades detonated below them. The sound of metal crashing downwards before smashing into the ground filtered up through the shaft. A light breeze escaped as the atmosphere in the room below worked its way up.

"It's a shame," the Irishman said before he grabbed the rope and lowered himself into the shaft. "I really liked that speech. 'Kill them all' and all that."

McCabe patted his Lee-Enfield as he watched the Black Visors descend the shaft. He had no idea what lay beneath them, but if he sensed an ambush or betrayal of any kind, he planned to gun down the Irishman first.

After he got a good look at his face.

CITY CENTRE, NEW BERLIN COLONY
17.03 MST
DAY 1

"...leaving ten guns remaining with full magazines. The following automated weapons are now completely out of ammunition. Gun emplacement numbers thirty-one, thirty-three, thirty-four, thirty-seven, thirty-eight..."

Generalfeldmarschall Seidel tapped his fingers nervously on the desk as his gaze moved from view screen to view screen. Since the Wehrmacht's eviction from the government district by the SS, he had been forced to relocate his headquarters to a nearby building.

It sat a fraction of the size of his old HQ, but he had to give reluctant credit to his subordinates for their effort. While New Berlin shuddered from the periodic attacks of the Jewish insurgents, his staff had hastily moved and reassembled his equipment, allowing him to tap into the external cameras outside the colony. He watched the British soldiers hold their ground despite his offer.

"...one hundred and eighteen and one-hundred and nineteen. The following automated weapons have been destroyed or rendered useless in the Allied assault. Gun emplacement's numbers thirty-two, thirty-five, forty—"

Seidel banged his fist on his desk. "Enough!"

The lieutenant giving his report winced and clasped his lips shut.

Sitting back in his chair, Seidel scanned the Allied activity on his screens. He had given them five minutes to surrender three minutes ago, and they appeared to be doing anything but that. He hadn't expected them to, yet a part of him hoped he'd broken their spirits. The automated guns played their part in giving the invaders a bloody nose. But if they threw themselves into another attack, it wouldn't be long until they realised that half the automated guns staring them down were completely out of ammunition.

"How long until our reinforcements arrive?" Seidel said as he reached for a cigarette.

The lieutenant cleared his throat and fidgeted with the papers in his hands. "The latest reports estimate they'll reach the colony within the next forty minutes or so. Allied airborne attacks have inflicted some damage, but Oberst Brandt reports that the Wirbelwind anti-aircraft guns have held their own."

Seidel lit his cigarette and took a long drag. Forty minutes. He needed to hold out for forty minutes until his returning Wehrmacht forces could grind the British into the blood-stained dust.

Checking his watch, Seidel noted that five minutes had fully expired, but the British forces held. They were hauling their wounded and dead from the battlefield and readying themselves for the next action. Seidel didn't dare authorise the guns to open fire on them without provocation, hoping they would delay their next move for as long as possible, buying the colony the time they desperately needed.

"Report from General Schulz, Herr Feldmarschall," another lieutenant said, appearing beside the other one and clicking his heels together. "The General reports that Jewish resistance has stiffened. The Volkssturm units under the General's command have, so far, been unable to penetrate any deeper into the ghetto. Repeated assaults on the enemy's defences have been beaten back. The General reports that without additional reinforcements or armour support, he may be unable to pacify the ghetto."

Seidel stood abruptly, causing the young officers to flinch. "He can have all the damned reinforcements he needs in forty minutes!"

He moved to the nearest window, waved away the officers, and set his sights on the government district on the opposite side of the street below. Already the SS had erected barbed wire fences and fortified gun emplacements along the perimeter of the colony's centre. Black uniformed SS guards stalked back and forth, their guns at the ready, and the helmets of the snipers on top of the buildings above lay clearly recognisable. With a single word, Reichsführer Wagner could unleash his armed goons on the Jewish populace and remove their intransigence once and for all. Yet, he and the rest of the high-ranking party members sat huddled behind their ring of steel while the colony burned.

Returning his attention to the screens in front of his desk, Seidel flicked his cigarette to the floor and stubbed it out with his boot. As he exhaled a cloud of smoke, he rapped on the desk again, wondering how long the British would wage their war of nerves. It would take one soldier to fall into range of an empty or damaged gun to realise how vulnerable the German colony stood.

"Herr Feldmarschall," General Franke said with a puzzled look on his face. "I've just received a report that a drop in atmosphere has been detected in one of the ventilation rooms connected to the refinery."

Seidel raised his hand dismissively and gestured the general away. "Let the civilians worry about maintenance.

69

I have no time for—"

The words died in his mouth. A long-forgotten titbit of information floated in his mind as he recalled a tour of the lower levels several years ago. Moving from behind his desk, he approached General Franke and guided him towards one of the many map-laden tables in the centre of the room. He pushed aside schematics of the colony's internal workings, scattering them to the floor until he found one that outlined New Berlin's ventilation and air filtration system.

"Where?" he demanded.

General Franke studied the report in his hands and traced his finger along a set of thin lines. He paused on a side room attached to the refinery, which led to an axis corridor connected to the eastern entrance's command complex. General Franke's eyes widened.

He snatched the nearest headset and thundered into the mic. "The British have gained access to the colony. Lock down the eastern entrance command complex. All available units, defend the command complex to the last man. The British must not gain control of the eastern entrance!"

Seidel stood back and glanced at his watch again. Thirty-eight minutes.

They just needed to hold on for another thirty-eight minutes.

REFINERY COMPLEX – EASTERN SECTOR, NEW BERLIN COLONY
17.12 MST
DAY 1

The Black Visors stood guard at the exit and waited for the small band of MEF to finish climbing down the shaft. McCabe signalled at the soldiers under his command to move into their order of march, and then he nodded towards the Black Visor leader.

Noid took point, quietly opened the airlock door, and stepped into the corridor beyond. Atmosphere hissed from the passageway as the small group of soldiers took up firing positions and crept towards either end of the dimly lit hallway. Once everyone filled the corridor and the door sealed behind them, the Irishman addressed McCabe.

"That way leads directly to the refinery," he said and pointed towards the southern corridor. "I'd recommend delegating some men to hold that entrance, so the Nazis don't try and hit us from the rear."

"Johnson, Horowitz, McManus, Sheik, hold that door at all costs," McCabe ordered. "Use the comm if they make a concerted effort to break through. Everyone else, prepare to move."

The Black Visors took the lead and jogged down the corridor at a quick pace, pausing once at the door that linked them to the control room complex. After ensuring the airlock was secure, the four Black Visors turned their backs on the MEF soldiers and, to McCabe's surprise, started removing their EVA suits. They slipped their black visor-tinted helmets off first, revealing face covering balaclavas with gaps for their eyes and mouth. McCabe opened his mouth to question their actions, but the Irishman got there first.

"There's atmosphere from here on out. I don't know about you, Sergeant, but I've had my fill of fighting in these bulky bastards."

The Black Visors snapped off the top and bottom sections of their EVA suit's, revealing unusual black and dark red khaki uniforms unlike the standard British battledress.

With a reluctant flick of his hand, McCabe disconnected his helmet and held his breath, half expecting a ruse. Seeing that none of the Black Visors were choking, he exhaled and took in a breath of New Berlin's air. It struck him as stale but undeniably breathable, so he nodded at his soldiers to proceed.

They stripped down to their battledress, stuffing their backpacks and pockets with the equipment and ammunition from their EVA suit's compartments. As they had rehearsed hundreds of times, they slipped their comm pieces from their helmets and placed them into their ears. Next, they removed the left-arm consoles from their EVA suits and fixed them to their left forearms over their uniforms. The MEF soldiers grinned from ear to ear at finally getting to remove the cumbersome EVA's and flexed their tired muscles in appreciation.

With their EVA suits discarded, the Black Visors ran through a quick check of their equipment before facing McCabe and the near-readied mass of MEF soldiers.

"Okay," the Irishman started and nodded towards the sealed entrance. "This leads into a corridor with several storage rooms and offices. We need to take the stairs at the end of the corridor and make our way across the upper level towards the entrance to the command centre. Chances are they've detected the drop in atmosphere from the way we came in, so they may be waiting for us. Ready?"

The Black Visors took up stances on either side of the door and prepared to move, but one of the MEF soldiers cleared his throat and spoke up.

"I just got one thing," Private Dobson said, glancing warily at McCabe. "Not a big thing but...you know...what do we call you? Like, say I see something you don't or a German is coming at you or something. Have you fellas got names?"

"That's not important," the Irishman snapped back.

"I think it is important," McCabe said, stepping closer to the MJ-12 operatives. "I get that you need to keep your identities secret, but if we're going into a firefight, you need to give us something to call you."

The Irish Black Visor shook his head in disbelief and glanced towards his comrades. They each returned his stare and shrugged their own shoulders in response. With a loud sigh, Noid faced McCabe.

"I'm Noid," she said and then pointed at her colleagues. "You can call that Irish son-of-a-bitch Dub. The stocky lad is Big Mo and the tall blonde with the great rack is Smack. We good now, people?"

The MEF soldiers nodded in agreement and lined up closer to the entrance. Dub and Noid took point. After a three-count, they sprang into action. Dub yanked on the door release, and Noid threw herself into the corridor first. Dub moved to follow her when a succession of shots rang out. Noid jumped back behind the cover of the door frame and pounded on her trigger while Dub took to his knee and blasted on his own Lee-Enfield.

"Move!" Noid screeched as she charged back into the corridor.

The Black Visors lead the way. McCabe counted three fallen enemy defenders from the initial engagement. Confirming they were dead, he kicked away their weapons. Without waiting to be told, the MEF advance party broke into smaller groups and cleared the vacated offices and darkened storage rooms. McCabe charged ahead, following the Black Visors towards the set of stairs leading up to the upper level.

A small group of Nazi soldiers appeared at the top of the stairway. They dropped to the ground and opened fire. Bullets whizzed through the air. Private Denny wailed when a bullet punched through his shoulder, sending him skittering across the corridor floor. His colleagues dragged him out of the line of fire as more enemy bullets riddled the ground where he had fallen.

Private Bingham threw himself behind the door frame of a vacant office and raised his Bren light machine gun to his hip. Squeezing the trigger, 7.62mm bullets burst from the weapon, forcing the Germans to clear the top of the stairs. Using the wall of the corridor they had emerged from as cover, the German soldiers continued to rain bullets down on them.

McCabe scurried from his cover in a bid to reach Bingham. Bullets cleaved through the air, but through sheer force of will, he braved the enemy lead and slid down behind the private. Ahead, the Black Visors grouped themselves on either side of the stairs, firing at the Nazis above.

Bingham slapped in a fresh magazine and prepared to unleash a short burst when McCabe stopped him. "We need to move closer," he said and squeezed his Lee-Enfield's trigger. "Those Black Visors are going to rush the stairs. We need to get suppressive fire on the Germans."

"Suicidal bastards," Bingham shouted back as he prepared to follow.

After signalling at the neighbouring MEF soldiers

to lay down cover fire, McCabe rushed from behind the doorframe and shot up at the enemy. A wave of bullets obliged the Wehrmacht defenders to seek shelter, and the MEF soldiers were able to move closer. Swinging into a cleared room at the bottom of the stairs, McCabe tapped at Bingham to take up a firing stance using the door frame for protection. The private raised his weapon again and squeezed on the trigger, battering the wall at the top of the stairs with a barrage of murderous lead. Careful to stay out of his line of fire, the Black Visors ran up the other side of the stairs with their weapons held high.

Managing to get a clear line of sight on the sheltering Nazis, they blasted on their Lee-Enfield's without mercy. One of the enemies slumped into McCabe's view and hit the ground at the top of the stairs. A grenade slipped from his blood-slicked hand and tumbled towards the MEF soldiers at the lower level.

"Grenade!" McCabe shouted and grabbed Bingham to drag him to safety.

The grenade exploded before the private could get to cover. McCabe roared when the strength of the blast sent him crashing into the room, but Bingham took the full brunt of the grenade's explosive fury.

Ears ringing, McCabe stumbled towards the smoking remains of the young soldier. Gazing into Bingham's lifeless eyes, he shook his head. Then he took a moment to close the private's eyelids. A rush of anger at the bloodshed burst through him, and he vowed revenge on the defending Nazis.

"We have the stairs!" Dub called out.

McCabe patted what remained of Bingham, and slinging his rifle, rose to his feet. He exited the room and experienced a wave of rage at the sight of the bodies of three more of his men. He pushed his emotions aside and, forcing calm, focused on the task at hand. He grabbed the stair rails and heaved himself up the stairs two steps at a time until he reached the top.

"Which way?" he asked, looking down at the bodies of the dead Nazis.

"Follow me," Noid said, nodding to the left.

With Big Mo toting a Bren light machine gun, the surviving MEF soldiers fell in behind the Black Visors. They moved quietly down the corridor, clearing every room as they went. When they reached the end of the hallway, McCabe ordered them to halt at the sound of boots banging on the tiled floor.

Using the wall for cover, Smack pulled out two grenades. She waited for the sound of the enemy boots to bound closer before ripping the pins out and hurling them. Distraught shouts burst forth after the grenades exploded.

The MEF invaders swung around the corridor and fired their weapons, cutting down any survivors. Enemy soldiers screamed as bullets punched through their bodies before collapsing to the ground in silence.

Like a well-oiled machine, the MEF soldiers and the Black Visors forged ahead as one. They screened the enemy dead and carried on securing the building. At the intersection of another corridor, Noid raised her hand, and the entire group stopped before going into all-round cover.

"Is this the place?" Dub whispered to her.

"Looks about right," she mumbled.

"The right place for what?" McCabe asked.

Big Mo took to a knee. "Resupply." He drew his knife and began jabbing it into the wall.

McCabe watched in confusion. He opened his mouth to ask what was happening when a chunk of the wall gave way. Big Mo redoubled his efforts and chipped out pieces of plasterboard until a secret compartment behind the wall crashed open. He swiped aside the excess debris and reached inside the wall. He pulled out a large metal case, and gently placed it on the ground in front of his colleagues. Wiping away the layer of dust, he took off one of his gloves and pressed his thumb onto the front of the mysterious container.

McCabe and the MEF soldiers looked on in amazement as the locks on the case clicked open. Big Mo lifted the lid, and, through the gap in his balaclava, the Black Visor smiled.

McCabe craned his neck for a better view. "What are those?"

Noid picked up the body of one of the weapons and slammed the butt-plate on before inserting the barrel. After fixing her sling, she attached the sight, slapped in a magazine clip and stood. "This," she said, with a hint of excitement in her voice, "is what we call a HK-17. Hybrid Killer in the house, baby. Come to momma." She cocked the weapon with single hand movement and reaching back into the case, began shoving as many magazines as she could carry into her pockets.

After assembling their own HKs, the Black Visors pulled equipment and backpacks from the crate. They attached strange headsets to their heads and lowered a single circular glass over their right eyes. The Black Visors took turns moving about and tapping at their headset controls before reaching for the last of their equipment.

"What is all this?" McCabe demanded. "How did you get this into the colony?"

"A friend left it here for us a long time ago," Dub said, flatly.

"God bless Intense Dan," Smack said with a smile.

"I miss the little dude," Big Mo chuckled.

Noid held up a padded black shirt, as if to change the subject. "This is body armour. Not as good as an Exo-suit, but better than nothing."

"Shut it with the references, Noid," Smack hissed.

Noid made to say something in reply when her gaze crossed the MEF soldiers surrounding them.

"Here," she said and tossed her body armour towards the nearest soldier. "You probably need this more than I do."

She nudged Dub in the ribs. Following Noid's lead, he flung his body armour to the nearest grateful soldier, as did Smack and Big Mo. Those that happened to be lucky enough to grab one dragged the black padded armour over their battledress and stepped closer to the front of the group.

"Disable particle chargers," Dub said to his colleagues. "Standard ammo only. Remember the rules of engagement. We get in, we get out, we go back home."

"Understood," Big Mo said and pressed a button on a

control panel on the side of his HK-17.

Smack walked to the front of the group. "Let's do it."

"Kill them all," Noid chimed back in a grim tone.

Dub faced McCabe and lowered his mysterious weapon. He unstrapped his water flask, took a quick swig and held it out to McCabe.

McCabe shook his head and waited for the Black Visor to return the flask to his belt.

"Okay," Dub said. "Last hurdle. The command complex is at the end of this corridor. They'll have sealed themselves in, so we're going to blow the doors, and then take the room. Have your men stay behind us and watch our backs."

After McCabe peeked around the corner to get a sense of direction, he gave his men their orders. They reloaded their weapons and prepared to move.

With a single nod from Dub, the assembled force swung around the corner and pushed on. When they reached the entrance to the command complex, they split into four groups. One covered the way they had come, and another situated themselves facing the opposite end of the hallway. The other two columns, each with Black Visors at the lead, hunched over at either side of the door.

Big Mo slipped a hand into one of his belt compartments and slid out a square rectangular device. He fixed it carefully to the centre of the door, pressed on the controls, and motioned at everyone to pull back. The two groups by the door wasted no time in withdrawing from the explosive and readied themselves to spring into action.

Ten seconds passed, followed by a deafening boom that engulfed the corridor, causing the lights to flicker. The brunt of the explosion burst into the room, tearing the reinforced metal door from its hinges with enough force to kill anyone unlucky enough to be within proximity of the blast. Dub and Smack were the first to jump into action, throwing themselves into the smoke-filled room. They fired their semi-automatic assault rifles in short bursts. Noid and Big Mo trailed close at hand, with McCabe the next to rush through the door.

Nazis showered bullets back at them, but the sheer volume of fire the renegade Black Visors sprayed forced them to seek cover. As McCabe stumbled through the doorway, a sharp, piercing sensation cut through his arm. Trying to push the pain aside, he slipped on the blood of someone obliterated in the explosion. Beyond his field of vision, a fist smashed him square on the jaw.

McCabe tumbled to the ground, unable to raise his weapon. A harsh-faced Nazi threw himself on top of McCabe. Saliva dripped from his mouth as he shouted in German. Hate-filled eyes drilled into McCabe. The solider pushed a knife towards McCabe's throat. McCabe shoved him back with his rifle.

Out of nowhere, Private Begley slammed the butt of his Lee-Enfield into the soldier's face. The enemy soldier crashed onto the tiled floor. Clutching his knife, he lifted it to defend himself.

Roaring like a madman, Begley raised the butt of his Lee-Enfield again and bashed it hard onto the Nazi's face. The Nazi tried to throw up his hands to surrender, but Begley pounded the butt of his Lee-Enfield downwards again and again, reducing the man's head to a bloody pulp.

McCabe dragged himself to his feet, and taking shelter behind a desk, prepared to fire.

Even with the MEF soldiers pouring into the command centre, the German defenders refused to budge. They fired from the far side of the room or stormed forward under a hailstorm of lead to engage in hand-to-hand combat. On McCabe's right flank, a ferocious-looking German pounced on Private Donovan, skewering him with his bayonet. McCabe turned his weapon and fired twice, shooting a hole in the side of the enemy soldier's face, causing him to slump back onto an overturned desk.

Bringing his weapon to bear on the enemy alive on the far side of the room, McCabe took careful aim. He pulled at his trigger as he advanced and took shelter behind another bullet-riddled desk.

Leading the charge and weaving between the storm of bullets spewing around him, Big Mo discharged his HK-17 relentlessly. For a man of his size, he moved with ferocious speed. He skidded to a stop behind some destroyed equipment for cover and lobbed a grenade at the Nazi holdouts.

The German defenders lunged for the grenade. One of them lifted it to throw it back, but it detonated in his hands, sending scraps of charred flesh and splatters of blood across the walls. The surviving Nazis screamed as shrapnel splinters punctured their flesh.

All the while, MEF bullets continued to crack at them.

"Surrender! Surrender!" a German soldier shouted in English. He dropped his weapons.

Three more joined their comrade as the Black Visors and MEF soldiers closed in from all angles. Each of the surrendering Nazis had fragments from the grenade embedded in their limbs and torsos. They raised their bloodied, shaking hands, and the Black Visors stepped in to strip them of their weaponry.

"Secure that door," Dub barked, pointing at another reinforced entrance opposite to the one they had stormed through. "That's the only other way these Nazi shite bags can get through."

Big Mo punched in a code to lock the door from the inside and positioned MEF volunteers on either side of the door.

McCabe removed his helmet and wiped his sweaty brow as he surveyed the remnants of his force. Four lay dead, struck down by bayonets and bullets. Six more were wounded, ranging from cuts and grazes to Begley getting shot in the leg. McCabe whispered words of comfort to the wounded lad as a medic worked to seal his wound.

McCabe took a moment to check the gash on his own arm, and standing up, inspected the damaged room. Desks and equipment were strewn about, smashed and bullet riddled. Twelve German soldiers lay dead, stretched across the wreckage, and their cowering colleagues huddled together under the watchful gaze of Noid.

"What should we do with them?" Noid asked McCabe.

"We'll secure them until we can hand them over to—"

Dub spoke over him. "Shoot them."

"Wait a minute!" Smack and McCabe said at the same time.

"That's not how we do things," McCabe snapped. "I don't

want our own boys getting captured and murdered when we go in to take the colony. We don't shoot prisoners."

Dub closed the distance between them.

McCabe returned the Black Visor's glare and made no sign of backing down.

"They're not prisoners," Dub said with a nod towards the terrified German soldiers. "They're baby killers, fascists, and genocidal maniacs. There's no Geneva Convention here on Mars, Sergeant. I say we kill them all."

"Kill them all," Noid repeated.

"No."

McCabe's answer caused the room to fall silent. In his peripheral vision, his soldiers stopped what they were doing. Some glanced over at him before locking their gaze on the Black Visors. Fingers inched towards triggers, while others moved closer to back him up.

"Private Donovan," he called out, without taking his eyes off Dub. "These German soldiers are our prisoners and will be treated with their rights as such. Their fate is in the hands of the courts, not ours. Escort them outside and guard them until reinforcements arrive."

"Understood, Sergeant."

Donovan moved towards the POWs and gestured at them to stand up. Urging them on, he prodded them with his riffle barrel towards the exit while the Black Visors looked on. The tension in the room eased slightly when the captives were brought into the corridor outside.

Dub continued glaring at McCabe, but after a slight shake of his head, he did an about turn and made his way to a nearby control panel. He clicked on one of the controls, causing a whirring sound to hum to life above them. The entire wall beyond the row of computers opened into a massive window, and a shutter on the other side lifted.

Lighting a cigarette, McCabe stepped closer to the window and explored the view of the colony beyond. Huge towers stretched from the streets below, almost scratching at the massive dome above them. Rows of houses lined the wide, vacant streets. Parks and dense patches of green dotted the landscape. A classic-looking structure sat bordered by imposing towers in the centre of the city.

"That's our objective," Dub said. "We need to reach the Command and Control building in the government district. But we may have a slight problem."

"Such as?" McCabe said in a cautious tone.

Dub beckoned him to step closer and pointed at something directly below them. Taking another drag on his cigarette, McCabe followed the Black Visor's gaze. Massing at well-prepared defences covering every angle around the main entrance stood hundreds of grey-uniformed Wehrmacht soldiers.

A sudden bang bounced off the window, causing him to jerk back out of instinct.

Chuckling, Dub extended his hand and rapped on the window with his knuckles. "That's solid flexi-plastic. Nothing short of a full-on particle blast will put a dent in that. They can take pot shots at us all day and we'll be fine."

"Shut up with the references, Dub," Smack murmured from across the room.

Dub turned to Smack and shrugged his shoulders in answer before focusing on the German soldiers below.

"Christ, without tanks or armour, they'll cut us to pieces if we try to get through the main entrance," McCabe said with a shake of his head. "There has to be another way in."

"There's a way of removing them as an obstacle, but I'm not sure you're going to like it."

"What have you got in mind?"

Stretching a hand towards the control panel again, Dub pointed towards a screen with three red switches.

"These switches control the three airlock doors of the main entrance. The one on the outside, the middle one that allows you to pressurise or depressurise the atmosphere depending on whether you're leaving or entering the colony, and the inner airlock the Nazis are massing to defend. How about we open all three and see what happens?"

OUTSKIRTS OF NEW BERLIN COLONY
17.37 MST
DAY 1

Private Peter Jenkins stayed unmoving as he lay on the rocky copper sand, watching Corporal Brown crawl ahead. Pausing, the corporal released the grip on his Lee-Enfield and extended a glove towards a hand-sized chunk of loose rock. After glancing at his section, the corporal pulled back his hand and threw the rock forward and to the right of their location. Midway through its flight, the automated guns guarding New Berlin's entrance flared up. They fired until the rock was reduced to sand. Then they fell silent again.

"Closer," Corporal Brown ordered.

Jenkins, his five platoon mates, plus their four French replacements inched towards the looming colony.

"I still don't get why they call him Mad Jack," Private Helms whispered to Private Woodward as they crawled. "Like, I haven't actually seen him go mad or look mad or anything."

"Maybe he's just barmy," Woodward replied in a hushed tone. "Did a stint in a nut house or something."

Corporal Brown raised his hand and the section stopped. Again, the corporal reached for a small lump of rock and threw it. The automated gun reacted a lot faster this time, spraying the air overhead with rounds until the rock disintegrated into fine particles of dust.

"I heard they call him Mad Jack coz he killed a bunch of Nazi prisoners after his company was cut to pieces during D-Day," Jenkins ventured. "I can understand that. I'd be pretty damn pissed if you lot were shot."

"Shut it, Jenkins," Helms snapped.

"Why are you ranting about us dying when we're staring down the barrel of a machine gun?" Woodward hissed. "Keep quiet or I'll clatter you across the ears, you pillock."

Jenkins shrugged off his colleague's comments and returned his focus to the corporal ahead. The veteran NCO selected another rock and threw it. He looked on as the automated guns belched a short burst of bullets before going quiet.

Corporal Brown cursed under his breath, picked up another rock, and flung it. This time no sound of heavy machine gun fire filled Jenkins's ears. He glanced at his colleagues as Corporal Brown tossed another volley of stones.

The enemy guns remained muted.

"Alright. Listen up," Corporal Brown said over the section comm channel. "That looks like it's it. The gun's run out of ammo, but we have to be sure. Jenkins, you're up."

Corporal Brown drew his knife and embedded it into the ground as a marker. They couldn't be sure, but all indications pointed to the guns being programmed to fire on movement within a three hundred metre range.

Trying to push aside his gut-wrenching nervousness, Jenkins slithered towards the knife and paused to look at the corporal.

"On your feet, lad," Corporal Brown ordered. "If you hear or see anything, hit the ground. We're right here."

"Yes, Corporal."

Fighting against every instinct in his body, Jenkins lifted his head and waited. The automated gun ahead lay fixed in his direction, but it remained subdued. With trembling hands, he pushed to his knees and again, paused. His heart pounded when he forced himself upright. He released a nervous exhale as he looked over the scarred battlefield around him. Most of the dead and wounded had been collected. Hundreds of pieces of damaged equipment and weapons dotted the red-brown sand where soldiers had fallen during the initial advance. Shuddering, Jenkins raised his rifle barrel and took a step towards the Nazi colony.

He fixed his gaze on the massive gun barrel eying him and continued moving in a slow, cautious pace. At any moment, he expected the automated defences to roar to life, but they made no sound or motion. His legs shook nonetheless. Fearing they could give out at any minute, and experiencing a wave of adrenaline, Jenkins broke into a full-on sprint towards the gun. His heart continued to bang like a drum.

Against all odds, he reached the weapon intact. Trying to catch his breath, he pulled two grenades from his belt. He tore the pins out, placed them on the body of the automated gun, and rushed for cover. The grenades exploded, destroying the housing of the weapon and causing the barrel to tilt downwards at an awkward angle.

"Clear, Corporal," Jenkins panted into his comm and waved his hands at his section.

With a path to the main entrance clear, columns of MEF soldiers jogged towards the huge, reinforced doors of the colony. They split into two distinct groups, taking cover on either side of the entrance but leaving a gap of several metres away from it. Within minutes, hundreds of soldiers lined either side with hundreds more flowing from the landing zone beyond the sandy dunes. Transports flew in from over the horizon, ferrying in soldiers stranded across the barren deserts of the red planet.

The surviving members of the officer core were the last to join the jumble of MEF battalions and divisions. Entire companies and battalions stood decimated, so much so that they allocated soldiers to whoever needed them most. Too few officers had lived through the various assaults by the Nazis forces, but those who did were impatient to take the fight into the heart of National Socialist power on Mars.

As Jenkins waited for the signal to begin the operation, he and his colleagues chatted idly about the plan to destroy the enemy waiting for them on the other side of the airlocked doors. The news that some of their comrades had seized the command complex, aided by the mysterious MJ-12 operatives, caused considerable excitement. After ten hours of fighting on a barren wasteland of a planet, Jenkins was eager to remove his helmets and breathe fresh air again.

From amongst the growing contingent of soldiers, Major Wellesley stepped away from the entrance and moved thirty metres back into the open ground. He held his hand high and waited as one of the transports circling above the colony began a slow descent towards his location. Studying his actions, Jenkins guessed that the major was organising transportation away from the battle zone. Instead, the bulky transport craft pulled to a halt, hovering a metre off the ground.

Turning about but keeping his hand held high, as if brandishing a sabre, Major Wellesley marched towards the main entrance. The transport crept after him, leaving a few metres between it and Major Wellesley, but made no motion to land itself.

"He's lost his marbles," Woodward mumbled.

"You reckon they'll pay us if we send Mad Jack to the funny farm?" Helms quipped.

"I still reckon he got that name from shooting those prisoners," Jenkins said as he watched Major Wellesley guide the transport closer to the main entrance.

The soldiers around him began jeering Jenkins as they always did, but he ignored them. He leaned in and followed the transport with his gaze. The passageway behind the main entrance leading to the colony certainly looked wide enough to fit four or five transports side by side, but height wise, the entrance appeared far too small. Even if the vessel landed and they found a way to tow the hulk in, the compartment that made up the main body of the craft stood far too high to fit.

Major Wellesley spent another minute or two aligning the transport to the centre of the main entrance before turning to the hunkering soldiers on either side. The transport craft hung behind him, making no effort to land itself.

"Soldiers of the Mars Expeditionary Force," the major called out, and his voice carried across all comm channels. "Today, we mark a historic day. A day like no other. A day of great sadness, pain, and death. We have come here to—"

"Christ, what's he chattering on about now?" Helms groaned.

"Shut it, Helms," Corporal Brown hissed over the section's private comm channel. "If the Major wants to make a speech, then keep your mouth shut. You don't have to listen, but you will pipe down."

"...an evil like no other," Major Wellesley continued, pounding his fists as if to hammer home his point. "We will scour this stain from humanity's soul by destroying the last traces of the Third Reich. We will—"

"This is boring," Woodward moaned to anyone who'd listen. "I'd rather be getting shot at then forced to listen to some blue blood cluck like an old hen."

"Woodward, shut up," Corporal Brown growled.

"...I say this to you now, men of the Mars Expeditionary Force, show no mercy. Let us avenge our fallen and the millions that lay in their graves back home. Kill the Nazi scourge. Kill every last one of them. Kill them all!"

Major Wellesley lowered his hands and placed them on his hips as he glanced from side to side. The gathered MEF soldiers looked back and forth to one another until some of the NCOs realised the senior officer stood awaiting applause. They clapped amongst themselves and nudged their subordinates into joining in, until a half-hearted wave of claps rang out in response.

"I wish he'd hurry up and let us get on with it," Helms said, reluctantly applauding. "I'm dying to get out of this suit and take a piss."

"As speeches go, it wasn't the worst," Woodward said. "Bit anti-climatic at the end, but I've heard far worse than that, I suppose."

With his chin tilted upwards, Major Wellesley stepped away from the main entrance and strolled to the right side of the massive, reinforced door. The transport continued to hover off the ground, with its landing thrusters gently whipping the sand beneath it.

"Get ready," Corporal Brown said. "The first door's coming up now. The second one will be right after, followed by the third. Hold your ground and make no movement until ordered. Is that clear?"

"Understood, Corporal," Jenkins and two dozen voices chimed back.

With a lurch, the massive external main entrance to New Berlin lifted upwards. Those who knelt closest to the entrance craned their necks to see if they could spot anything of interest inside, but Jenkins and everyone else behind them waited quietly. It took ten seconds for the fortified airlock door to fully raise itself.

"Here comes the second door," Corporal Brown called out.

A wave of nervous anticipation spread through Jenkins as he waited. He glanced at his colleagues. They checked and rechecked their weapons, wished each other luck, and whispered muted prayers of protection to whatever divine power they held dear. Taking a deep breath, he tightened his gloved grip on his Lee-Enfield and turned again to observe the hovering transport, trying to figure out its mission.

"Second door is up," Corporal Brown called out. "Last door is coming up now. Everyone, stay down and don't move until ordered to do so."

Jenkins murmured his understanding and gazed down at the sandy ground, mentally preparing himself. His hands trembled at the thought of what lay ahead.

Several more seconds passed until the sand outside the opened main entrance door whipped about as if dancing in a gentle gust. Scraps of paper and small pieces of debris floated past when New Berlin's atmosphere seeped out of the open entrance. Alarms wailed, heralding that all three airlock doors sat open.

Without warning, the heavy machine guns on either side of the transport exploded to life. Jenkins shuddered at the ferocity of the guns as they pelted continuous waves of rounds into the colony. The transport fired off two of its missiles, causing chucks of concrete and scraps of metal to escape the colony on the back of the venting atmosphere. The Allied vessel swung from side to side, spewing non-stop death into the German lines. The pings of enemy bullets scratched the thick armour of the transport, but the craft remained undamaged. It fired off two more missiles, quickly followed by another two until its guns went quiet. Then it backed slowly away from the main entrance before beginning its ascent to the skies above.

"Third door is down," Corporal Brown called out. "Prepare to move."

Jenkins rose to his feet.

"Fix bayonets."

Jenkins unsheathed his bayonet and attached it to the end of his Lee-Enfield rifle in a smooth, well-practiced movement.

"Second Battalion," Major Wellesley cried out over the battalion comm channel. "Advance!"

With a roar, Jenkins and the first wave of attackers rushed from their positions and spilled into the tunnel connecting the three airlock doors that led to the colony. He burst into a sprint, hurrying as fast as he could towards the one airlock door that remained down. Rubble and torn scraps of metal blanketed the floor giving him a taste of the devastation unleashed upon their enemy. When they reached the final airlock door, Jenkins studied the splatters of blood and torn pieces of flesh strewn across the ground. He shivered at the thought of experiencing such a violent death.

When the soldiers of the Second Battalion reached their destination, Jenkins took his place in the front rank with the rest of his company. As the second airlock lowered behind them to pressurise the room with breathable atmosphere, he primed himself for an impending attack. Along with everyone else in the front rank, he lowered himself to the ground and took up a firing stance. Those behind him lowered a knee. They rammed their rifle butts into their shoulders and raised their barrels. What heavy guns and RPG's they had with them, they cocked and flicked off safeties.

The second airlock thumped shut. With a hiss, the atmosphere pressurised into the compartment. Jenkins studied the read-out on his EVA suit's left arm consoles and confirmed the presence of breathable air right as the final airlock door began rising.

With bated breath, Jenkins looked on in anticipation as a gap of light appeared from under the final airlock door. He prepared himself for an immediate attack, but no bullets rang out at the first rank. No grenades lashed out. When the airlock reached waist height, Jenkins and the rest of the first rank of soldiers, led by their NCOs, hurried in to seize what defendable positions they could find.

Jenkins followed his comrades and surged into the open. As soon as his boot touched the cracked concrete ground, he found himself mesmerised by the huge buildings that dominated the skyline.

"Move it, Jenkins, you soft headed twat," Woodward shouted as he shouldered into him.

Without retorting, Jenkins pushed on and surveyed the scene around him. Hundreds of German soldiers lay slumped over lumps of twisted debris that looked like it had once been a series of defences. Their bodies were hacked to pieces by the transport's machine guns and torn off limbs and clumps of bloodied flesh stained make-shift barricades.

His stomach churned at the barbaric horror and bloodshed. He experienced little remorse for what those enemy soldiers represented, yet he couldn't help but feel a tinge of sadness from the looks of horror stretched across their contorted faces. They had died watching their colleagues being carved apart by high-calibre rounds, powerless to do anything about it until they fell to the same onslaught.

"Serves the silly buggers right," Helms said and signalled at Jenkins.

On the corporal's command, Jenkins jumped into a small crater. He pushed the splattered remains of an enemy soldier out of his line of sight and taking up a firing position aimed towards the street directly ahead. Another road lay behind and to either side, seemingly following the perimeter of the dome. Several worn buildings with German words scrawled outside them sat on their immediate flanks.

When the airlock door slammed shut behind them to allow in the next batch of MEF invaders, the Second Battalion created overlapping arcs of fire, covering every possible direction the enemy could attack them from. Smaller groups of soldiers stormed into the derelict buildings, while mortar teams began setting up their 60mm and 81mm mortars.

The barren street ahead lay devoid of activity. Jenkins shifted his gaze across his field of vision but saw no signs of enemy soldiers. The silence that engulfed this section of the massive city hung heavy, although, in the distance, pillars of smoke rose and the sound of small arms fire continued from the Jewish insurgency.

After checking his left arm console and confirming the breathable atmosphere, Jenkins unclasped his helmet and removed it. He took a careful breath of air and found himself surprised at the sweet-smelling fragrances. During the absence of enemy counterattacks, Jenkins removed the cumbersome EVA equipment. He grinned at finally getting to relieve himself of its burdens.

"Contact front!" a voice called out.

Jenkins focused his gaze on the street ahead. In the distance, working its way towards them, he spotted what looked to be an armoured vehicle. Rows of Wehrmacht soldiers clung to its side or jogged alongside it, ready to throw themselves into battle against the Mars Expeditionary Force.

A wave of nervousness tingled through Jenkins's stomach as he lowered his gaze to his rifle's sight and took a deep breath. The sound of roars echoed from arriving reinforcements, further bolstering the MEF lines on both of Jenkins' flanks.

The battle for control of New Berlin colony was about to begin.

2KM NORTH OF NEW BERLIN COLONY
18.14 MST
DAY 1

Oberst Wilhelm Brandt stood atop his panzer and looked towards New Berlin as they crossed the track across the northern mountains. Tapping at the side of his streamlined EVA suit's helmet, he increased the magnification of his view for a closer look at the invading Allies. Several of their aerial craft hovered over the colony's dome, doing close flybys or no doubt collecting intelligence on troop movements. Others flew in a near-continuous loop, likely unloading supplies or men before setting off again. Two of the enemy craft paused from doing a standard patrol around the colony and made a beeline for his convoy.

Behind him lay the remnants of New Berlin's Second and Fourth Panzer Divisions. Like everyone else, he thought it had been a misunderstanding, or even an ill-timed joke about the Allies' arrival. Hours away from the nearest colony, the magnitude of what was happening struck when the reports started flowing in.

In a vain attempt to make better time, General Vogel had ordered them to abandon their heavier, sluggish vehicles and equipment. They piled as many soldiers as they could into the faster troop transports and set off to defend their home. Then the Allied air attacks began.

From out of nowhere, the highly manoeuvrable Allied craft launched blistering attacks on the German forces. Tanks and transports packed with men burst into fiery infernos under enemy missiles. The general's skilful direction of the anti-aircraft weapons on some of the modified panzers had been enough to stave off complete destruction. And for that defence, General Vogel had paid with his life.

Pressing his helmet's controls again, Brandt signalled Major Huber.

"Yes, Herr Oberst," the major said.

"Detach your task force. Tear out the enemy's throat."

"Yes, Herr Oberst," Major Huber replied. "Germany above all!"

One of the columns of panzers on the left flank of the convoy immediately broke off. Rows of panzers peeled away and made for the open ground, heading on a direct course for the Allied positions east of the colony. Cheers went up from the soldiers hanging from the transports attached to the main convey. They shouted and urged on their brethren who marched with pride to their own destruction.

Brandt hardened his heart to any swell of emotion. He took no joy in sending men of the Wehrmacht to their deaths, let alone men he had trained and led for a decade. Yet, their sacrifice stood as a necessary one. If the main convoy had any chance of stepping foot in the colony and bolstering their besieged comrades there, a blood sacrifice was required.

"Commence anti-aircraft fire," he commanded.

The rows of modified panzers with anti-aircraft weapons blared to life. Shells burst into the air towards

91

the approaching Allied craft. Anti-aircraft flak flew across the Martian sky, causing the Allied vessels to break into evasive actions. One of them peeled off and headed towards the smaller taskforce. The other ship spun about, executing reckless manoeuvres in a bid to target the main convoy.

Even as anti-aircraft shells exploded around it, the enemy craft dove towards them. Standing on top of the lead tank, Brandt held his nerve as the Allied vessel pounded towards his lead panzer. From behind him, high-calibre machine guns roared to life, unleashing torrents of furious bullets at the oncoming craft.

He gritted his teeth as he watched, smiling as the enemy craft turned after being hit. It spun about like a lame duck, eager to make an escape, but the German guns showed no mercy. They kept firing until smoke burst from the flailing craft and it finally exploded in a flash of flame and burning metal.

The anti-aircraft guns continued to fire in support of the task force, even as the main convoy turned away from them. Brandt's group made a beeline for the northern entrance to New Berlin, but Brandt's gaze remained focused on his brothers-in-arms. The task force had fended off the Allied craft and managed to inflict enough damage, forcing the vessel to withdraw. No doubt panic would be spilling through the Allied lines when they saw dozens of panzers on a direct course for their exposed soldiers. What Allied craft lingered in the area, descended like birds of prey on the task force, missiles and guns firing, and the German weaponry responded in kind.

"Germany above all!" Major Huber cried out over the comm channel again.

The men of the Second and Fourth panzer divisions cheered as their colleagues disappeared behind the dome's perimeter. After vowing to honour the memory of the brave soldiers he had sent to their deaths, Brandt turned his thoughts to the task at hand.

Just like every other senior Wehrmacht officer, his suspicions of the activities of the SS grew with every passing second. He had listened to the reports of the SS-dominated fleet's suicidal actions in stunned silence. Even more worryingly, he heard that in some theatres of the conflict, the SS had withdrawn their forces entirely. He had fought alongside the SS in the last war and although he didn't share their ideological extremes, he held a grudging admiration for their fighting abilities and their attitude towards the Jews.

As the northern entrance of the colony came into view, the cries of the panzer task force reverberated through his ears. With luck, they could fight off the Allied craft and drive right into the heart of their soldiers. Every invader who died at the steps of New Berlin brought the colony what it needed most—time. Time to deploy his reinforcements, time to dig in their defences, and time to mobilise a massive counterattack.

The reinforced outer metal doors of New Berlin's northern entrance ascended slowly as the convoy grew closer. A sense of relief washed over Brandt, even as the last of the task force fought on. Against all odds, against Allied air attacks, the Second and Fourth panzer divisions and thousands of infantry soldiers had arrived home.

They would never again leave New Berlin, one way or another.

PART 3

KILL THEM ALL

**OUTER DISTRICT – EASTERN SECTOR, NEW BERLIN
COLONY
19.21 MST
DAY 1**

Private Jenkins snarled when a German soldier vaulted into the crater he and Private Helms used as a foxhole. He tried to raise his Lee-Enfield to fire, but the Nazi jumped on him and grabbed at his face, pushing him backwards. Lifting his knife, the Nazi struggled to bury it into Jenkins's flesh. Screaming, Jenkins shoved back, creating space between them. The German growled and threw himself forwards again, but Jenkins reacted first. He levelled his Lee-Enfield at the advancing enemy and thrust the bayonet into his chest.

The Nazi soldier cried out in pain, but he still tried to lunge at Jenkins. The two men struggled and fought for control of the Lee-Enfield.

Lashing out with his knee, Jenkins caught the Nazi square in the groin. He snatched back his rifle and swung the butt of the weapon as hard as he could, knocking the wounded German to the floor of the foxhole. Without even a moment's thought, Jenkins stabbed the bayonet tip into the chest of his enemy repeatedly until the life drained from his eyes.

To his right, Helms pinned another Nazi against the side of the crater. He raised his entrenching tool and smashed the edge of the instrument against the German's skull, causing him to drop dead at his feet. Helms struck again and again, splashing chunks of skull and brain matter across his face. Between them, Private Woodward lay unmoving. His vacant gaze looked off into the distance, and his guts hung across his lap from where the grenade fragments caught him.

Somewhere to his left, Junior Sergeant Boris Alexeev cursed in Russian, long before the hulking Red Army NCO appeared. Cracks of gunfire and explosions enveloped the struggling MEF soldiers as they withstood yet another German counterattack. One of the buildings ahead of Jenkins's foxhole split apart and tumbled to the ground from another volley of MEF mortar bombs. The entire scene in front of him showed dozens of advancing Germans blanketed in a cloud of concrete and shrapnel. Men, allied and enemy alike, wailed.

"That'll show you," Helms shouted as he pulled his entrenching tool from the shattered skull of the dead Nazi. "That's for Woodward, you stupid kraut wanker." Helms buried the entrenching tool into the soft ground of the foxhole, and grabbing his rifle, took careful aim ahead.

Catching his breath, Jenkins dragged the fallen body of the enemy soldier at his feet and pushed it out of their make-shift defensive position. He took up his Lee-Enfield and looking on as the cloud of debris ahead cleared, saw a half-dozen silhouettes charging towards them.

Jenkins clicked in a fresh clip, and peering down his rifle's sight, he fired. A Volkssturm soldier tumbled to his knees, clutching his chest. Jenkins pulled the trigger again and caught him right in the jaw, and the soldier flopped back onto the ground. Shots rang back at him from the other Volkssturm soldiers, determined to avenge their fallen comrade. Ignoring the hailstorm of lead slicing the air, Jenkins steadied himself and pulled on the trigger. He butchered the Volkssturm when they tried to rush his foxhole, clearing enemy activity around the immediate vicinity of his position. While scanning for another target, he caught a blur of motion in his peripheral vision. Junior Sergeant Alexeev appeared for a moment to Jenkins's left, seeking shelter behind the bullet-riddled ruins of a gutted building. The Soviet NCO pressed a fresh magazine into his AK-47 and raised his weapon to fire. The muzzle of his AK-47 flashed in the dimming light, casting an eerie glare across the Russian's grim face. Swearing loudly in his native language, he charged ahead, fearless in the face of the advancing Wehrmacht soldiers.

The sound of German artillery shells whistling overhead forced Jenkins to duck. The ground rocked and shook from the sheer quantity of the enemy rounds. Men shrieked as shrapnel sliced through their bodies. Forcing his head up, Jenkins spied four Volkssturm soldiers in their mismatched uniforms move against his position. He lifted his weapon in time to drop one, but the remaining three attackers opened up on him. Beside him, Helms screamed when a bullet caught him in the face. Grasping at his bloodied jaw, he stumbled backwards and hit the ground.

Slipping another clip into his Lee-Enfield, Jenkins pushed himself back into a firing position.

The three advancing Germans continued to crack bullets at him as they took turns covering one another. The ground around him pinged, forcing Jenkins to act. Controlling his breathing to steady himself, he took careful aim at the lead soldier. He squeezed the trigger and watched the bullet fly wide.

With a bloodied face, Helms scrambled back beside Jenkins and began firing.

The lead Volkssturm soldier crashed to the ground, clasping at a hole in his stomach. The remaining two braved the blizzard of MEF lead and surged towards the crater in a suicidal bid.

"Crazy pricks!" Helms shouted like a wild man as he hammered on his weapon's trigger. With bullets whizzing and grenades exploding around him, he stood like a heroic monument, defiant in the face of impending death.

Jenkins witnessed Helms's relentless trigger pulls drop

German soldiers, and then Helms's chest exploded in crimson. He opened his mouth to scream, but by the time his body hit the floor of the foxhole, the life in his eyes had evaporated.

Another series of whistles streaked over the foxhole, forcing Jenkins back down. Even with a full-blown battle raging around him, the sound of his breathing filled his ears moments before the artillery shells struck. Mounds of dirt spewed into the air as the enemy artillery strike pounded the ground around him. The deafening sound of buildings bursting apart thumped against his eardrums, punctured only by the high-pitched screams of the wounded. Trembling from the sheer ferocity of the sustained enemy assault, Jenkins drove himself to get back up again.

Twenty metres ahead and to his left, Junior Sergeant Alexeev sheltered in the remains of another disembowelled building flanked by four other MEF soldiers. To his hard right, Private Byrd from D-Company stumbled around in a daze, carrying his detached left arm in his right hand. Jenkins watched in horror as blood squirted from the stump, leaving behind a crimson trail. He opened his mouth to call to the wounded soldier right when enemy bullets battered Byrd's chest.

Shouts from the rear caught Jenkins' attention. He risked a glance back and spotted reinforcements advancing from behind his crater, refilling the foxholes and defences they had seized from the German forces. Medics raced under constant enemy fire, tending to the wounded and dragging them to any shelter they could find.

A sudden movement from the edge of his vision took Jenkins by surprise. Fearing the enemy had flanked him, he spun about, ready to strike with his bayonet. He stopped as soon as he spotted the familiar patterns of British battledress. It took a further moment for him to recognise the soldier who leapt into his foxhole. Major Wellesley!

Stunned at seeing a senior officer so close to the action, Jenkins opened his mouth to speak. The major placed his hand on Jenkins's shoulder and pushed him back into a firing position.

"The enemy's that way," Major Wellesley said, while studying the enemy lines in front of him. "There's a good lad."

An unnerving silence blanketed the battlefield, interrupted by sporadic shots from the surrounding areas. The wounded muffled their cries of pain, desperate not to be picked off by a sniper in the unexpected lull in fighting. Jenkins scanned the enemy lines. German soldiers darted back and forth behind their defences.

"They're trying to buy time for their panzers, the cheeky buggers," Major Wellesley mumbled.

Jenkins tried to control his breathing as he tracked the actions of the Nazi soldiers ahead. His entire body shook, but strangely enough, he didn't experience fear. His heart went numb to the death and destruction he had witnessed over the last few hours. The ache of his limbs and the exhaustion that crept up on him in waves told him he was alive.

"Right," Major Wellesley said aloud. "We'll need a lot more armour piercing grenades and anti-tank rounds. Can't let Fritz get too cocky now, can we?"

Unsure if he was expected to answer, Jenkins risked a quick glance up at his superior officer. The major stared at the Germans ahead of them. Rows of MEF soldiers continued to mass behind whatever protection they could find as they prepared for their own moves against the defending Germans.

"You there," the major said in an abrupt tone.

After a long moment's pause, Jenkins fired another glance at the major. This time, Major Wellesley gazed down at him. He held his left hand extended out towards Jenkins, holding a polished metal flask. "Drop of scotch?"

Caught off guard by the gesture, Jenkins shook his head. "No, thank you, sir."

"Good lad," Major Wellesley said and slipped the hip flask back into his pocket. "Can't have a dull head while fighting the enemy. What's your name, young man?"

"Private Jenkins, sir."

"Ah, Jenkins. I knew a Sergeant Jenkins once. Bought it

at Normandy. Fine fellow. Salt of the earth. Any relation?"

"No, sir," Jenkins said with a shake of his head.

"Good, good," the major replied and returned his attention to the German lines.

To their left and right, groups of soldiers moved forward under the cover of dozens of guns. Jenkins observed one group running to join Junior Sergeant Alexeev in the smouldering ruins of the German building. He didn't recognise who led the platoon on the right, but he spotted anti-tank grenade attachments fixed to some of the soldier's Lee-Enfield's.

"Right." Major Wellesley pulled out his Smith and Wesson revolver. "We're about to go over the top, young Jenkins. Ready to take the fight to Jerry?"

"Yes, sir."

The major reached for a chain around his neck and placed a whistle between his lips. Giving a final glance at the soldiers on both flanks, he blew hard into the instrument. A long, shrill tone rang out, repeated throughout the area by other officers.

Dozens of Bren light machine guns blared to life, showering the enemy lines with lead. Volleys of Lee-Enfield rounds pounded the Nazi defenders as the MEF stormed forward, hurling grenades as they ran. Without so much as another word, Major Wellesley leapt up and threw himself into the firefight.

Surprised at his actions, Jenkins followed close at his heels, stumbling over the dead that littered the ground around his foxhole. The smell of sulphur, burning hair, and excrement filled his nostrils as he shoved ahead. Pushing the stench from his mind, he made his way towards the crumbling buildings on the left. Major Wellesley appeared oblivious to the bullets that sliced through the air, cutting down the MEF soldiers by the dozen.

Against all odds, the soldiers of the Mars Expeditionary Force thrust deeper into New Berlin.

EASTERN SECTOR - NEW BERLIN COLONY
20.43 MST
DAY 1

"Get down!" Sergeant McCabe yelled and pushed Private Wallace to the ground.

The German panzer wheeled towards them with a seemingly unstoppable fury. Before it could bring its guns fully on them, Privates Messi and Donaldson leaned out of their hideaways. They fired the anti-tank rounds from their modified Lee-Enfield's and ducked back down. The grenades struck the side of the panzer, grinding it to a halt. Hatches opened, allowing dense black smoke to seep from the panzer as its crew tried to escape. All were gunned down by the waiting MEF soldiers.

The news of German reinforcements arriving had spread like wildfire. After seizing the eastern entrance and key strategic points in the surrounding area, the soldiers of the Mars Expeditionary Force had made quick progress in gaining a toehold in the colony. While reinforcements continued to gush in, the forward units made a cautious advance, moving in strength to seize control of the adjacent streets. In haste they established command posts, sniper nests, mortar positions, field hospitals, and make-shift defences. With minimal Nazi resistance, the jokes started spreading that the end was nigh for the last remnants of the Third Reich. The rank-and-file genuinely believed the Wehrmacht to be on the verge of surrender.

Then the panzers struck.

The merciless German tanks and the waves of Wehrmacht soldiers that sheltered behind them pummelled the MEF lines on the left and right flanks. For a horrifying period, it looked like the German pincer movement could wrest control of the eastern entrance from the Allies. Such an action held the potential of leaving thousands of British and French troops isolated, cut off from reinforcements, and surrounded. Dread hung as heavy in the New Berlin air as the raw and pungent smell of death.

The quick deployment of every single anti-tank weapon they could find, steal, or pilfer saved the day. While most of the MEF armour had been destroyed in orbit, they held a numerical advantage on the Nazi forces within New Berlin. The MEF also held one ace up their sleeve that McCabe guessed the Germans hadn't anticipated: air superiority within the colony itself.

Too big to fit through the main entrance, the MEF units outside had moved against the external landing pad in a bid to get the transports inside. Along with support from MEF divisions within New Berlin, they seized the hangar bays beneath the colony, allowing them to bring in the transports. From what McCabe heard, it remained a time-consuming process just to get one of the craft into the domed city, but it struck him as well-worth the effort. Even one of those transports could annihilate an entire enemy platoon or battery with the push of a button.

As if on cue, one of the atmospheric troop transports jetted overhead to the cheers of the MEF soldiers hiding in the battle-damaged street. The transport rolled about as it avoided enemy anti-aircraft fire before launching two of its own missiles in reply. A heavy line of smoke rose from whatever the transport had struck. Checking that no other panzers approached, McCabe dusted himself off. Keeping his head down, he sprinted from his position.

He twisted between the large chunks of concrete that covered the street and leapt into a nearby crater. He nodded at Private Swift as he slid down the side of the pit, skidding to a halt at the bottom. McCabe turned his gaze towards the officer in the unusual uniform speaking into the long-range transmitter. He had anticipated seeing a lot of strange things in the battle for Mars. Never in a million years did he expect to be placed under the command of a West German officer.

Like every other British, French, and American soldier, McCabe had been surprised to learn of the presence of a West German delegation back in the Atacama Desert base in Chile. Seeing Germans in military uniforms, when West Germany had no official military, caused concern amongst the rank-and-file. Even more so considering the end of World War Two was less than a decade ago. Although the fresh-faced enlisted men were most likely young boys when the war ended, all the NCOs and officers looked old enough to have served in Hitler's Wehrmacht. Military discipline, the obvious need for German translators, and the fact that the West German delegation were to remain unarmed kept the simmering tensions at bay.

Yet, Nazi guns showed no discrimination when gunning down British, French, American, or West Germans alike. Like everyone else, the West German contingent had come under relentless attack since crash landing on Mars and stood side by side with their MEF allies. With every soldier needed in the fight to destroy the last fragments of the Third Reich, the MEF leadership not only turned a blind eye to the West Germans arming themselves from the Nazi dead, they utilised their experience and eagerness to atone for their country's past sins.

McCabe kept his distance from the West German officer until he finished his transmission. It bothered him to be so close to someone who probably had British blood on his hands from the last war. Yet, he took his orders like everyone else. Mad Jack had instructed him and a small group of MEF soldiers to bolster the strength of the company-sized West German contingent. Like it or not, McCabe had a job to do.

The West German officer put down his handset. "Ah, Sergeant McCabe, report."

"Oberst Henke," McCabe said, trying not to grit his teeth as he spoke.

The West German officer held up his hand, stopping him from proceeding. "I appreciate the gesture, Sergeant, but you may refer to me as Colonel. Please instruct your soldiers to refer to the men under my command by their English ranks, where applicable. Continue please, Sergeant."

"Very well, Colonel," McCabe said with a slight nod. "We took out the last panzer. It looks like the transports are taking care of the rest. Recces have confirmed there's several companies' worth of Wehrmacht and Volkssturm in the surrounding areas. They're not advancing, but we are cut off. If we are to attempt a breakout to re-join the MEF lines, I'd recommend we do it sooner rather than later and before the enemy strengthens their defences. What are your orders...sir?"

Colonel Henke motioned for McCabe to follow him.

They climbed to the top of the crater and glanced around. Dozens of MEF positions guarded their area of control, and there were no signs of enemy activity. However, the sounds of missile strikes continued to rock the colony from MEF transports pummelling the Nazi defences and their panzers. With no enemy in sight, Colonel Henke signalled for McCabe to sit back down at the edge of the crater. He studied McCabe a moment as he slid a hand into his trench coat pocket. He whipped out a packet of crumpled cigarettes and, holding his hand aloft, offered one. For a heartbeat, McCabe considered refusing but unsure of when he could restock his own supply, he accepted one. Colonel Henke lit their cigarettes with a match, took a few rapid puffs of his own and exhaled a cloud of smoke.

"Orders from Major General Hamilton. We are not to return to MEF lines. Instead, we are to proceed to the tram station in the Potsdam district west of here." After placing the tip of his cigarette between his lips, Colonel Henke reached inside his trench coat again. He slipped out a map, unfolded it, and pointed out their current location before tracing his finger towards their objective.

McCabe examined the map in detail and glanced at the crumbling buildings that surrounded them to orientate himself.

"It's roughly a kilometre ahead," Colonel Henke said as he tapped ash from his cigarette. "The Major General advised he will provide as much aerial support as possible, but as you said, Sergeant, we're surrounded on all sides, so we may need to fight our way through."

"Understood, sir. What are our orders once we reach this tram station?"

Colonel Henke grimaced as he stubbed out his cigarette on the ground.

"Our orders are to hold the station and render any assistance needed to a small group of MJ-12 operatives currently located there."

"The Black Visors," McCabe said with a frustrated sigh.

Colonel Henke nodded. "The Black Visors, Sergeant."

Although McCabe couldn't help but begrudgingly admire the Black Visors' ruthless determination in achieving their goals, he still didn't trust them. As soon as they had seized control of the command complex at the eastern entrance, the small group of masked MJ-12 operatives had melted away like ghosts without so much as a word. Even thinking about them caused his suspicions to rise. He couldn't put his finger on what bothered him, but more lay to this secretive group than met the eye.

After a short meeting with the other NCOs and officers, the understrength company of MEF and West German soldiers prepared to move. McCabe took control of the mostly MEF-filled lead platoon and laid out their plans and objectives. While the noise of battle raged around them like a brutal thunderstorm, the West German contingent and their MEF allies pushed deeper into the colony.

PERIMETER OF THE CITY CENTRE – EASTERN SECTOR
21.52 MST
DAY 1

As New Berlin's artificial weather system cast the dark shadows of night across the colony, Oberst Brandt thought over the events of the last few hours. The savagery of battle made him feel alive; years had passed since he had engaged in a real life-or-death struggle. The simmering anger that burned within him since evacuating Berlin a decade ago had boiled over. Although he would have enjoyed exacting his revenge against the Red Asiatic hordes instead, the rebelling Jews and the British soldiers made just as good targets.

Carving a swathe through the perimeter of the Jewish district, he had authorised his forces to fire indiscriminately. Entire buildings lay obliterated in their wake as his panzers rammed volleys of shells into the already dilapidated structures. At any other time, he would have allowed his panzers to steamroll over the area to drive home the message of National Socialist hegemony, but he had his orders. Moving beyond the Jewish ghetto, he led the vanguard of the attack on the British right flank. At one point, he could taste success as he pushed the invaders from the colony. Then their desperate, near-suicidal counterattacks began.

As much as he'd never admit it in public, he admired the Allied fighting spirit. Even in the face of superior German armour, the Allies fought for every inch of ground. They hurled wave after wave of their soldiers at the panzers and ground the German advance to a halt with frantic anti-tank grenades and missiles from their heavily armed aerial transport vessels. It had been a good fight, pitting German against Britisher in close-quarter combat while his panzers showered them with shells and bullets. Even with the Allied aerial craft bombing them in endless waves, he remained positive that the force of National Socialist convictions could deliver victory to them.

And then that fool Generalfeldmarschall Seidel intervened.

Rather than let him achieve glory and bring honour to the Führer, that dithering dotard ordered Brandt to not only halt his attacks, but to withdraw his forces to defend the centre of New Berlin. To make matters worse, Generalfeldmarschall Seidel split up his panzer divisions to use them for static defence rather than utilising them for steamrolling through the enemy lines. Sitting atop his panzer, camouflaged amongst the rubble of his blazing city, Brandt studied the group of advancing enemy soldiers through the lens of his binoculars.

"It looks like a few platoon's worth of soldiers, Herr Oberst," Captain Fischer said, lowering his own binoculars momentarily. "Perhaps an under-sized company. They must be cut off."

"Indeed," Brandt said as he tracked their movements.

Away from the prying eyes of the aerial craft that dominated the New Berlin skyline, the Wehrmacht units under his command sheltered in abandoned shops and factories. Those who had lived through their first battle with the British remained impatient to avenge their fallen. Under any other circumstances, he would have granted them their wish, but the generalfeldmarschall's orders stood explicitly clear. Brandt was to hold his position and engage the enemy only if fired upon.

"It looks like they're heading in the direction of the Potsdam district," Captain Fischer continued. "I've received reports of other groups moving in that direction. We have several evacuation centres there for our civilians. Perhaps they mean to avenge themselves on our citizenry, Herr Oberst? Surely, Generalfeldmarschall Seidel will allow us to intervene on such grounds."

"You would think," Brandt grumbled.

He rested his binoculars on the panzer hull and reached for his radio's handset. He switched the frequency to the generalfeldmarschall's command post, relayed his findings and requested orders. Static interference crackled and popped until a shaky, distorted voice appeared on the other end. In the background, an explosion from an Allied missile attack temporarily cut the transmission. When the signal returned, the terrified officer at the command post relayed Generalfeldmarschall Seidel's orders. They were to do nothing more than continue to protect the defensive lines around the centre of the city until the Allied airborne attacks could be halted. The civilian population evacuated into the colony's centre needed to be safeguarded at all costs. The counterattack being planned was to be led by Brandt's rival—Oberst Weber.

Brandt found himself ordered again to do nothing. Slamming down his transmitter's handset, he cursed under his breath. He ran a hand under his chin and scratched his skin as he thought. After a moment, he raised the binoculars to his eyes again. The advancing under-strength company continued on their course parallel to his position. Like a predator ready to mete out a death blow, he could lash out at them, catch them in his claws. But unless they turned towards him, he remained unable to engage. The frustration within him growing, he lowered his binoculars and turned to Captain Fischer.

"I will not have my hands tied behind my back while our city burns. Ready the men to move. It's time to get our hands dirty."

Without delay, Captain Fischer sprang from the panzer and sprinted towards the closest factory. Seconds later, German soldiers poured from their hideouts, brandishing their weapons. While Brandt turned his panzers about to cut off the Allied advance, the infantry men broke down into smaller groups to hit the unsuspecting British company from the flanks and rear.

With his gaze scanning the sky above for signs of Allied aerial craft, his panzers lumbered down one of the ravaged streets. He listened to the movements of the infantry on his comm, plotting out their locations in his mind. With luck, they could sneak through the alleyways that lined the Allied approach and set up an ambush to cut them to pieces. Spurring his panzers onwards, he watched German soldiers creep closer. His lead panzer ground to a halt near the intersection connecting to the street the unsuspecting British found themselves traversing. After confirming everyone stood ready, he gave the order, and his panzers drove forward again.

Raising his pistol, he smiled when his lead panzer wheeled about and turned right into the head of the Allied invaders. Stunned British soldiers froze at the sight of so many armoured monsters storming towards them. The panzers boomed to life.

Shells sent the British soldiers scurrying for cover and burst those too slow to react to pieces. Machine gun fire blared with unrepentant vehemence as the infantry units on the flanks let loose their grenades. Like gazelles being hunted by a pack of starved predators, the Allied force swung about from side-to-side unsure of where to concentrate their fire.

Ushering the infantry behind his panzers onwards, Brandt leapt down onto the rubble-strewn ground. Bullets pinged around him as the British company panic-fired at the Wehrmacht soldiers attacking them from all directions. Heart thumping, Brandt ignored the bullets whizzing through the air, took aim with his Luger, and fired a single shot at a British soldier, who hit the ground, clasping at his neck. From the left flank and the rear, his infantry units advanced with their bayonets fixed, stabbing and slashing at the enemy. Men from both sides fell to the destructive flurry of lead or the wave of sharpened blades fixed to the end of rifles.

After a few short minutes, the skirmish ended. The bodies of British soldiers lay mangled across the ruined street. Limbs sat severed atop rubble, and chunks of flesh and blood dripped from the walls of broken shops and burnt-out houses. A handful of British soldiers who had thrown down their arms and surrendered stood encircled by the men of the Wehrmacht.

Taking off his hat to wipe his brow, Brandt moved in closer to inspect his prisoners. He holstered his weapon as he approached and stopped at the feet of a soldier wearing a colour sergeant's stripes. The NCO wheezed as he struggled to breathe. His left hand covered a gaping wound in his stomach, and he stretched out his bloodied right hand. As if studying an oddity, Brandt glared down at the wounded man.

The prisoner muttered something over and over again.

"What is he saying?" Brandt asked, turning to Captain Fischer.

"He's requesting a medic and asking for help."

Brandt returned his attention to the wounded colour sergeant. "I see." Taking to a knee, he extended his gloved left hand towards the British NCO. "Come on," he said softly, knowing the soldier didn't understand him. "Come on. I'll get you some help."

The British colour sergeant nodded in earnest when his hand connected with Brandt's. He forced a smile across his pained face and continued chattering in his bastard tongue as Brandt pulled him up. The smile faded the moment Brandt thrust his blade into the colour sergeant's chest. With shock stamped across his face, the prisoner looked down and blinked at the knife buried deep in his flesh. Smiling, Brandt twisted his blade, and the light faded from the prisoner's eyes.

"There's your help." Brandt released the body and let it slump back onto the hard ground.

The captured British soldiers all started shouting. Even with bayonets and barrels aimed at them, some of them made to lunge at their captors.

Wiping the blood from his knife, Brandt nodded towards Captain Fischer. "Well, what are you waiting for, Captain?

Execute them."

Grinning from ear to ear, Brandt returned to his panzer to the sound of a volley of shots.

COMMAND AND CONTROL BUILDING, GOVERNMENT DISTRICT
22.29 MST
DAY 1

Reichsführer Wagner marvelled at his creation. Anna Bailey's chest rose and fell where she lay on the trolley. Her eyelids were closed as if in a peaceful slumber. His gaze worked their way over the curves hidden beneath her hospital gown and rested on the delicate features of her face. Although her new Hollow body looked identical to her wounded, original body, something had changed. She looked angelic.

Slipping off the glove on his right hand, he took a step closer. With his fingers trembling in anticipation, he extended a hand towards her soft porcelain skin. The need to touch her grew stronger, urging him on. The moment his fingertips could feel the warmth of her cheek, Anna let out a sigh. With her eyes closed, she fidgeted, as if searching for a more comfortable position. Wagner snapped his hand back and nearly laughed. Feeling like a schoolboy caught red-handed, he pulled his glove back on and beamed down at his prize.

"There's no need for games, Miss Bailey. I know you're awake."

Wearing a smile as warm as the kiss from a summer sun, Anna opened her piercing blue eyes. She stretched her limbs before resting her head against her shoulder like a pillow and gazed up at him. A surge of longing rushed through Wagner as he drank in the sight of her. Yet he knew her well enough to know she was attempting to manipulate him. Even as she tried to tease him with her gaze, out of his periphery vision, he noticed her index finger probe the strap restraining her left hand.

"I'm surprised you don't have a new medal pinned to your chest, Herr Reichsführer." A small smile crept across her face. "After all the lives you've taken to achieve your goals, I would have thought the Führer himself would be here in person to reward you."

Wagner placed his hands behind his back and smiled. "This has never been about rewards, Miss Bailey. This is about humanity's future. Everything we have achieved together brings us one step closer to unlocking the potential that we as a race have long since forgotten."

"And the Jewish laborers you experimented on," Anna said, her voice hardening. "Will they be remembered?"

"Casualties of war," he said in a calm voice.

Reaching across from where he stood, Wagner pulled out a chair. After placing it so that he sat directly in Anna's eyeline, he took his seat. She looked longingly at him, and yet, buried beneath those deep blue eyes, he sensed her rage. If at any point she could free herself, he held no doubt that she'd snap his neck like a twig.

"Have you ever met any of the so-called native humans that live on Mars, Miss Bailey?"

"Briefly, Herr Reichsführer."

"These Natives have a saying. 'We have always been here.' Have you ever heard this expression?"

"I can't say that I have."

Wagner nodded at that. For a moment, he thought back to his days of being a schoolteacher. Long before the war and the Nazi party; before fate and providence sent him on his hallowed journey. It felt like a lifetime ago, yet he missed shaping the minds of the next generation. More than anything, he wished he could make Anna see the truth, like the pupils he had educated. If only she knew what her sacrifice meant for humanity and how humankind would benefit.

"Some of my colleagues believe this expression merely states the obvious," Wagner said, "that humanity has always lived on this planet. That alone opens another series of questions as to how two branches of the same species could evolve on two separate worlds, does it not?"

"I suppose so, Herr Reichsführer. One I'm sure you and your learned colleagues have solved over the last decade."

"Quite so. However, I take this phrase to mean something

entirely different. That everyone is doing exactly what they should be doing at the right place and the right time. You and I have always been in this moment, Miss Bailey. We were always destined to be here and play our respective parts."

Now Anna smiled back. Even when she checked the straps that held her down for weaknesses, she maintained her flirtatious behaviour. Every gesture and movement she made was calculated to influence him. He sensed it from the way his heartbeat increased at the sight of her bare shoulder or the way she bit the inside of her lower lip from time to time; she'd glance away as soon as he caught her.

Despite her games, the need for her to understand him overpowered his own biological urges. In all the universe, he had never known a woman like her. In the old world, he could never be with someone of Jewish descent, but they stood on the brink of a new epoch. If he could make her understand her place, then she could decide that place lay at his side.

Wagner shifted his gaze to the ground. "I know I have hurt people. I know you have witnessed this and have experienced some of this cruelty first-hand. But everything I have done was meant to save lives in the wars to come. Imagine a world where soldiers cannot be killed, Miss Bailey. One where all their experience and training can be saved, ready to be shared with another generation of soldiers. In time, we may be able to develop a system of bringing soldiers killed on the battlefield back to life. This is one of the reasons behind the Hollow Programme, to usher in a new era of warfare."

"I can see you are passionate about this," Anna said, focusing the full force of her attention upon him. "Even I must admit, transferring consciousness from one body to another has endless military capabilities. But the idea of my experiences and memories being shared with others is, quite frankly, offensive. They are mine and mine alone. As for dying, every soldier knows what they sign up for. The fear of death has kept me alive on more occasions than I care to remember. Remove that and all you'll have are pigs willingly marching to the slaughter."

"You still don't understand," Wagner said with a shake of his head. "You still can't see."

Wagner rose to his feet and moved across the room towards one of the desks. He removed his hat and gloves and placed them neatly side by side on the desk. Next, he pulled off his trench coat, folded it, and sat it across the back of one of the chairs. Then he spun about and unholstered his sidearm. Anna studied the weapon in his hand before he placed that, too, on the desk.

Wagner slipped a hand into his pocket and produced a set of keys. While he ordered his thoughts, he fidgeted nervously with the keys. After a brief moment of hesitation, he took a few paces towards Anna's trolley, the keys dangling from his finger.

"The natives of this world tell a story," he began. "A story that predates our own remembered history. A story of a great war between the ancient masters and the lesser worlds, one which transformed this once-rich paradise into the barren hellhole we call Mars. This war was fought with weapons of unimaginable destruction, but on the ground, soldiers were required. These soldiers needed to be resilient, obedient, and utterly devoted to their just cause. The natives say that many of these soldiers came from Earth."

He peered down at Anna's face, searching for any sign of genuine interest. He saw what she wanted him to see, but in her eyes, he sensed her fury and disbelief.

"A fascinating story, Herr Reichsführer."

Taking a step closer to the foot of her bed, he held the jumble of keys out. After flicking through them, he selected one and inserted it into the lock that restrained her right foot. With a careful turn the lock sprung open. Anna moved her ankle from side to side, lifting it slightly, clearly unsure why he would take such a risk. With one limb free, she became more dangerous than the average prisoner. He glanced up at her again, and curiosity furrowed across her brows.

"As the war raged, the ancient masters, the false gods of our history, faltered. They turned their eyes upon our world, a planet filled with primitives, once obedient to the false gods but now in open rebellion. They unleashed their vengeance, but the people of this world paid the price. The so-called natives, an advanced race in their own right, took pity upon our child-like ancestors. They sacrificed their own home world that ours may live."

Leaning across her, he unlocked her left ankle. She pulled her legs in closer to her. At any point she could lash out, locking him in a vice-like grip before snapping his neck. Instead, she studied him, her eyebrows narrowing.

"With the lesser races on the verge of winning, the old gods retreated to their heavenly lair, turning their backs on the fallen and leaving them to their own devices. In time, all memory of their presence was forgotten or removed, save for myths and ancient stories. Civilisations that had thrived on Earth, bringing us knowledge and enlightenment not seen again until this century, collapsed into the dust. We descended once again into savagery, everything we had once been forgotten to the mists of time."

Pacing to the head of the bed, Wagner gazed down at his captive. With a deep breath, he leaned across her to free her left hand. At any point, she could sink her teeth into his neck and tear out his throat. With her left hand free, nothing stood in her way of choking him or striking him hard enough to knock him unconscious. But she moved her free hand to her stomach and rested it there while she watched him.

"According to the natives, the old gods are rising again. These so-called Annunaki have awoken from their ancient slumber and cast their greedy eyes on what was once theirs. They covet their place in the universe. While this is happening, our people are busy fighting pointless wars based on race, resources, and territory. We are not ready, Miss Bailey. But thanks to my work, we will be."

With another twist of his wrist, Wagner freed the last of Anna's restraints and took a step back. She sat upright on her trolley and caressed her wrists. He took another step away, giving her the space to swing her feet off the trolley. Watching him, she moved forward and stood in front of him. She stretched her limbs and rotated her joints.

"I have one final question for you, Herr Reichsführer."

She flexed her fingers into fists. "This talk of old gods I take to mean aliens of some sort. Is that correct? Surely this is the stuff of legends."

Wagner chuckled. "Why, of course, Miss Bailey. There is no such thing as aliens, that I am aware of. Only humans killing other humans. The way it's always been."

Anna took another step towards him until she stood within arm's length. The scent of her hair invigorated him, and the sight of her face so close to his set his blood on fire. If he was to die, he could think of no other sight in the world to be his last.

"Well," she said, pushing a strand of hair behind her ear, "I would like to say this has been a pleasure, Herr Reichsführer, but, quite frankly, you're a monster. I don't agree with torture myself, but I would indeed enjoy making you suffer for as long as possible. Luckily for you, I've had quite enough of your company, so I shall bid you adieu, you Nazi pig."

She lunged.

Wagner didn't see the blow coming but sensed a momentary blur. He turned to see her fist had halted centimetres from his face.

He smirked.

In disbelief, Anna whipped her fist back and lashed out with the other. It looked like a deathblow if Wagner had ever seen one, but her hand froze again before it could strike him.

He turned his back on her and paced across the room towards his hat, trench coat, and gun. The soft patter of her feet sounded when she raced to leap at him or snap his neck. After he reached the desk, he spun about and pulled on his trench coat.

Anna's face boiled red with fury, and she lashed out with her limbs, but her every attack was blocked from connecting to his body by an unseen force. She screamed as she exerted her reserves of energy to tear him to pieces but to no avail. He slipped on his gloves and hat and picked up his sidearm. He held it out towards her and offered no resistance when she snatched it from his hand. She cocked it and aimed the weapon right at his forehead, but as her finger inched for the trigger, her entire hand started trembling. Written across her face was her desire to kill him and the growing frustration at being stopped by some invisible entity.

"Sit," he commanded.

Without hesitation, she took a seat on the nearest chair. He snatched back his weapon and holstered it. Wagner grinned as she sat there, her hands resting on her knees. Her head tilted slightly upright, and she gazed straight ahead, unmoving, like a well-trained dog.

"You're a Hollow now," Wagner said. "Devoid of soul and free will. Your personality, memories, and training remain yours, but you are mine to command now. You are the first of many, Miss Bailey. You are the mother of hundreds of thousands of unborn children that will inhabit bodies even more advanced than yours. You and your kind will take humanity into the next era. Your progeny will help us forge a new identity. One where we are no longer Aryan, Jew, Saxon, or Slav. One where we are all Terran."

Frozen on her seat, a single tear trickled from Anna's eye.

POTSDAM DISTRICT, 4KM FROM THE CITY CENTRE
22.54 MST
DAY 1

Tracer rounds leapt out from the darkness and pounded towards the MEF. Men relayed enemy locations when they bounded between the heaps of rubble, firing as they ran. Towards the end of the street, McCabe could see the entrance to the underground Potsdam tram station.

"Contact right!" Sergeant McCabe exclaimed when a new wave of German fire opened up on them. "Two hundred metres. Suppressive fire now!"

The MEF armed with Bren light machine guns belched lead at his order, showering the advancing Wehrmacht soldiers. The men of the MEF and their West German allies ducked behind what cover they could find and kept the pressure on the Nazi forces trying to flank them. The Germans tossed grenades at them from the darkness, causing ripples of flame to dance across the surreal night.

McCabe raised his Lee-Enfield, and aiming at one of the enemy soldiers, fired twice, catching him in the torso. With flailing arms, the Nazi soldier hit the ground, but two more of his colleagues rushed from the nearby alley and fired back at McCabe.

Bullets filled the air, downing anyone not fast enough to find cover on the ravaged street. Howls of distress from friend and foe alike carried in the air, mixing with the oily smell of burning panzers and smouldering apartment blocks, giving the scene a hellish disposition. As the Germans flowed out from the shadows, they yelled and cursed when they threw themselves at the soldiers of the MEF.

"Sergeant McCabe," Colonel Henke called over the comm. "Your platoon is the closest. We must link up with our forces at the Potsdam station. Move First Platoon to the objective. We'll cover you."

"Understood, sir," McCabe said with a nod before turning to his men. "First Platoon, on me".

McCabe turned to face the enemy, and lifting his weapon again, he squeezed the trigger. Bullets leapt from his rifle towards the advancing Nazis. He ducked down to reload. Enemy lead pinged over him. Somewhere to his left, Germans shouted at one another, and he wondered if the Wehrmacht had just realised they were mostly fighting their own countrymen. Those from his platoon crawled and crouched their way over to the shell of the panzer he sheltered behind. They kept their weapons on the enemy, firing back as they awaited instructions.

"We need to join up with our soldiers in the station," McCabe roared at Corporal Boggs and the West German Corporal Maier. "I'll take Section One, you two lay down as much cover as possible. Once we have the entrance secured, Boggs, you and your boys follow, and then you, Maier. Understood?"

"Yes, Sergeant," they said in unison.

With a nod of good luck, McCabe tapped the soldier nearest to him on his shoulder. He emptied his ammo clip before bolting towards another pile of bricks from an eviscerated house. He landed with a rough grunt and turned to confirm his section followed close behind. Aiming his Lee-Enfield at the Germans, he let off another series of shots. With his section huddled behind what shelter they could utilise, he reloaded and glanced back at Corporals Boggs and Maier. At his signal, both sections opened up, laying down suppressive fire to give Section One some cover. Taking a deep breath, McCabe leapt up and, keeping his head low, charged towards the tram station.

As he ran, he dodged behind piles of debris, as well as Allied and Nazi dead. He ducked behind chunks of brick and fired back at a small group of Germans when they burst from the shadows. Pausing to reload, he took a deep breath before pushing on again. Even in the darkness, his senses sharpened to the noise and signs of movement. Despite exhaustion from the day's exertion, he bellowed his approach at the MEF positions as he and his section ran for cover.

McCabe landed between four grubby looking MEF soldiers. "Who's in charge here?"

They glanced around at one another in between taking pot shots. After deliberations carried out entirely by confused looks, the soldier nearest McCabe answered. "I think you are, Sarge." The tired-looking private slipped a fresh clip into his Bren.

Grunting, McCabe glanced down at the steps that led into the underground tram station. "Have we many lads down there?"

"Not sure, Sarge," the private said in between unleashing controlled bursts from his Bren. "Sergeant Paxton led a platoon from Eighth Battalion down there about a half hour ago. Haven't heard from them since, but Jerry hasn't come gunning for us, either, so not sure what's happening."

"Are the Black Visors with them?"

"Yeah, Sarge. Four of them altogether. A paddy, a paki, and two skirts, if you can believe that."

"Wash your mouth out, sunshine," McCabe growled.

The private spat on the ground and held McCabe's glare. A flurry of bullets pounding the ground around him pulled his attention back to his Bren's sights.

117

McCabe slapped a fresh clip into his Lee-Enfield and gestured at his section to follow. Ready for whatever lurked below, they stormed down the stairway and took up positions at the entrance to the tram platform. Peering through the small window on the double doors, he spied a single tram on the tracks to his left and what looked like ticket stands and small confectionary shops to the right. He counted at least ten bodies in Wehrmacht uniform slumped along the platform, stripped of their weapons. Bullet holes dotted every wall. After dividing his section to split and take the left and right flanks respectively, he pushed through the doors.

Rushing towards the tram, checking for signs of friend or foe alike, McCabe's blood turned to ice at the sound of a gun cocking. He spun about and came face to face with the familiar black and red uniform of a Black Visor. From her size and stature, he instantly recognised Noid. Signalling at his men to stand down, he lowered his weapon and approached her.

"You should really check behind doors when you're clearing a room, Sergeant," she chided and holstered her sidearm. "Be wary of little people like me."

"Where's Sergeant Paxton?" he asked as his section spread out, heeding Noid's warning and checking the remainder of the platform.

"There's an emergency exit on the opposite side of the platform," she said with a nod in the direction. "The Germans tried to take us by surprise, so he did his job. I think he's dead, but some of his boys are in place. It's a shame. I quite liked him."

A flush of anger rushed through McCabe at Noid's tone. Everything that the MEF experienced since crash-landing on Mars was like a game to the Black Visors. Outside, men were dying to fulfil whatever MJ-12's secretive objectives happened to be. Sergeant Paxton and his men had given their lives to hold their position, but for what?

"Who's in charge here?" he demanded.

"Who do you think?" Dub called out.

Turning about, McCabe spotted the balaclava-wearing Irishman as he exited the tram. With his strange semi-automatic weapon dangling at his side, the leader of the Black Visors strolled up to him and came to a stop a few steps away.

"A pleasure to see you as always, Sergeant McCabe," the Irishman continued, extending his hand in greeting.

Ignoring him, McCabe opened a channel to Colonel Henke and confirmed they held the platform. Within minutes, the surviving MEF and their West German allies filled the platform and fortified the tram station's defences for the inevitable Wehrmacht counterattack. Twelve of their number lay dead, and another twenty sported a variety of injuries, some near fatal. As soon as they had the tram station fully secured, Colonel Henke and his officers pulled the surviving NCOs and senior privates together. Lighting up cigarettes, they gathered near the tram for a meeting with the Black Visors to decide on their next course of action.

After seeing yet more British casualties stretched across the cold floor, McCabe's temper flared again. Death walked hand in hand with soldiering, but the aloofness of the MJ-12 operatives bothered him. Not just their interaction with the mysterious human back at the Russian Liberation Army base, but the things they said and how they said them ate away at the back of his mind. Similar to having a word on the tip of one's tongue, yet not being able to say it, he couldn't place what irritated him about their behaviour, but he needed answers.

"We're on a bit of a time limit," Dub said, checking his watch, "so let's keep this brief. Big Mo is rigging up one of the trams as we speak. We're going to take it to a station near Alexanderplatz. There's an access tunnel outside the station. If we take it, it'll lead us to the sewers. From there, we can bypass the Wehrmacht and SS patrols and move directly into the government district. After that, my team will do the rest. We just need you to keep the back door open."

"Won't there be patrols blocking us from using the tram system?" Colonel Henke said while checking his own map of New Berlin.

"Possibly," Dub conceded, "but that's a risk I'm willing

to take and why we need your men. This is the most direct route to the government district. The only other option is to go above ground, and that means fighting our way through a couple of Wehrmacht and Volkssturm divisions. My hope is that the continued Jewish insurgency, as well as the MEF's advance, will keep their forces below ground to a minimum."

Colonel Henke rubbed his chin and shook his head, seemingly unconvinced with the answer.

"This will work," Dub pressed. "Even if we do run into a patrol, it'll be considerably smaller than what we'll face above ground. We need to get to the government district before the SS turns on the Wehrmacht. Otherwise, it'll be a bloodbath."

The assembled NCOs and officers eyed one another. Sensing his moment to force the Black Visor's hand, McCabe cleared his throat and asked the burning question that ate away at him since they first crossed paths.

"Why?"

"Why what?" Dub snapped back.

"Why are you so determined to lead an understrength company, completely cut off from reinforcements and supplies, right into the heart of Nazi territory. What are you after?"

Dub fired a quick glance at his comrades, like he was seeking a prompt before he returned his full attention to the British sergeant. He remained quiet for a few seconds longer, blinking his eyes as if processing the question.

"That's MJ-12 business, Sergeant. It's need-to-know and right now, you don't need to know."

"I say we do need to know," McCabe said, unable to mask the rising fury in his voice. "Before I take my soldiers any farther, I want to know what they're going to fight and die for."

"Sergeant," Colonel Henke said in a conciliatory voice.

McCabe ignored the colonel. The anger within him boiled over and burned through his flesh. The faces of his men killed aboard the USAF North Carolina flashed in front of his eyes. He saw dozens more, all young men with no families, gunned down by RLA weapons and the automated defences of New Berlin. No one would mourn them at home. No tombstones would be erected for them, no parades thrown on the streets of London. They died frightened and alone, millions of miles from anything resembling home. The least they deserved was the truth.

"Have we got a problem here, Sergeant?" Dub said, turning his body towards McCabe.

"You're damned right we have a problem," McCabe spat back. "I saw you with that strange-looking human. I heard what you spoke about. Since we've crossed paths, I've listened to every word you've said. Particle weapons. Flexi-plastic. Exo-suits. MOF. All of it. You always seem to know what's about to happen next, and I want to know why. I want to know the real reason my men have died on this godforsaken rock."

"Sergeant," Colonel Henke said again, his voice firmer.

He took a step closer, but McCabe ignored him again and kept his gaze locked on the Irishman, refusing to back down. With every passing second, his anger bubbled and grew like a volcano threatening to explode.

"Colonel Henke," Dub said, finally breaking eye contact with McCabe. "MJ-12 has authorised us to—"

"I don't give a flying damn!" McCabe thundered, cutting across him. "That's another thing. What in the hell type of Irish accent is that? Both my parents are Irish, and I sure as shit don't recognise it. Same as your three little cohorts over there. I can tell they're English, but never in my life have I heard accents like that, and I've been stationed in every part of Britain that has an army base. I say you're all a bunch of damned liars."

"Sergeant McCabe!" Colonel Henke shouted. "You are out of line. You will cease this immediately."

McCabe turned his rage on Colonel Henke, who glared back at him, but McCabe didn't falter. They could line him up against a wall and shoot him for insubordination, but he refused to play along anymore. His men relied on him to lead. He asked nothing of them that he wouldn't do himself, but this was a step too far.

"No."

McCabe's curt answer caused the platform to fall

deathly silent. The NCOs and officers stood rooted to the spot, shocked at his behaviour, especially towards a senior officer. A flicker of surprise cut across Colonel Henke's stony features, but quickly faded. McCabe knew that most of the officers of the make-shift company came from the West German delegation, but three-quarters of the NCOs happened to be British. Half of the private soldiers wore British or French battle dress, equally divided amongst the West German platoons.

McCabe glanced over the faces of the officers and NCOs that surrounded him. From their worried expressions, he feared their platoons had overheard everything. On the periphery of McCabe's vision, British and French soldiers moved quietly closer to one another while turning to face their West German comrades. Whereas minutes ago, they had fought side by side, McCabe sensed an invisible canyon cut its way through the company. Rifles moved from shoulders to hands, and fingers caressed triggers.

As the tension grew, one of the West German officers reached for his pistol and made to apprehend McCabe, but Colonel Henke raised his hand to keep the officer in place, stopping the situation from boiling over. McCabe flicked his gaze from side to side. The wrong move could spark bloodshed.

Clearing his throat, Colonel Henke held his palms open and gestured towards the officers and NCOs. He completed a full circle, driving home the need for calm until his gaze rested on McCabe.

"Sergeant McCabe," Colonel Henke said in a calm but firm tone. "While I encourage input from all officers and NCOs under my command, never forget that I am your commanding officer. As such, I will ask the questions, not you. Disregard my orders again and I shall report it directly to the relevant MEF authorities and have you court-marshalled for insubordination. Do I make myself clear?"

Before McCabe could respond, Colonel Henke switched his focus to Dub. "My senior NCO has a point. Too much has been asked of us with too little information. I will not commit any more of the men under my command without knowing the reasons or the objectives. As commanding officer, you may report me and me alone to your superiors, should you wish. I accept full responsibility."

In a single move, the colonel had publicly reprimanded McCabe for his actions and pushed his demand for answers of the Black Visors. The soldiers who had nearly turned their guns on one another seconds ago now concentrated on the four MJ-12 operatives.

Dub stared them down. His gaze moved across them one at a time. His hand wasn't far from the pistol strapped to his waist.

"Dub, we're running out of time, mate," Big Mo whispered, loud enough for everyone to hear.

Dub rubbed his temples. "Christ almighty. Fine." He threw a glance back at his colleagues before facing the crowd of MEF and West German officers and NCOs. "There's things we can't talk about, and if that costs us your support, so be it. The reason we're here is two-fold: to rescue the person Sergeant McCabe saw us with earlier on. Gya, a leader of the Native Martians. The second asset is a former British MI6 operative named Anna Bailey. Right now, she's being held in a secure location within the Command and Control complex in the government district. It is imperative that we rescue her before the SS turn on the Wehrmacht. And, believe me, they will turn on them."

"How do you know they'll turn on their own people?" McCabe pressed.

Dub glanced back at his colleagues. They gazed back at him and shrugged. Dub wheeled about to continue speaking, but then Smack chimed in.

"Because the SS want to surrender to the MEF. In order to do so, they need the Wehrmacht destroyed. They're hoping you'll bleed them dry first. When they're weak enough, the SS will make their move."

"But that makes no sense," Colonel Henke said. "There have always been historic tensions between the groups, but never any open hostilities. The SS are sworn to serve the Führer until death. They would rather die than break their oaths."

"They'll do as he bids them, and right now, that's what the bastard wants," Noid said from Dub's side. "There's technology on this planet that's worth far more than fighting the last battle in a long-since ended war."

McCabe folded his arms. "Such as?"

"Sergeant, please!" Dub exclaimed. "Did you not hear me? There's a woman, one of *your* country's operatives, being tortured and held by the SS. Time is of the essence. I'll answer any other questions you have when I can, but right now time is running out. Are you with us or not?"

The NCOs and officers glanced at one another, whispering under their breath at the nuggets of information. Colonel Henke turned to focus his concentration on McCabe, and they studied one another. As much as he didn't trust the Black Visors, McCabe couldn't see any other options. They were already behind enemy lines and if they chose to disobey orders, they'd still have to fight their way back. He remained unsure about their plan, but something about the way Dub spoke about the imprisoned MI6 operative struck him as genuine. After a few moments of silent deliberation, McCabe gave Colonel Henke gave the slightest of nods. The colonel remained quiet for a few seconds before answering.

"We're with you," Colonel Henke said. "Although I have a slight amendment to your plan. One which I believe will increase the odds of the success of our mission. However, given the recent...tension and the hostilities outside, I'm reluctant to suggest it."

"Go on," Dub said, his eyes narrowing to slits.

Colonel Henke spun about and waved his hand. A West German private sitting amongst his colleagues jumped to his feet. With a large bag slung over his shoulder, he raced to his commanding officer's side. Clicking his boots, he placed the bag at the colonel's feet. He took a step back and saluted before scurrying off.

"God forgive me," Colonel Henke muttered under his breath. He knelt over the bag and unzipped it. With a heavy sigh, he placed a hand inside and pulled up a Wehrmacht uniform, taken from one of the dead that littered the tram station. "I will order my soldiers to don these uniforms.

Should we run into any patrols, we may be able to convince them we are on their side."

An uneasy silence passed over the MEF and West Germans again, until Dub shattered it.

"Fine. Great plan," he said. "Grab your gear and let's move. Time is running out."

The understrength company sprang into action. Leaving enough soldiers behind to hold the station, the rest piled into the waiting tram.

With tensions momentarily subsided, McCabe, the MEF, the Black Visors, and the West German delegation set off to find Anna Bailey.

CITY CENTRE, WEHRMACHT COMMAND POST
23.27 MST
DAY 1

Generalfeldmarschall Seidel glared out the window of his command post and stared over at the colony blanketed in darkness beneath him. Standing on the roof of the building he had occupied to oversee the battle left him vulnerable to lurking snipers, but he didn't care. In less than a day, the Allies had not only survived the attacks in orbit but had fought their way into New Berlin. Whether by Allied or SS bullet, he wasn't long for this world.

In the distance, the flashes of muzzle fire lit up the night as ally and enemy alike battled for ownership of the colony's streets. Even with panzers and waves of reinforcements, he remained unable to halt the enemy's momentum, no thanks to their heavily armed aerial craft. High above him, where the dome reached its zenith, one of those craft hung there, no doubt relaying the position of his Wehrmacht forces so they could pound them with mortar, artillery, and missile strikes. Beneath him, his men were dying in their hundreds and he stood powerless to stop their slaughter.

Seidel removed his hat, and rubbing his tired face, he paced over to the far side of the roof. Staring at the iron ring around the government district, he felt the gaze of the SS snipers upon him. He imagined them reporting his appearance to their direct superiors, who in turn would pass the message further up the chain of command.

In his mind's eye, he pictured Reichsführer Wagner smiling at the news as he sat behind his comfy desk. With a single word, he could order Seidel's death and put him out of his misery. As if tempting fate, Seidel pulled out a cigarette from his cigarette box and lit it. He puffed on it in contentment, holding the cherry of the cigarette for all the world to see. Even a bad sniper could home in on such a giveaway.

The fatal shot never came. A smirk crossed his face as he again thought of Reichsführer Wagner ordering no action to be taken, knowing full well he'd suffer more alive than dead. Taking a step closer to the ledge, he peered over the edge into the streets below. Hundreds of figures packed the cordoned off streets in front of the government district, wandering aimlessly or hollering for protection. Evacuated civilians from the poorer outer areas of the colony mixed with the slightly more affluent ones driven from their homes by the raging Jewish insurgency. Sobs and wails filled the chilly night air, giving the burning colony a nightmarish feel.

Each of them cried out to their god-like messiah to deliver them from the savagery of the approaching Allies, but their words fell on deaf ears. Hidden behind rows of barbed wired, reinforced concrete, and thousands of fanatics, the Führer refused to hear them. The man who had led their country to destruction before promising a new life on this alien world remained oblivious to his people's suffering. Like back in the old country, people were nothing more than pawns to him, disposable tools to be utilised and discarded at a whim, useful to further his own delusions.

"We only have ourselves to blame," Seidel muttered.

At any other point in his life, to say such a thing, let alone think it, would be treason. Yet that didn't change it from being true. Deep down, he believed everyone in the colony was starting to realise it. They had run from their mistakes once before. Now, their sins had caught up with them, and they would suffer the same fate as their countrymen had a decade ago.

Seidel shook his head, flicked his cigarette to the ground, and then pulled his hat back on. He tightened his trench coat against the chill manufactured from the colony's artificial weather control system and moved at a brisk pace towards the stairwell. He swung the door open and walked down the steps back towards the hustle and bustle of his command post. When he stepped inside, a dozen hands raised in salute. He casually waved his own hand, allowing them to return to their job of co-ordinating the faltering defence of New Berlin.

Trying his best to appear confident of their final victory, he made his way around the rows of desks and map-laden tables towards his own desk in the corner. He paused to study the various mounted monitors and watched in real-time as the battle raged. So far, the Allies had carved out a salient around the eastern entrance. But with every passing second, their offensive pushed closer and closer to the city centre. Soon, civilians with nowhere to run would find themselves caught in the crossfire between German guns and those of the invaders.

With a heavy heart, Seidel lit up another cigarette as General Schulz approached his desk. He dismissed his salute before the young general even made the attempt and sauntered towards his window to peer down at the crowds below.

"The latest reports, Herr Feldmarschall," General Schulz said in a despondent tone. "Reinforcements have helped us contain the Jewish rebels, but even with panzer support, they continue to harass our forces. They appear far more organised than we originally suspected."

"Of course, they are." Seidel exhaled. "They've had a decade to prepare for this. Think about that. A decade under the watchful eye of the SS to not just build but equip an army. What does that say to you?" He turned to see General Schulz's jaw drop.

"With all due respect, Herr Feldmarschall," General Schulz choked out. "To say such a thing—"

"And yet I have said it," Seidel said, cutting across his subordinate. "How else could a group of slaves organise and make such extensive preparations without the SS knowing? Hell, the SS could have armed them, without letting the Jews know, of course. They probably sent some of their agents to pose as wealthy, connected, and sympathetic members of the public eager to free the Jews and overthrow National Socialism. If I were Reichsführer Wagner and wanted the Wehrmacht bled slowly before being gutted by the enemy, that's how I'd do it."

General Schulz averted his gaze. He raised his hand to his mouth and coughed into it, as if to break the tension. Lips trembling, he lifted his gaze to Seidel. "If what you say is true, Herr Feldmarschall, then we are truly doomed."

A dark cloud hung over ahead as they realised the true extent of their downfall. Whether it took hours or days, they stood on the brink of destruction.

Seidel rose to his feet and opened his mouth to speak when an avalanche of machinegun fire ripped through the night. The panicked screams of the civilians in the streets below filled the command post. Thinking it had to be the enemy's aerial craft on a brazen strafing run, he rushed to the window and searched the night skies. Seeing nothing, he lowered his gaze and saw the muzzle flashes of dozens of SS guns. On the street, hundreds of bodies lay unmoving on the cold concrete.

Seidel was turning to bark orders when the windows of the command post shattered. General Schulz hit the ground with a roar, grabbing at his shoulder, and Seidel dove out of the way. Bullets riddled his desk. Staying out of the shooters' line of sight, he reached for the wounded general and pulled him to safety.

Officers and radio operators slumped over their desks when bullets blasted across the room, carving them to pieces. Blood spatters stained equipment. Machinery hissed and fizzed from the onslaught. Screams of shock replaced the wails from the civilians below as the SS turned on the Wehrmacht and the citizenry they had sworn to protect.

The SS had unleashed the dogs of war upon their own people.

**NEAR THE POTSDAM DISTRICT – EASTERN SECTOR
04.56 MST
DAY 2**

"Jenkins. Jenkins. Wake your lazy arse up."

Blinking his heavy eyelids open, Private Jenkins cradled his Lee-Enfield close to him as his senses flared back to life. Feeling like he had gotten a few minutes sleep, he checked his watch to see that it had been closer to two hours. Looking up at Private Morse, he nodded his head and lifted himself up from leaning against the cold concrete wall. Keeping his head low, he stretched his tired legs. He stepped over the bodies of his sleeping colleagues and crept quietly through the shell of the gutted beerhall.

In the distance, sporadic gunfire echoed throughout the night. The strange chill in the air sharpened his senses as he pushed onwards, passing rows of fatigued soldiers stealing what little sleep they could until the next Nazi attack. Crossing the roofless beerhall, he made his way towards what had once been the front door and paused to look up and down the street.

MEF soldiers sheltered in craters made from artillery shells or behind overturned automobiles. They sat in balconies overlooking the street and behind piles of wreckage from bomb-damaged shops and apartment blocks. In the distance, what looked like muzzle flashes came from the massive ornate building in the centre of the German colony. Jenkins wondered what daredevil MEF outfit had attacked so deep into enemy-controlled territory.

"Jenkins," Corporal Brown hissed at him in the darkness. "Over here. Double time."

Keeping his head low, Jenkins darted towards the crater and dove in. He landed beside the corporal, and raising his rifle, he pointed it directly ahead. The street remained deathly quiet, but a curious sensation swept over him that, somewhere in the shroud of night, unseen eyes watched their every movement. He glanced back at the corporal, nodding to show he sat alert and at the ready, Corporal Brown sank back into the crater. Laying his Lee-Enfield across his knee, the corporal fought to supress a tired yawn. He lifted a flask nestled at his feet. He unscrewed the lid, and after pouring himself a cap full of tea, he sank his helmeted head into the concrete wall of the crater. When he raised the tea to his lips, a call cut over the battalion's comm channel.

"Looks like we got movement," Private Kelly said from the forward observation post.

"What have you got, Kelly?" Sergeant Richards responded.

"Not sure. Maybe a dozen or so people heading towards our lines. Could be civvies. I can't see weapons, but it's fairly dark, Sarge."

"Sniper One," the sergeant said. "Have you eyes on them?"

"Confirmed, Sarge," Lance Corporal Prescott answered. "Looks like a dozen all right. No weapons that I can see, but some of them are in uniform."

"Could be deserters," Kelly said with a tint of hope in his voice.

"Wait One," Sergeant Richards said in reply.

The comm channel fell silent. Jenkins's gaze shifted from side to side, scanning the blackened street ahead, but he couldn't see anything.

"All units," Sergeant Richards spoke again. "We have a flare coming up. Keep your noggins and arses down and don't move."

The various Second Battalion units covering the street chimed in their understanding. Anyone with even the remotest possibility of being visible to an enemy froze like a statue and stayed low. Overhead a flare from one of the mortars in the rear erupted in an orange glow. Like a falling star, it streaked through the gloomy New Berlin skyline, casting an eerie hue across their positions and the streets ahead.

"It's kids," Kelly exclaimed. "I count fifteen of them. Some of them look young enough. Some of the older ones have Hitler Youth uniforms on, it looks like. Still no weapons that I can see."

"Definitely bairns all right," Lance Corporal Prescott

confirmed. "No signs of weapons, either. Looks like they've spotted our lines, though. They've started to pick up the pace."

From the murky veil covering the end of the street, Jenkins spotted shadows moving towards them. He raised his eye from his sight as he watched them change from ghoulish silhouettes to child-sized figures ranging in height and size. He couldn't make out their faces or any details about them, but his suspicions grew as to why children would be wandering about in a warzone at this early hour.

"If they see us, why are they running?" Jenkins said aloud, without thinking. "For all they know, we're a bunch of blood-thirsty murderers. Who runs right at the barrel of a gun?"

"You do, Jenkins, you plonker," Kelly said.

Muffled laughter crossed the comm channel.

"Knock it off," Sergeant Richards growled.

Beside Jenkins, Corporal Brown pushed himself up to gain a better view of the approaching children. His brow furrowed when he glanced down at Jenkins, as if dissecting his words. The children kept running. Some of them held their hands over their heads in surrender.

"Halt!" Corporal Brown roared and gestured with his hand.

Jenkins returned his gaze to the sight. "I don't like this, Corporal." He moved his weapon from side to side, searching for anything resembling a weapon, but he saw no signs of guns hanging from any of them, only backpacks.

"Does anyone speak German?" Corporal Brown asked with desperation in his voice.

"Halt!" he called out again. "Halt! Stoppen-zei! Stop! Halt!"

The group of German children either didn't understand the corporal's words or didn't care. They made no sign of slowing down as they peeled off into smaller groups, running towards the various foxholes and craters manned by the men of the MEF.

Two young girls wearing mismatched Volkssturm uniforms made straight for Jenkins and Corporal Brown. They held their hands high as they raced closer and closer.

When they closed in proximity, Jenkins spotted something in his sights.

"What's that in their hands?" he asked as his heart pounded. "What are they holding onto? Christ..."

"They're holding detonators—"

Confused conversations died in balls of fire. The stony faces of the children disappeared in smoke and flame when they detonated the bombs strapped to their backs across the MEF lines. A brief spurt of panic fire erupted before Jenkins found himself thrown back into the side of the crater. His eyes stung and watered from the flash of light. A ringing pounded through his head. Gasping from breath, the pain hit him, and he tried to scream. His mouth opened, and air escaped his lungs, but the ringing remained all he could hear.

Whether seconds or minutes passed, Jenkins couldn't be sure. His vision returned. He noted the outline of his Lee-Enfield and picked it up. To his right, he spotted Corporal Brown leaning against the side of the crater, cradling a bloodied right hand. Streaks of blood mixed with the dark black soot that crusted his face. His mouth lay opened, as if he was screaming in agony, and his hand shook.

Jenkins tried to say the corporal's name, but with the ringing in his ears bashing through his skull, he wasn't sure if the word escaped his lips.

Dazed from the flashes and the pain that reverberated through his body, Jenkins unclipped his water flask from his belt. He grabbed at the stunned corporal's wrist and poured the water over the wound revealing a long cut. The corporal winced, but the gash didn't look deep. He unstrapped Corporal Brown's helmet and splashed more water across his face. He wiped his face gently with his sleeve and uncovered several smaller cuts, thankfully none of which looked serious. After seeing that the corporal happened to be more shocked than wounded, Jenkins forced himself to look over the edge of the crater.

The children no longer existed. One of the two girls who had advanced on his position lay motionless on the cold ground in front of him. Her eyes looked upwards at an angle. Blood leaked from a hole in the side of her tiny skull. Scraps of leather boots, pieces of seared meat, and scorch marks were all that remained of her partner.

As the ringing in his ears receded, the anguished howls of men came to him. Shaking from the pain in his limbs, Jenkins turned from side to side to survey the damage. Three of the foxholes that had contained two men apiece lay empty. Thick clumps of bloody matter soaked the piles of debris that had sheltered them hours ago from one of the Wehrmacht's earlier counterattacks. The singed remains of children and soldier alike smeared the ground. Embers of scorched uniforms fell from the sky like snowflakes.

The stench of burnt hair invaded Jenkins's nostrils as he clawed out of his foxhole. To his right, Private Griffiths sat with his blood-stained hands resting on his knees, sobbing. All that remained of Private Kelly dribbled from his tattered battledress as Griffiths' eyes bulged from his head in confusion. Private Roberts stumbled from his position behind Griffiths. A waterfall of crimson seeped from the stumps where his hands used to be. He turned to face Jenkins, revealing a burnt face devoid of a nose and lips. Then he collapsed.

Medics and the soldiers resting in the beerhall streamed out, awakened by the commotion. They rushed to their colleagues, dragged the wounded to safety, and refilled the defensive positions. The sound of explosions swept over the entire eastern district of New Berlin. Jenkins winced at the pops and bangs emanating from streets on both flanks.

Still dazed, he offered no resistance when someone lifted him to his feet. The sound of gunfire increased in tempo until even the roars of the wounded were drowned out. Up above, a transport streaked across the colony's skyline. It unleashed a payload of furious missiles on an unseen target closer to the city centre.

Jenkins looked on as the aerial craft dodged the enemy anti-aircraft fire, until it didn't. The side of the craft lit up like the morning sun. Within seconds, it rolled about before plummeting downwards and disappearing behind New Berlin's towering apartment blocks.

"Contact Front!" someone shouted, and those hands

released him to snatch up a weapon.

One of the medics beckoned him from the ruins of the beerhall. Jenkins shook his head and waved the medic off. Raising his Lee-Enfield, he stumbled back towards his foxhole. Inside, he took aim alongside Corporal Brown.

UNDERGROUND TRAM LINES, 1.5KM FROM THE CITY CENTRE
05.49 MST
DAY 2

Sergeant McCabe blinked as light stung his eyes. His ears rang out in a high-pitched sharp whistle, and his head pounded like a drum. His arms and legs throbbed. Groaning, he lifted his head up.

"Easy," Noid whispered. "Easy, Sergeant."

He turned to look up at her. A few seconds passed until his pain-addled brain registered that his head rested in her lap, and her left hand cradled him. Embarrassed that he had fallen asleep on the Black Visor, he made to sit up, but she held him in place.

"Relax, Sergeant," she said in an unusually soft voice. "Everything's fine. You just took a blow to the noggin."

McCabe lifted a bloodstained hand to rub his face, unsure if he was dreaming. The pain that rippled through his body told him otherwise. With curiosity eating at him, he peered into Noid's eyes. For the first time, no unbridled contempt leaked from them.

"What happened?" he asked and fidgeted for his water flask.

With her free hand, Noid unstrapped her own. She unscrewed it and held it out for him. Her gloved fingers lingering on his hand for a second longer than expected.

"You don't remember?" she asked. An uncharacteristic smile emanated from the cut-out in her balaclava.

"No. Where are we? What happened?"

"We hit a mine," she said with a casual shrug. "Blew the whole front carriage to pieces and nearly flipped the others over. The Germans hit us straight away. I was trapped under some wreckage when they stormed in to get us.

You bayonetted one Nazi dickhead and clubbed another to death before pulling me free. When you were dragging me out, you got winged by a piece of shrapnel. I had to haul your arse to safety."

Flashes of broken memories flickered in McCabe's mind. He had a vague recollection of the scene, but the images remained jumbled and distorted from the ache carving through his skull.

"How many did we lose?" he asked, dreading the answer.

"Four," Noid said with a slight shake of her masked head. "Another three injured. It turned into a running battle to get to safety. Those Nazi bastards kept on coming. Thankfully, it's like a maze down here, so we managed to shake them off for a while. But for all intents and purposes, they have us pinned down. It's only a matter of time until they tighten the noose."

McCabe tried to sit up again, but his head spun.

"Easy," Noid said as she guided him into a sitting position. "You don't have a concussion, but that was some blow to the head."

His eyes refocused as he leaned against the cold concrete walls of the underground tram lines. Noid reached into her pocket and slipped out two cigarettes. She placed the butts in her mouth, lit them with her lighter, and then handed one to him. Trying to ignore the pulsating ache bashing through his cranium, he smiled his thanks and took a few quick drags.

Noid flicked ash onto the filthy ground. "I took these off a dead German."

Despite himself, McCabe couldn't help but smile at the mysterious Black Visor.

Catching his glance, she cocked her head and exhaled cigarette smoke. "Something funny?"

"Yes, actually," he said and tapped the ash from his own cigarette. "This is the longest conversation we've had without you reaching for your gun."

Noid chuckled to herself before quickly bringing her hand to her mouth to muffle the sound. She lowered it again, but her smile remained. "This conversation isn't over yet, Sergeant."

They finished their cigarettes before tossing the extinguished butts away. Despite the dull pain throughout his body, McCabe dragged himself to his feet. He nodded his thanks to Noid for her unexpected kindness and slung on his Lee-Enfield. After slipping in a fresh clip, he made his way past small groups of West German soldiers huddled together until he found Colonel Henke.

The colonel confirmed Noid's story about the ambush and the subsequent clashes with the enemy. Colonel Henke ordered him to check on the Black Visor's progress with finding a way out of the underground tram tunnels. A few paces into his journey, he came to a halt when a call came through on the division's common comm channel. He listened to the report ordering all advancing units to be on the lookout for a downed atmospheric troop transport. Thanks to the intermittent jamming from the Nazis, he couldn't make out the full details, though. He tapped on his left arm console and checked the readouts as he tried searching for the crashed transport's transponder signal. If the craft had landed behind enemy lines, that left the West German contingent and their MEF allies as the closest group to render assistance.

As he made his way back down the underground tunnels, McCabe looked over the small pockets of wounded soldiers stretched out along the tram lines. Most of the injuries were minor, but some lay unconscious with worried medics refusing to leave their sides. He lit another cigarette as he lingered at an intersection. A nearby patrol pointed out the tunnel to reach Dub and Big Mo's position. Nodding his thanks, he unslung his weapon and threw his cigarette away before stalking along the tram lines.

It didn't take long for him to locate the two Black Visors at a point where the tunnel curved to the right. Dub lay sprawled on the left-hand side, his body concealed by the thick metal beams of the tram line. Only his eyes and the muzzle of his HK-17 stood visible, but in the dim lighting, McCabe doubted the enemy would be able to make him out until it became too late. From somewhere ahead, the sound of Germans whispering back and forth to one another echoed through the tunnel. On the right, Big Mo knelt on a prayer mat, out of the line of sight of prying eyes. His lips moved in silent prayer.

"Don't interrupt him, Sergeant," Dub said in a hushed tone, without taking his gaze off the tunnel ahead. "He gets cranky if he misses his prayers."

Finishing off, Big Mo stood, carefully folded his prayer mat, and placed it gently into his backpack. "Forty years and it's still not funny, asshole," Big Mo mumbled as he slung his weapon into his hands.

"It's still funnier than your impression of me. Don't think I don't hear you trying to imitate my accent every time I have my back turned, you muppet."

"And I'm the cranky one," Big Mo said with a smile.

"Gentlemen," McCabe interrupted before anyone else could get a word in. "This isn't the time. The Germans are on the way."

"I wouldn't be too concerned," Dub said in a dismissive tone.

"Oh? And why not?"

"Because I don't think they speak English. I shouted loud enough for them to hear that we booby-trapped the tunnel ahead. I don't speak much German, but I think they shouted something back about my mother."

McCabe made to speak when a high-pitched creaking noise emanated from above them. Lifting his Lee-Enfield, he readied his finger on the trigger. He relaxed when he saw the black and red uniform of another Black Visor. From a hatch, Smack made her way down a rusted metal ladder fixed to the side of the tunnel. She jumped the last few steps, landing with ease, and swung her HK back into her hands.

"Any joy?" Dub asked, his gaze locked on the tunnel ahead.

"Sergeant," Smack nodded at McCabe in greeting before answering Dub. "I think so. The hatch opens onto an alleyway on a side street. I couldn't scout around, but it looks like it's pandemonium out there. Civilians running in every direction. Best guess is we're about a klick or two out from the government district. I have no clue how we're going to break in, though."

"Leave that up to me," Dub replied.

"Yeah, 'cause this plan worked out well," Big Mo muttered.

The words had barely escaped Big Mo's mouth when a string of explosions rocked the tunnel. The three Black Visors and McCabe flinched and readied their weapons. The dull lights of the underground tunnel flickered as dust trickled from the concrete roof.

Within seconds a medley of pained wails resonated through the tunnel as the German patrol set off the boobytraps. Smaller secondary blasts drowned out those agonised cries as bullets from panic fire struck the concrete wall. Shrill screams pierced over the sound of frantic orders being shouted by NCOs as the advancing Germans halted to render aid to their wounded colleagues.

"That's what you get for insulting my mother, you racist pricks!" Dub called out.

Bullets lashed at the concrete wall of the tunnel in response, away from Dub's position.

"C'mon." Smack turned to McCabe. "We need to move everyone up while we can."

"Understood," he said with a nod. "Just one thing, though. When we get topside, we need to keep an eye out for a downed transport. The American pilot could still be alive."

"Not our problem," Dub snorted and raised himself into a kneeling stance.

"I say it is our problem," McCabe barked. "Some of those pilots are kids, and they're risking their necks for us. I won't leave any of them in the hands of those Nazi butchers."

"Bollocks to that," Dub roared as he rose to his feet and whirled around to face him. "We have a mission to complete, and we're running out of time. We need to get to the government district before it's too late."

Anger coursed through McCabe's veins like molten lava. Even with the enemy a few hundred metres away and no doubt regrouping for an assault, Dub irritated him more with every passing moment. McCabe closed the distance between them, never taking his gaze from the Black Visor.

"We are not leaving anyone behind enemy lines," McCabe roared.

Smack raised a hand and stepped between them.

"You two need to knock this off now," she shouted. "It's like I'm babysitting children! Dub, back the hell down and stop acting like a stubborn git. Sergeant McCabe is right; we can't leave a pilot behind. They'll string him up if they catch him."

Dub glared at Smack like a scolded child. She met his gaze head on, refusing to look away, until Dub averted his eyes and fidgeted with his HK-17.

McCabe couldn't help shining a victorious smirk at seeing Dub put in his place. As soon as it appeared, Smack fired her laser-like stare upon him, wiping it from his face.

"I don't know what you're smiling about, Sergeant," she snapped. "You're a grown man and a senior NCO. You should know better. Now, contact Colonel Henke and let's get moving. Do I make myself clear?"

An unmistakable shudder of fear worked its way through McCabe when he found himself on the receiving end of Smack's ferocious glare. He had known many tough and headstrong women in his lifetime, but none compared to Smack and Noid. He had seen them in action. Although it stung his pride to even think about it, he didn't doubt that they could take him down should they so choose.

"Yes, ma'am," he said. He activated his comm and relayed Smack's findings to the colonel.

Smack turned her attention to the tunnel ahead while they waited for the company to join them. Dub remained standing but waited until Smack stepped out of earshot before turning to McCabe. "You know what, Sergeant?" he said in a hushed tone. "I'm starting to take a serious disliking to you."

"Do something about it," McCabe growled back.

"When this is all over."

"Until then."

They eyed each other for a few seconds longer and only broke eye contact when the rest of the company arrived.

MITTE DISTRICT COMMAND POST, CITY CENTRE

06.37 MST
DAY 2

The senior officers of the Wehrmacht stood in uneasy silence around a single table. The field officers wore uniforms stained with the blood of their enemies and their own soldiers. The staff officers, wearing cleaner uniforms, looked haggard and worn. Each of them stood motionless with their chins tilted upwards, avoiding Generalfeldmarschall Seidel's gaze.

He curled his hands into fists. "Children."

No one spoke a word. Only the sound of artillery smashing the buildings closest to the government district seeped in from beyond the bunker they utilised as their new headquarters. Some of the officers barely breathed, no doubt hoping to avoid his fury.

"Children," he snarled. "Children strapped with bombs. Children. *German* children."

The door to their meeting room creaked open.

A young lieutenant pushed into the room with a cart laden with tea and coffee. Oblivious to the tension, he made his way around the table and placed the first tray in front of Seidel.

"Children!" Seidel bellowed, spittle flying from his mouth.

He grabbed the tray, and flung its contents across the room, drenching the stunned lieutenant with hot coffee. The lieutenant's cries of shock disappeared when Seidel banged the wooden tray against the table. After three impacts, the tray splintered, sending wooden shards in every direction. Seidel glared at each of his officers in turn.

"You vile, wretched cretins! How dare you? How dare you!?" he screamed, causing some of the officers to wince. "I will know who gave that order. I will know the name of the man who sent those children to die such pointless deaths. I will know who sacrificed German children on such a foolish, idiotic attack doomed to fail. *Who*?"

The trembling lieutenant scampered from the room like a scolded dog. Everyone else remained perfectly still. The building shook from the impact of an enemy shell landing

140

somewhere near their makeshift headquarters. The lights flickered, threatening to die, but stabilised. The screams of wounded civilians outside reverberated through the walls of the bunker.

"They sacrificed their lives for Germany!" Oberst Brandt called out. "Those children gave their lives for the glory and honour of the fatherland!"

Seidel turned his gaze on the panzer commander. Moving from where he stood, he paced around the table. The sound of his boots clicking against the concrete floor remained the only sound in the room. "So, you gave the order, Oberst Brandt?"

"No, Herr Feldmarschall."

"But you know who did?"

"No, Herr Feldmarschall. I believe the children of the Volkssturm and the Hitler Youth acted out of patriotic fervour and commitment to their—"

Seidel held up a hand, muzzling Brandt. Without breaking eye contact, he unholstered his pistol and cocked it. He kept the weapon at his side while his eyes bored through his subordinate. A slight tremble betrayed Brandt's stoic disposition.

"Herr Feldmarschall," a voice said from a few metres away.

Seidel turned his interest towards Major Roth, who stepped a pace forward from his fellow officers. With his gun at the ready, Seidel moved towards Roth and paused in front of him.

Roth cleared his throat and reached for the files under his left arm. He selected one and held a single sheet of paper aloft.

Seidel holstered his still-cocked weapon and snatched the paper.

"One of my operatives retrieved this from the body of a Volkssturm commander," Major Roth said. "Several more have since fallen into my possession. It is an order signed by the Führer himself ordering all available Volkssturm and Hitler Youth units to launch an immediate attack upon the enemy lines. The order explicitly states that you and the Wehrmacht chain of command are not to be informed or consulted. My sources within the SS confirm that this order is authentic."

Seidel examined the paper in his hands. He read and re-read the text before his gaze rested on the signature at the bottom. Just as Roth had said, the order looked to be signed in the distinctive scrawl of the man they had sworn loyalty to. Too stunned to do anything else, he crumpled the paper up in his hand. As his mind raced with the implications of being officially subverted in such a way, he made his way back around the table to his original position. The second he took his seat, the door to the room swung open again.

A young, grim-faced corporal entered and hesitated at seeing so many officers standing at attention. He fixed his eyes on Seidel, crossed the room, and saluted before handing over a dispatch from the front.

Dazed from the revelation, Seidel gave an absentminded flick of his hand after accepting the dispatch. He unholstered his pistol again. He rested it on his leg and opened the dispatch. His tired eyes analysed the contents as he leaned back into his chair.

Seidel lowered the paper in his hands as he recited the key points of the dispatch. "The SS have carved an exclusion zone around the government district. They are firing on civilian and soldier alike. We have most of the surrounding areas evacuated, but the Allies are maintaining their thrust towards the city centre. Civilian casualties are mounting due to the sustained artillery and aerial bombardments."

"We should continue to do our duty," Oberst Brandt said. "We have sworn an oath to the Führer to give our lives in defence of the Reich. We should fight till the last man and the last bullet. The strength of our arms and the purity of Aryan blood shall render us the final victory."

Seidel gazed at Brandt, while his mind explored the few options left to take. He picked up his pistol again and placed it on the table in front of him. He turned his focus to the weapon and shook his head slightly from side to side. Outside, another series of booms shook the ravaged streets. The piercing howls of the wounded followed close behind.

"We have been betrayed by the Führer," he whispered. "The SS have turned on us all. They concealed the arrival of the Allies and destroyed their own fleet, rendering us defenceless. They said nothing while we continued with our exercises, leaving the colonies ripe for the picking. They armed the Jews. They withdrew their forces when we needed them most. They have turned their guns on us, the last defenders of the Reich. To compound their treason, they are content with letting the German people suffer. This, I cannot abide."

General Schulz took his place at Seidel's side. "Herr Feldmarschall, it is entirely possible that the SS are staging a coup against the Führer. It would certainly explain their actions and why he and the other ranking party members stay silent on the matter."

"Possibly," Seidel said with a sad nod of his head, "but it doesn't change the fact that we are in a hopeless situation. Our forces are being hacked to pieces. Our civilians are suffering. Any prolongation of the fighting merely draws out the inevitable. New Berlin is lost to us."

Another round of blasts erupted from outside their command post, as if bolstering his words. The lights flashed on and off as the officers exchanged uneasy glances. From their faces, Seidel could see most of them agreed with him, even if they refused to say so publicly. The junior ones, and Oberst Brandt in particular, trembled in rage at his words. Their faces burned red in anger at his admission.

Seidel slid a hand into his trench coat and produced two sheets of paper with neatly typed text. With a shaking hand, he fumbled for a pen in his pocket. Finally locating it, he looked down at the words in front of him. He took a deep breath and scrawled his name across the bottom of both documents.

"General Schulz."

"Yes, Herr Feldmarschall," the man said with a click of his boots.

Seidel picked up one of the papers and, extending a hand, passed it to his subordinate.

"As ranking officer of the Wehrmacht and my second-in-command, this document confirms your authority in my absence. I and I alone accept full responsibility for any questionable actions carried out under my leadership."

General Schulz threw his gaze over the paper in his hand.

"This document," Seidel continued and lifted the second paper, "orders all units within the New Berlin defensive zone to ceasefire with immediate effect and to obey all orders issued by you to surrender to the Allies."

A series of gasps broke out from around the room. Some of the younger officers forgot themselves and banged the table in frustration, seething that such words could leave a German officer's mouth.

Seidel ignored the ruckus as he took his pistol from the table in front of him. "History will not remember my deeds on the eastern front, nor my defence of the fatherland. Instead, I will forever be remembered as the man who lost New Berlin within a single day. Such is the will of Providence, gentlemen. Heil Hitler!"

Without hesitation, Seidel raised his gun, placed the barrel in his mouth and pulled the trigger.

MITTE DISTRICT COMMAND POST, CITY CENTRE
06.48 MST
DAY 2

A single shot rang out, blasting brain and skull fragments across the wall behind Generalfeldmarschall Seidel's chair, and his lifeless body flopped backwards.

A surreal calmness enveloped the room as everyone stood transfixed at the sight.

After a few heartbeats, General Schulz pocketed the documents. Dazed at the sight of his commanding officer slumped awkwardly across the chair, he grabbed a tablecloth draped from a nearby table and placed it over the generalfeldmarschall's head.

He turned about to see Oberst Brandt and some of the younger officers storm out of the room, slamming the door behind them. Some of the senior officers fumbled for their pistols and made to stop them when Schulz halted them.

144

"Let them go," he said and sighed. "General Franke. Assist me."

Schulz turned and stood over Generalfeldmarschall Seidel's corpse and waited for Franke to join him. He cast his gaze over the bloodstained tablecloth and nodded at Franke to take the generalfeldmarschall's feet. Schulz shook his head in disgust as he eased his hands under his superior's shoulders.

"We lift on three," he said to Franke. "We'll take him to the basement."

"Yes, Herr General."

After counting down, the two men lifted the body. Blood and brain matter from the generalfeldmarschall's gaping wound poured onto the floor, splattering Schulz's boots. The senior officers flocked around their deceased commanding officer and threw their arms under his body, keeping him steady. A sombre-faced captain standing at the door swung it open, snapped to attention, and saluted. The grim funeral procession slowly made their way into the corridor and marched in time through the command post. Officers and adjutants stood up from behind their desks and put down their radio headsets. The room fell quiet as they watched Schulz and the other generals plod past them.

A series of explosions from outside the command post nearly caused Schulz to lose his footing. He steadied himself at the last minute and nodded at his subordinates. They eased their way down the basement stairs, careful to keep their grip on their fallen commander.

Once they reached the basement floor, General Franke led the way towards an unoccupied corner. Schulz cast his gaze over the three dozen civilians sheltering there, along with the hundred or so soldiers too wounded to continue the fight. A priest and a blood-stained nurse walked between the rows of the wounded offering what little assistance they could. Both came to a halt as their gaze fell on the Schulz and the officers before resting on the body they carried.

With all eyes on them, Schulz and the procession lowered Generalfeldmarschall Seidel's body onto the dusty floor. On Schulz's order, they came to attention and saluted their commanding officer one last time.

General Franke leaned in close to Schulz and whispered. "Perhaps you should say something, Herr General."

"There is nothing left to say," Schulz said with a sad shake of his head. "He was a soldier. Now he is dead. If we are lucky, we will meet him again in Valhalla."

After allowing another few seconds to pass in silence, Schulz glanced over at Major Roth.

"Major Roth."

"Yes, Herr General."

"Find a white flag and the nearest group of Allied soldiers. Discover who the ranking officer is and tell them it is our desire to secure a ceasefire, with the intention of ending hostilities within the colony."

"Yes, Herr General." Roth clicked his boots and after raising his arm in salute, he exited the room.

With a casual wave of his hand, Schulz dismissed the lingering officers and glanced down at the lifeless body of the generalfeldmarschall. He had spoken truth in his final words. Despite his best efforts, Generalfeldmarschall Seidel would always be the German officer who lost New Berlin in less than a day.

Unfortunately, Schulz would bare the same fate. He may not have been responsible for losing New Berlin, but he would forever be known as the man who surrendered it.

PART 4

WOE TO THE VANQUISHED

2KM FROM THE CITY CENTRE – EASTERN SECTOR
10.04 MST
DAY 2

Despite weakened bodies and tired minds, Private Jenkins and the remaining members of the Second Battalion marched through the battered streets. In the hours that followed the Nazis' use of child suicide bombers, vengeance had walked closely with the men of the Mars Expeditionary Force. Immediately after the enemy's cowardly offensive, non-stop mortar and artillery strikes against the Nazis had begun. The sound of bombs and shells whizzing overhead filled the air, as did the thunderous crash of those explosives smashing the city centre. With hardened hearts, Jenkins and the MEF maintained their offensive against the Nazis, determined to make them pay for the losses of so many friends and colleagues.

Leaving the outer districts and moving closer to the city centre, Jenkins saw more signs of civilians caught in the crossfire. The bodies of men, women, and children lay where they had fallen, often mangled alongside defending Wehrmacht or Volkssturm soldiers. Rows of houses lined the streets, riddled with bullet holes from the brutal fighting. Medics continued to pull the corpses of MEF soldiers from the piles of charred wood and brick that littered the streets, mainly those of the Fifth Battalion who had spearheaded the recent offensive. But while they marched, something far more sinister spurred on Jenkins and his colleagues.

As the companies of Second Battalion pushed through the tattered German streets, more and more Jenkins witnessed bodies swinging from lampposts. Most of them looked like old, haggard men and elderly women. All bore bruises and cuts, giving a glimpse into the pain they suffered in the moments leading up to the nooses wrapping around their necks. Some had swastikas cut into their flesh. Hand-written signs hung from their lifeless bodies with a single word written on it.

Judenrein.

"Cleansed of Jews," Junior Sergeant Alexeev mumbled from beside Jenkins as the endless stream of the dead swung in a light breeze.

To his left and right, small teams of soldiers in Polish uniforms worked their way methodically up the street. They smashed open house windows, and lobbed grenades into them before kicking the doors in and spraying the house with machinegun fire. Several groups of German civilians who had survived the recent battle found themselves herded together by battle-weary MEF soldiers. Jabbing at them with bayonets, the soldiers of the Fifth Battalion urged on the wailing civilian population.

When a transport swung into sight in the far distance, Jenkins turned away from the bodies swaying on either side of his path. He closed his eyes, wishing to unsee everything he had experienced over the last twenty-four hours. The faces of his fallen comrades raced in his mind. Some killed aboard the USAF North Carolina in the cold, darkness of space. Others by Nazi bullets, bombs, bayonets, and knives.

Forcing his eyelids open, he saw the corpse of a young girl dangling from one of the lampposts ahead. Her vacant eyes stared into the anger and horror that built inside him. For a heartbeat, he thought he heard the young girl's final pleas as she begged her tormentors to set her free. In a million years, Jenkins couldn't imagine any circumstance where he'd kill a child. Yet the brutes who built and ran New Berlin had sent her and hundreds of others to the gallows with ease. As the anger continued to boil deep within him, his gaze sank to the sign strung around her tiny neck.

Judenrein. Cleansed of Jews.

As the Second Battalion reached an intersection in the street, the sounds and sights of fierce fighting grew sharper. A platoon of Fifth Battalion soldiers covered defensive points along the crossroads, their rifles raised. Some positioned themselves behind the twisted husks of destroyed panzers. Others used the bodies of dead Nazis like sandbags, propping them across one another to create a savage defensive wall.

Following Junior Sergeant Alexeev's orders, Jenkins and the rest of the company darted across the street. They slowed when they reached the relative safety of the houses flanking them on either side. Fewer bodies swung from the lampposts this close to the frontlines, but macabre figures rocked gently in New Berlin's man-made breeze for as far as the eye could see. Marching on, Jenkins passed small groups of Fifth Battalion soldiers clustered outside the bullet-riddled houses. Each of them wore uniforms stained with blood and dirt. They puffed on cigarettes and sipped on tea atop piles of stone and broken bricks. Several of them lounged up against dead German soldiers, their vacant stares looking through the Second Battalion reinforcements.

Towards the middle of the street, commotion rang out long before Jenkins could locate the ruckus. A small group of MEF soldiers surrounded a much larger group of German POWs. The captured Nazis held up their hands in surrender, and the MEF corralled them towards the front of a burnt-out, roofless house. A dozen of the younger captives looked like boys, many younger than Jenkins. Tears streamed down their faces as MEF bayonets prodded the air in front of them. Four of the older men in Volkssturm uniforms spoke in rapid bouts of German. Jenkins couldn't decipher their words, but from the tone of their voices and the expressions on their faces, he guessed their words as pleadings for mercy.

Standing on top of a small pile of rubble in front of the POWs, a British sergeant kept pointing towards the stream of bodies hanging along the street. His face burned red and spittle flew from his every word.

"Judenrein!? Judenrein?" he screeched like a madman. "I'm a Jew. How does it feel now, you German cockroaches? We're going to cleanse Mars of *you*."

Despite the shouts and pleas of the captives, the sergeant leapt down from his perch. With hatred engraved across his face, he moved to a waiting private and snatched up a flame-thrower. Hoisting the pack onto his back, he aimed the nozzle at the group of POWs and urged the MEF soldiers back. Cries of panic broke out as most of the Germans fell to their knees in terror, begging for mercy in broken English.

Unsure of what to do, Jenkins opened his mouth to say something. Before he could even think of what words to use, a hand as hard as steel clasped his shoulder. He turned to see Junior Sergeant Alexeev towering over him. His granite-cool eyes pierced through Jenkins, and he shook his head at the captured POWs. Then he released his grip from Jenkins's shoulder without uttering a single word, but Jenkins understood the unspoken order and said nothing.

The tear-filled pleadings of the Nazi POWs reached a crescendo, and the sergeant with the flame-thrower squeezed the trigger. A cloud of fire spurted from the weapon, enveloping the screaming POWs. The sergeant waved the hell storm of flame from side to side, ensuring he bathed every one of the prisoners in his vengeance. Figures covered in a flare of red and orange unleashed soul-piercing screeches as they collapsed and writhed on the ground.

Satisfied, the British sergeant released the trigger and basked in his handiwork. Most of the Nazis lay motionless as the flames devoured their flesh. One or two thrashed in the fires as their organs cooked and boiled. A nearby soldier aimed his weapon to put them out of their misery, but the grim-faced British sergeant shook his head.

Jenkins said nothing as he passed the sight of roasting prisoners.

Chatter broke out amongst the lead platoons as soldiers commented on the grotesque sight. Officers within earshot repeated Major Wellesley's words, stifling any further discussion on the treatment of Nazi POWs.

"There's no Geneva Convention on Mars, lads. They kill civvies and murder our boys, and we'll reap our pound of flesh. Kill them all!"

"Kill them all!" Jenkins and the Second Battalion mumbled back in what was becoming their new, unofficial motto.

At the end of the street, Jenkins halted in their designated staging area for the up-and-coming offensive. The rallying point looked to be blanketed in rubble, as if the houses that once stood there had been pounded into oblivion. On all sides, mammoth apartment blocks towered over Jenkins. Many had British, French, Soviet, and American flags dangling from them, showing their occupation by the Mars Expeditionary Force. White flags of surrender flew from hundreds of apartments as the civilian population abandoned their former masters in the hopes of leniency from the new overlords of New Berlin.

Standing in the middle of the staging area, a solitary woman leaned a rifle against her shoulder. Junior Sergeant Alexeev signalled Jenkins and his platoon to move towards her while the various companies formed up into all-round cover. To Jenkins's surprise, Major Wellesley trotted along beside them, falling into the right of Junior Sergeant Alexeev. The two men spoke in hushed tones.

The woman slung her rifle and paced towards them. She wove through the stacks of debris, her skinny fingers gripping the strap of the weapon slung across her back. Pulling her soiled, tattered jacket tight with her free hand, she halted a few metres away. Wisps of auburn hair escaped the confines of her cap and danced in the breeze over her gaunt face. With a hard stare, she cast her gaze over the assembled MEF soldiers until she spotted Major Wellesley.

151

"You British certainly took your time," she said in a heavy Polish accent.

"These are extraordinary times, Miss...?" Major Wellesley prompted.

"Zofia."

"Miss Zofia, my name is Major Wellesley. Allow me to introduce—"

"We have no time for pleasantries," Zofia snapped. "The Army of David stands ready to strike at the heart of the Nazi pigs." She turned her left arm for all to see, showing a handmade flag of Israel wrapped around her coat's sleeve. "Those of us who have survived this hell have yearned for this moment since before the start of the war. No more talk. Action."

Several of the platoon members threw each other various looks. Junior Sergeant Alexeev sent a watchful gaze across the platoon, quieting everyone it came upon.

Major Wellesley brought his hand to his mouth and cleared his throat. Lowering it, he wiped some imaginary dust off his arm and spoke again. "Miss Zofia, Major General Hamilton has asked for me to extend his personal gratitude for the effort your fighters have put in to distract our mutual enemy. Your Jewish insurgents have fought bravely against an enemy many times your number, but now is the time to let us do our jobs. If your fighters can step aside and let us—"

"No."

The word reverberated off the walls of the surrounding apartments. Jenkins found himself leaning to the side, eager to get a better look at the Jewish freedom fighter.

Her steely eyes refused to break contact with the major as she stared him down. She raised her right hand to her mouth, and inserting two fingers, she let out a shrill whistle that cut over the machinegun fire.

In a single co-ordinated movement, rows of fighters streamed out of doorways and underground cellars hidden amongst the wreckage.

Jenkins and the Second Battalion soldiers turned their weapons on the unexpected arrivals but lowered them at Major Wellesley's command. From all sides, hundreds of armed men, women, and children trudged through the cracked bricks and wood.

Jenkins was most struck by how scrawny they stood in appearance, especially the children. Their clothes looked rag-like and handmade, in most cases using sackcloth. Many of them didn't have shoes, and their faces were caked in a thick layer of grime. Their gazes blazed with unbroken determination as they fell in behind Zofia.

Jenkins examined the weapons at their disposal. Many of the men, women, and older children carried rifles and light machine guns captured from the Nazis, although some sported older shotguns and pistols. Children, as young as four or five, carried backpacks filled with ammunition or Molotov cocktails. Each of them wore homemade helmets and the same flag of Israel wrapped around their left arm.

"The Army of David is mobilising all across the front," Zofia spat at the major, with contempt dripping from her voice. "We will fight the Nazis. You may join us, or you may try and stop us, but you will have to kill every last one of us. The Nazis take no prisoners, so we do not surrender, and we will never stop."

Shaking his head, Major Wellesley called for a radioman when Zofia turned her back on him and waved her soldiers towards the front.

"Where are you going?" Major Wellesley called after her. "I'll need Major General Hamilton's authorisation to allow some limited form of—"

"You talk too much," Zofia shouted without turning her head back towards him. "We'll be in the vanguard when you have your authorisation."

A cheer went up from the Army of David when they marched towards the frontlines, while a flustered Major Wellesley began barking into his handset.

FREDRIKPLATZ, 1.5KM FROM THE CITY CENTRE
11.32 MST
DAY 2

Sergeant McCabe accepted a mug of tea from one of the West Germans. He took a sip and started pacing around the abandoned Nazi church. For the last few hours, he and most of the company had sought refuge in it from the increasing chaos outside. After they emerged from the underground tramlines, this building sat as the closest one to their location. Initially, he thought it a bad idea to bunker down in a place of worship. A part of him half-expected desperate souls to interrupt them as they sought solace in this trying time. But on the streets of New Berlin, things continued to escalate at an alarming pace. The sounds of battle had increased in tempo closer to the government district. It didn't take long for the scouts to see the Wehrmacht and SS soldiers engage in intense gun battles with each other.

To make matters worse, the adjacent streets had remained thronged with people. Confused and terrified civilians ran in every direction, searching for safety but finding none. The SS gunned them down if they approached the government district, and the Wehrmacht tried to keep them hunkered down in the city centre. All the while, MEF shells and bombs burst around them. The Wehrmacht had since restored a fraction of order and cleared the surrounding streets of civilian activity, but the tension and fear hung heavy in the air.

After confirming that his platoon kept doing what they should be doing —eating, standing guard or sleeping — McCabe sipped on his mug of tea and glanced up at the stained-glass windows behind the church's altar. He examined images of Jesus's life on display and shuddered at Hitler's likeness being used in his stead. Swastikas replaced church crosses and covered every wall. Out of morbid fascination, McCabe flipped through the book the Nazis used as their version of the Bible. Although his written German wasn't as good as his verbal skills, he was horrified to see the changes the Nazis had made to the gospels. Everything had been rewritten to fit the National Socialist agenda, with Hitler made out to be mankind's saviour and salvation.

Lighting up a cigarette, McCabe returned to his pacing. In his peripheral vision, he spied Wehrmacht uniforms approaching him. Out of instinct, he reached for his

154

Lee-Enfield but stopped himself when he identified the soldiers of the West German contingent. With the situation deteriorating outside, sending the West Germans out to scout in captured uniforms was the only way to move without being detected.

"Sergeant McCabe," Colonel Henke called out from across the room.

Falling in behind the patrol, McCabe crossed the church and joined the West German commanding officer. The colonel sported his own captured uniform but looked disgusted at the thought of having to don it again. In truth, it bothered McCabe just as much. He couldn't help but question the leadership and judgement of someone whose former army had committed such gross atrocities in the war. Despite his misgivings, he grudgingly couldn't fault the colonel's actions so far, although he kept a close eye on him.

The Black Visors joined the small group of British, French, and West German officers and NCOs. Even hiding behind his balaclava, McCabe could sense the agitation emanating from Dub. Whoever this MI6 operative Anna Bailey happened to be, the Black Visor leader appeared beyond impatient to jump into action and rescue her.

Dub flashed McCabe a cool glare before turning his focus to the colonel.

"Here's what we have so far," Colonel Henke said as his fingers moved across a map. "Our patrols have confirmed that the Wehrmacht have withdrawn from any contested areas around the government district. Although there have been several reports of both sides exchanging fire over the last few hours, the SS have made no serious move to advance beyond their current positions."

"It'll happen," Dub said. "Both sides will try and gut each other, and soon. You can count on it."

Colonel Henke nodded politely and returned his attention to the map.

"It appears a Nazi operation launched in the early morning has failed. I believe that's why the MEF artillery, mortar, and aerial bombardments have increased. It seems that an MEF offensive is underway, with the main thrust of the attack having recently broken through Nazi defences roughly three kilometres east of our current location."

The NCOs and officers mumbled words of thanks and patted each other on the backs in celebration. If their allies kept up the momentum, they could reach the centre of New Berlin within hours and end the bloodshed.

"What's it like in the areas around here?" Smack asked.

"Some patrols but not many. It looks like civilians have been moved to the underground bunkers, and most of the units have been evacuated to bolster the lines. There's rumours that the Jewish insurgents are mobilising to link up with the MEF and launch their own offensive from the east and north-east."

"Have we anything on the pilot?" McCabe queried. "Any updates if he's alive or dead?"

"Yes," Colonel Henke said. He gestured at a nearby waiting soldier and took a slip of paper from the scout. After skimming its contents, he gazed at the map again. It took him a few seconds until he pointed out an area close to their church base. "My patrols have discovered the crash site roughly a kilometre north of here. Rumours are that a pilot survived and was moved to a site several streets across from where we are. Unfortunately, none of my soldiers have been able to get close enough to confirm this without arousing suspicion. My plan is to lead a team and investigate it for myself."

"That's far too dangerous, sir," McCabe said. "A few soldiers wandering around is one thing, but a colonel enquiring about a POW may be too much. I'll lead a team to check. You said it yourself, the streets are deserted. I'll stick to these back alleys, have a quick peek, and if it's our boy, I'll bring him back safely."

Colonel Henke rubbed his chin.

McCabe knew they had a limit on how many uniforms they had and could use with going undetected. Even in a city as large as New Berlin, it stood as a fact that no new arrivals had come to the colony over the last decade. The slightest misstep or misspoken word could cost them all their lives.

"Very well, Sergeant," Colonel Henke said after

deliberating. "Lead a small team and report back."

"We'll go," Smack volunteered out of nowhere. "We're no use to anyone sitting here."

McCabe eyed her and the rest of her associates, but he nodded his consent. He took the map from Colonel Henke, and removing any unnecessary equipment from his belt, he checked his ammunition supply. He selected two other West German soldiers to accompany him, and stepping in beside the Black Visors, he walked towards the side exit adjacent to the alleyway. After the sentries confirmed the all clear, McCabe and the Black Visors jogged at a rapid pace toward the end of the alley. Without prompting, the Black Visors moved into all-round cover when he scanned the street. Several buildings lay blackened and charred, but he could see no signs of enemy activity. Breaking into small groups, they raced across the street into the opposite alley, covering each other as they ran.

They repeated that exercise several times, stopping to allow small groups of forlorn-looking Wehrmacht soldiers to pass them as they trudged towards the frontlines. After crossing several streets, they located the area marked on the colonel's map. From the outside, it looked to be a small grocery shop off one of the side alleys. The windows and doors remained intact, but no goods sat on display in the cracked shop window. McCabe peered through the glass and seeing no signs of movement, he led his team to the rear of the shop. Again, as the group covered each other, he crept to the single pane of glass in the back door and peeked through.

Anger rushed through him at the sight. Four dishevelled and inebriated German soldiers swigged bottles of wine and laughed in merriment. In the centre of the room, a young pilot stood on a rickety stool with a noose around his neck. The Nazi soldiers had torn the US Airforce shirt from his body, revealing a bruised chest. Standing on a chair beside him, one of the Germans held a funnel to the pilot's mouth and poured the contents of the wine bottle in as the pilot struggled and shook, unable to resist with his hands bound.

Laughing, the German discarded the empty bottle,

allowing it to smash to pieces on the floor. He removed the funnel and chuckled again when the young pilot threw his head forward, splattering the contents of his stomach onto the floor and gasping for air. When the German picked up another bottle to do it again, McCabe got a look at the pilot's bruised and disorientated face. He immediately recognised the captive as Crewman Lockhart.

Furious at the treatment of the young man, McCabe signalled his orders to the waiting Black Visors. Dub and Noid took positions on either side of the door with their HK-17s locked and loaded. Noid reached a hand towards the doorknob and, as quietly as she could, twisted it. But she shook her head to show it was locked, so Dub pulled his right leg back. He crashed his foot against the door with enough force to break it open. Noid leapt into the room, bringing her weapon to bear on the Germans. Dub trailed close behind. As McCabe jumped into the shop, the Black Visors fired in cool, methodical fashion.

Noid cleared the right side of the room, tapping her trigger twice. She shot the first soldier in the back and caught his colleague square in the head when he spun around in surprise. Dub blasted the soldier pouring wine into Lockhart, sending his body hurtling backwards onto a nearby table. The last soldier, far stockier than the others, snatched at his own weapon and dashed behind the captured pilot for cover. Dub dove forward, hit the ground with a roll, and swung himself into a crouched firing stance. He fired once, catching the enemy soldier in the stomach and knocking him into an empty display.

Making a beeline for the young pilot, McCabe slung his weapon. He grabbed at Lockhart's legs, terrified the chair he perched on would give out at any second.

While Noid and Dub worked on clearing the other rooms of the shop, Big Mo drew his knife. He slipped it under the rope and gave it one clean slash to cut Lockhart free. Smack and McCabe gripped the captured pilot under his arms and eased him to the ground. Lockhart's battered head bobbed up and down as an uninterrupted stream of vomit poured from his mouth, pooling across the floor. Smack patted him on the back while keeping him from collapsing face-first onto the lake of sickness.

"Place is clear," Dub said when he returned to the room, Noid close behind.

"It's going to be okay," Smack said in a soothing tone to the young pilot.

Lockhart's body shuddered and trembled in reply. He groaned in between coughs and spluttered the alcohol forced into his body. A thick stream of saliva fell down his chin as his arms and legs continued to shake.

"Animals," McCabe cursed as he too patted the traumatised lad.

"You got a name?" Smack asked.

The young pilot groaned again. He moved his lips as if to answer, but another waterfall of vomit sprayed out.

"I know him," McCabe answered. "He's one of the pilots from the North Carolina. His name is Lockhart."

Out of the corner of his eye, he spied Smack's body flinch, as if struck. He looked up out of curiosity. Even with the balaclava concealing most of her features, her eyes were wide open in surprise. She turned to gaze up at her colleagues. The mood in the room changed as the other three Black Visors shifted closer to the vomiting pilot.

"No shit," Noid exclaimed as she took to a knee.

Oblivious to the waves of vomit around her, she leaned in and gently tilted the young pilot's face up. Lockhart gave her a vacant stare back as he raised a hand to his mouth. He wiped the mess from his lips and chin and squinted at the masked strangers surrounding him.

"Cap-Captain Lockhart," he grunted and spat onto the ground. "I...I have a sh-ship now. That m-makes me a... captain."

"Captain Lockhart," the four Black Visors exclaimed at the same time.

Surprised at their sudden change in attitudes and the softening of their tones, McCabe looked over each of them. "You know him?"

Big Mo took McCabe's place and helped the bruised pilot to his feet. "He's one of us."

Noid and Dub turned their wrath on the remaining wounded Nazi, guarded by the West Germans. They stomped across the room, and Noid ordered the two guards to lift the Nazi to his feet. The wounded soldier begged and pleaded for his life, but the Black Visors were in no mood for mercy. While the West Germans held him up, Dub and Noid slung their weapons and drew their knives. Like animals pouncing on wounded prey, they drove their blades into the injured German with savage ferocity. They stabbed and hacked until they stood dripping in his blood.

The West German soldiers released their grip, allowing the dead prisoner to slip to the floor. McCabe expected them to leave it at that, but Dub took to a knee. Using the point of his bloodied knife, he carved lines into the Nazis forehead. McCabe recognised a bloodied Star of David cut into the soldier's skin when the Black Visors sheathed their knives and snatched at their HK-17s.

"Reicher son of a bitch," Dub screamed and kicked at the disfigured corpse. "You string up pilots. Do you shoot people in their beds, too? You scumbags killed Nordie."

The Black Visor leader lashed out with his foot again, booting the dead soldier. With his teeth bared in a ferocious snarl, he drove his foot down repeatedly, further bloodying the mangled body. While Dub seethed with rage, Noid placed her hand on his arm, causing him to stop. As if jolted back to reality, he shook his head and nodded at his colleague. Chests heaving from the frenzied attack, the two MJ-12 operatives re-joined their comrades and assisted with aiding Lockhart.

Dub thumped his chest. "Kill them all."

"Kill them all," the three Black Visors replied together.

They pulled the tatters of Lockhart's shirt over him, and Smack let him sip water from her flask. With Smack and Big Mo carrying him, the Black Visors walked towards the door. McCabe took point after glancing over the battered pilot.

"We have him, Sergeant," Dub said in an authoritative tone. "He's one of us."

Lockhart groaned again as his groggy head rolled from side to side. With his eyelids half closed from intoxication, he tried to focus on the masked soldiers around him. A strange smile cut across his face. "I...I kn-know you, d-don't

I?" he mumbled. "I...I dr-dreamt...dreamt...dreamt..."

"You're one of us," Smack whispered.

"We have always been here," Big Mo said, with a hint of sadness in his eyes.

Lockhart laughed at that. Then his body shook again with another bout of dry retching.

Confused by their cryptic conversation, McCabe opened his mouth to speak when Noid's cool gaze stopped him. "Questions can wait, Sergeant," she muttered. "Right now, we need to get back so we can carve up some more Nazis. Lead the way."

Deciding not to force the issue, McCabe said nothing as he reached for the door. Answers could wait. Right now, they had to get Captain Lockhart medical attention.

COMMAND AND CONTROL BUILDING, GOVERNMENT DISTRICT
13.56 MST
DAY 2

Anna Bailey stood as rigid as a statue. Reichsführer Wagner admired her as if she were a piece of art deserving to be on display in one of New Berlin's galleries. His gaze soaked up every contour of her body in the skin-tight jump suit he had ordered her to change into. While the lab technicians and scientists scurried around him, running various tests and scans, he wanted to admonish them for not appreciating the full glory of their work. So many people sacrificed, so many lives lost, and yet everything had been worth it. He savoured the moment as he would a fine wine.

When his team finished their last series of checks, Wagner moved closer to his prize. The fragrance of her hair sent a tingle of electricity through his body. His sheer proximity to her caused him to tremble as he brought his lips close to her ear.

"You may relax now, Miss Bailey."

Her shoulders slumped with immediate effect. Fingers flexed and curled into fists. She snapped her head around to face him, her burning eyes drilling through him.

Smiling, Wagner took a step back as she continued to stretch her muscles.

"Do I have the honour of knowing what this particular test is about, Herr Reichsführer?" Her voice no longer sounded soft and feminine. She made no effort to flirt with him or toy with him to gain an advantage. All that emanated from her was an unbridled hatred.

She started pacing the room again as she often did before she fought the guards. Her gaze moved across the working technicians and scientists. Slight nods of her head made Wagner guess she was listing off how and in what order she planned to murder each of them if given the chance.

"Of course, I'd be happy to enlighten you, Miss Bailey," Wagner said with a polite nod. "Our next test will be one linked to the internal programming of your new Hollow body."

Anna tilted her head, returning her fiery gaze to him. "Internal programming?"

"Yes. It makes you not only more compliant to my orders, but it has some interesting applications, which could revolutionise how we fight future wars."

"Fascinating," Anna hissed in response.

"It is," he said, beaming back. "I'm surprised you can't hear it whispering to you right now, beneath the surface."

Anna stopped in her tracks and faced him. Every muscle in her body tightened, as if fighting her invisible restraints. Her face flashed red, and her eyelids fell to slits.

"Hear what?" she demanded.

Wagner leaned in closer to her until their eyes became level. He smirked as she maintained her efforts, fighting a useless battle to free herself from his control.

"The Voice of God," he whispered.

A rap on the reinforced window stole his attention. He spun about and saw two waiting SS officers standing outside the lab. He clapped his hands in delight and ordered the rest of his team to exit the room. With a spring in his step, he walked into the open area in the centre of his laboratory and gestured at Anna to follow. Seething, she marched in a mechanical fashion and halted as soon as he commanded.

"It looks like we're about ready to begin," he said, unable to mask the excitement in his voice. "But first, I have a few questions for you. You will answer them honestly. Do you understand?"

"Yes, Herr Reichsführer," Anna responded in a flat tone.

"Good. First, tell me... How many times have you met or seen a member of these so-called Native Martians?"

"On three occasions. The first was shortly after I arrived here. The other times were during some point in my incarceration. I never interacted with them, and I'm not sure if they even saw me."

"Excellent." Wagner rubbed his gloved hands together. "Tell me... Based on your limited knowledge of these Natives Martians, what are your impressions of them?"

"They appear to be human, although taller and slenderer. I've overheard them speaking German and what I assume is their own language. They seem fit, healthy, and friendly with your people. I can't offer any more insights, Herr Reichsführer."

"They are a most hospitable people, Miss Bailey," Wagner said as he circled her. "In all the years we have shared this planet, there has never been a single incident of violence between our races. They have never posed a threat to our existence on...what is it they call this place?" He snapped his fingers as his brain searched for the term. "Ah, yes. Big Red."

Wagner halted directly in front of his prize. With a savage grin, he reached for his Luger and cocked it. He took Anna's hand in his, and turning it over, he slipped the pistol into her palm. He stepped to the side and raised his hand towards the guards and staff observing him through the reinforced glass.

"One final question, Miss Bailey. I am sure you're not going to like this, but for the purposes of our test, I need to know. Tell me... What do you hate more than anything?"

The hand holding the pistol shook slightly. Anna clenched her teeth and locked her jaw, as if to keep the words to herself. Her face glowed red from the effort of fighting the programming that dominated her mind. Her resistance died quickly.

"Insects," she blurted out. "I hate insects."

Some of the watching technicians and scientists chuckled at that, but a single glare from Wagner quieted them.

The door to the lab swung open, and two burly SS soldiers stepped through. Behind them a tall, hooded prisoner sauntered forward, his wrists and ankles shackled. Two more soldiers brought up the rear and guided the prisoner to where Wagner indicated. They whipped the hood from the prisoner's head, revealing the thin and angular face of a Native Martian. Adjusting to the light, the native lowered his gaze and squinted as he glanced around the room. He spoke confused words in his own language, but Wagner ignored him.

"Miss Bailey, what do you see in front of you?"

"A Native Martian, Herr Reichsführer."

"Good."

He walked over to one of the nearby controls and typed in several commands. After checking the read-outs on his screens, he turned his focus to the audience outside.

"For the purposes of this test, I will be verbalising exactly what is going through the test subject's mind. The Voice of God programming will do this internally and without the subject being aware of it. Right now, Anna is in Standby Mode. Next, I will move her to Assessment Mode. Beginning test."

Wagner pressed a final button on his console and then spun about to face Anna. She stood as rigid and unflinching as before, with the gun resting in her hand.

After spotting the pistol, the terrified native kept uttering words of mercy, but they fell on deaf ears.

"Who are you?" Wagner asked.

"My name is Anna Bailey. I am a Terran soldier."

"What is your core drive, Miss Bailey?"

"Protect Terra."

"What is Terra?"

"Terra is life. Terra is home. Terra is everything. Terra must be protected. Protect Terra."

"Good. Good!" Wagner exclaimed and clapped his hands.

"Now, Miss Bailey, what do you see in front of you?"

"I see a Native Martian male, approximately 1.9 metres in height and 60 kilogrammes in weight. He appears shackled and unarmed."

"If I ordered you to shoot him, would you, Miss Bailey?"

"Yes, Herr Reichsführer."

"Would you experience guilt or regret afterwards?"

"Yes, Herr Reichsführer."

Beaming with joy, Wagner turned to the console. He worked his fingertips across the controls again, and glancing up at his eager audience, he flicked a switch. "I'm initiating Combat Mode now."

He swung about and took a few paces closer to Anna. He peered from the native and back towards her. Her penetrating gaze was fixed on the panicking prisoner in front of her.

"Now tell me what you see?" Wagner asked.

A momentary look of disgust flashed across her face, but the rest of her body stood rooted to the spot. The tempo of her breathing increased.

"I see an insect-like creature with eight legs and a torso. It appears to be approximately 1.9 metres in height, but I cannot ascertain its weight. All eight points of its legs appear razor-sharp. Its head is human-like but contains sharpened teeth."

The technicians and scientists started clapping, but Wagner held up a hand to hush them. Marvelling at his creation, he placed a gloved hand on her shoulder.

"That creature is an enemy of Terra. Exterminate it."

"Protect Terra," Anna said and raised the pistol from her side.

With no outward signs of hesitation, she took aim and squeezed the trigger. Bullets struck the native in the centre of his chest, causing him to crash backwards onto the ground. Crimson blood squirted from his wounds as he flailed about, screaming in his native tongue. Anna stalked towards him, took aim at his head, and fired a final shot. The native's skull exploded across the floor, finishing him off.

With a flick of Wagner's hand, the waiting SS guards

grabbed at the prisoner's punctured body. A trail of blood streaked across the polished floor as they dragged him from the lab. Grinning in victory, Wagner took back his pistol, uncocked it, and slipped it into his holster. He gave a slight bow as his audience applauded him, and placing his hand on Anna's arm, he led her back to her original position.

"I'd say that went quiet well," he said to muffled laughter from his team outside.

He tapped on his console again, and removing several disks, he placed them in a brown envelope marked as URGENT. One of his staff members entered the room, took up the package, and hurried down the hallway.

Focusing on Anna again, Wagner brought his lips close to her ear. "You may relax now, Miss Bailey."

Her body slumped again. This time, she stumbled back a few paces. She raised her hands as her gaze shot back and forth, scanning the room.

"What in God's name was that thing?" she shrieked as she backed into the far wall.

"That, Miss Bailey, is the future."

CITY CENTRE DEFENSIVE LINES
15.45 MST
DAY 2

The sound of non-stop gunfire filled the air as Private Jenkins jumped behind a blazing panzer for cover. A torrent of bullets lashed out at the MEF from Nazi defences up ahead. To his left and right, the Jewish insurgents known as the Army of David crept forward. Carrying mostly German equipment and weapons, they made co-ordinated movements as they rushed towards the barricades, taking turns to lay down covering fire. Oily-smelling smoke choked the air from the burning carcasses of panzers. The bodies of Nazi, Allied, and Jewish fighters blended, blanketing the cratered street.

Braving the enemy rounds bashing into the twisted panzer shell, Jenkins aimed his Lee-Enfield. He pointed it at the German lines and tracked a small group of

Volkssturm defenders foolishly throwing themselves into the blizzard of MEF bullets. Jenkins curled his finger on his rifle's trigger and emptied his ammo clip, dropping two of the Nazis. The other three fell to the Allied onslaught.

The terrifying screech of a transport missile sounded a split second before the enemy line disappeared into a ball of flame. Broken bodies spiralled through the air from the deadly payload. Machinegun fire tapped out at the MEF, but at a fraction of the volume from moments ago.

"Forward!" Zofia's voice pierced the avalanche of noise around Jenkins.

The Army of David fighters let out their own savage cheer as they pulled themselves up and pressed on. Men and women alike charged towards the burning Nazi trenches, and children were not far behind them. Junior Sergeant Alexeev appeared on Jenkins's right flank, his AK-47 on full-automatic. The surviving Nazis laid down as much fire as they could, but with most of their line in ashes, it looked to be a hopeless attempt. Jumping to his feet, Jenkins joined in the mad dash and fired his Lee-Enfield at the same time.

As they neared the German lines, several of the Army of David fighters hit the scorched ground from the enemy's bullets. Even wounded, they clutched at their weapons, shooting at point blank range with their dying breaths.

The children sheltered behind their adult wards. They lit their Molotov cocktails and chucked them at the German emplacements. Many of them died alongside their adult protectors, but the Nazis paid dearly. Wehrmacht and Volkssturm soldiers exploded in flame when the Molotov cocktails struck them. They rolled about on the ground, screaming as the fire seared their skin and uniforms. The Jewish fighters ignored them and vaulted into the enemy trenches.

Following close behind the first wave of Jewish attackers, Jenkins reached the Nazi lines when Junior Sergeant Alexeev did. The hulking Russian swung his AK-47 to the left and right, tapping on his trigger with precision. German soldiers crumpled around the Soviet NCO before two Volkssturm soldiers caught him off guard.

One grabbed the Russian from behind, and another tried to skewer him with a bayonet. Snarling, the junior sergeant kicked out his foot, catching the approaching Nazi in the stomach. Jenkins threw himself forward and ran the point of his bayonet into the back of the Volkssturm soldier who gripped Junior Sergeant Alexeev from behind. The enemy combatant shrieked. He released his grip and dropped to the muddy trench floor. Jenkins thrust his weapon downwards repeatedly until the German died in as much agony as Jenkins could inflict.

Junior Sergeant Alexeev grunted something in Russian, which Jenkins guessed to be some form of thanks. Then he turned about and pushed towards the sound of enemy gunfire.

On the left flank of the Nazi lines, Jewish fighters swarmed the remaining holdouts. Moving towards them, Jenkins fired twice as enemy reinforcements tried to join the fray. He caught one Nazi in the head and another through the chest. He pushed on, leaving them on the ground where they lay.

Two more Wehrmacht soldiers landed in the trenches ahead and turned their guns on the Jewish fighters. They blasted their weapons, cutting down men, women, and children without hesitation.

An elderly man, clasping at his wounded chest, crawled along the street and out of their line of sight. He pulled out a grenade, rolled into the trench in front of the Nazis, and landed at their feet. Shouting something in German, he held up the grenade for them to see. In a flash, all three men disappeared, leaving splotches of scorched meat and blackened limbs in Jenkins's path.

Stumbling from the force of the explosion, Jenkins ran a quick hand over his chest to check for wounds. Not feeling any, he shook himself off before darting past the singed and torn pieces of the men that lined the trench. He continued towards the sound of Nazi guns. Three young girls appeared above him. One raised a rifle, but she lowered it a moment later at seeing his stained British battledress.

The girl with the rifle started to speak when bullets

rang out. She rammed the butt of the weapon into her shoulder. Like an expert, she took aim, exhaled, and pulled the trigger. The screams of wounded men told Jenkins her bullets found their mark. She said something to her two friends and nodded towards the Nazi machinegun emplacement. An eyeblink later, she tumbled backwards with a shriek, clutching at her throat. Her friends screamed. They lit Molotov cocktails and flung them over the trench. Seconds later, two burning Nazi soldiers plummeted onto the ground in front of Jenkins. Their limbs flapped as they burned. Jenkins plunged his bayonet into their chests, wounding them further. As they writhed and screeched from the flames chewing their sizzling flesh, Jenkins ran past them.

After hauling himself out of the trench, he watched the Jewish fighters overrun the last Nazi machinegun. They hacked the soldier to pieces with hatchets before swinging the light machinegun about to face the next Nazi defensive line a hundred metres away. A solitary panzer rolled in from one of the side streets, shielding several Wehrmacht soldiers from the MEF onslaught. When the barrel of the lumbering monstrosity swung towards his direction, Jenkins dove into a nearby crater for shelter. The light machine gun in the hands of the Army of David belched out lead in short, swift bursts at Germans foolish enough to fall into their sights. The panzer boomed once as it fired a shell, and it obliterated the fighters with the light machine gun.

Like ants swarming a picnic, Jewish fighters converged on the tank. As if oblivious to the concept of fear, they charged the Nazi weapons head-on. Dozens of them collapsed to the ground from bullets that cleaved through their bodies. Several Jewish insurgents leapt onto the hull of the panzer. Some of them used it as a firing position to blast at the Wehrmacht soldiers seeking shelter behind it. Others smashed their Molotov cocktails off its armour in a vain effort to slow its advance.

An MEF team carrying captured panzerfausts signalled at the surviving Jewish fighters to scatter from the top of the panzer. Shots rang out, engulfing the enemy panzer in flames and causing it to lurch to a halt. Hatches swung open when the panzer crew tried to escape, but the waiting Army of David soldiers struck them with Molotov cocktails.

Jenkins dragged himself up and fired his Lee-Enfield as the MEF and their allies continued the push against the enemy.

Overhead, a transport swung low and unleashed another pair of missiles on the Nazi lines. Flaming death ripped through the German trenches as the attackers attempted to break their enemy's spirit. Without faltering, Jewish units forged ahead, dying in droves as they sought to tear out the throats of their oppressors. Trying to lay down covering fire for them, Jenkins and his colleagues struggled to keep up with the Army of David's unstoppable drive.

Using the burning panzer for cover against German bullets, Jenkins slipped in a fresh clip and prepared to move. When he was about to swing himself around the hunk of burning metal, a bloodied Wehrmacht soldier knocked him to the ground with a savage punch to the jaw. Dazed from the unexpected attack, Jenkins looked up. He rolled out of the way when the Nazi lunged his bayonet downward. The blade embedded in the ground where he had just been.

Jenkins thrust his weapon upward, but the German soldier blocked it with his own rifle and slashed again. The tip of the blade cut across his cheek, and pain tore through Jenkins's face. Roaring in anger, he grabbed at the Nazi's rifle and shoved the barrel away. Keeping his grip on his opponent's weapon, Jenkins forced his Lee-Enfield forward again, but he missed when the German sidestepped his attack.

With a snarl, Jenkins rose to his feet and used his momentum to pin the Nazi against the side of the battle-scarred Panzer. A glare of hatred tore into Jenkins, and the enemy combatant smashed his head forward, catching Jenkins on the forehead. As his eyes watered, Jenkins barely had time to swipe with his Lee-Enfield before the Nazi tried to gouge him again.

As Jenkins grappled with his adversary, a series of

deafening explosions carving through the Wehrmacht's lines sent them both crashing to the ground. They landed on their backs, but immediately tried to grab at each other. The German soldier managed to throw himself on top of Jenkins and grabbed his throat, but Jenkins used his enemy's momentum against him and flung him onto the ground. The Nazi tightened his hand around Jenkins's throat, but with Jenkins on top, he pressed his advantage.

While fighting off the German's attempts to unseat him, Jenkins moved his own hand to his enemy's face. With the Nazis grip on his throat choking him, Jenkins inched his thumb towards the soldier's eye. He gave a savage thrust and pressed his thumb into the Nazi's eye socket. The eyeball burst under the pressure.

The Nazi soldier screamed, and his body shuddered in pain. His grip around Jenkins's throat loosened, so Jenkins snatched at the knife on his enemy's belt. He slipped the knife loose and shoved the blade into the German's throat. The enemy soldier gurgled as he choked on his own blood, driving Jenkins to twist the knife until the Nazi's body fell limp. He pulled his bloodied thumb out of the German soldier's eye socket and collapsed back against the panzer.

Jenkins glanced down at the blood-stained knife in his hand and wiped it on the dead German's trouser leg. He slipped the blade into his own belt and picked up his Lee-Enfield when a small group of MEF soldiers surged into view. Major Wellesley fired his pistol and took to a knee to reload when Jenkins dragged himself to his feet.

"You there," the major called out. "Jenkins! Are you injured?"

Jenkins ran the back of his hand across his cheek and examined the small trail of blood.

"Not seriously, sir."

"Then let's hop to it, Private. The enemy lies ahead!"

"Yes, sir."

Up ahead, the Army of David crashed into the Nazi trenches yet again, refusing to slow down their momentum. As bullets bit through the smoky air, Jenkins fired at any target that he could see. MEF soldiers fought viciously to gain ground, and the defending Nazis shot back at them from positions mere metres apart. Both sides lobbed endless waves of grenades at each other, until a thick fog enveloped the lines.

Jenkins rolled into the nearest section of the Nazi trench, startling two wounded Jewish insurgents. The old men nodded to him after seeing his uniform. Speaking in German, they pointed towards the sound of fighting. Jenkins rushed past them and came across the bodies of several MEF, Army of David, and Nazi soldiers alike. Each of them bore horrific wounds from combat. He supressed a shudder at the pained expressions written across their faces and continued his advance.

Three Germans landed in the trench ahead of him. Jenkins dropped to a knee and unleashed what was left in his clip. He caught two with the first barrage. The last he wounded in the stomach. Needing to reload, Jenkins charged before the German soldier could raise his weapon. He punched his bayonet into the Nazi's chest and twisted the blade. Then he ran the bayonet through the dying man until the light faded from his eyes. After sliding in a fresh clip, Jenkins made to carry on when the ground shook in a thunderous earthquake.

A sequence of booms sounded. Pillars of smoke, dirt, and shrapnel shrouded the trenches in front of him. Jenkins tumbled to the ground from the force of the detonations. Moaning, he pulled his battered body upright. A moment later, enemy soldiers rushed his trench. He lifted his Lee-Enfield and shot two at point blank range, forcing the others to pull back. The surviving Germans shouted at one another as two grenades landed beside Jenkins. He dove towards them and threw the devices out a split-second before they exploded. Pain cut through him when small pieces of shrapnel ate into his skin. Stunned by the noise and the pieces of metal dotting his arms, he barely had enough time to bring up his rifle before two more Nazis threw themselves into the trench.

He caught the first Wehrmacht soldier with a shot to the face, sending his lifeless body crashing into his colleague. Without a clear shot, Jenkins surged towards the surviving soldier and slashed at him with his bayonet. The edge of the blade sliced across the German's face. Jenkins aimed again and smashed its point straight through his enemy's throat. He twisted the bayonet, and pulling the blade out, he reached for the edge of the trench.

With his entire body aching, he rolled out and crawled towards the nearest cover he could find. He sheltered behind chunks of metal jutting from the ground, his body numb to the pain and exhaustion. As bullets raged above his head, Jenkins peeked towards the next line of enemy defences.

Just as before, the Army of David were intent on leading every thrust. MEF soldiers trailed close behind, eager to utilise the Jewish insurgents' seemingly unrelenting drive. British, French, Irish, Russian, and American flags, dangling from radio antennas, waved in the artificial wind. Company after company advanced with unyielding determination as the invading forces pushed deeper and deeper into New Berlin, ever closer to the centre of the city.

Willing himself to move, Jenkins pushed to his feet again.

A series of shrill whistles pierced the air.

"All units hold positions and cease fire. Repeat, cease fire."

Jenkins blinked at the words coming across the MEF's common comm channel. The sound of fighting abruptly died off, lowering to sporadic shots. Even the German defenders ceased firing. Unsure of what was happening, Jenkins broke into a mad dash and dove into the latest series of trenches seized by the allied forces. On either side of him stony-faced Jewish warriors of all ages kept their guns trained on the enemy lines. Dragging himself up, he took a vacant spot beside the Army of David fighters. He aligned his eye to his Lee-Enfield's sight.

An unnerving stillness descended across their portion of New Berlin. In the distance, he could hear the constant blasts of machinegun fire, but that too sounded fainter. Artillery shells no longer howled overhead. Jenkins considered asking the Jewish insurgents if they knew what was happening, but then he spotted it.

From around a street corner on the left, a German officer

emerged brandishing a large white flag in his left hand. Flanked by two other soldiers, he kept his right hand up to show he held no weapon as he marched. The Army of David fighters broke into angry exchanges at the sight, but none made any move to shoot at the approaching Germans.

A strange sense of hope washed through Jenkins. After a day and a half of fighting, could it be over?

Could the Germans be surrendering New Berlin?

CITY CENTRE DEFENSIVE LINES
16.51 MST
DAY 2

General Schulz fidgeted on the rickety seat in the back room of what two days ago had been one of hundreds of grocery shops dotting New Berlin. For over thirty minutes, the Allies kept him and his retinue waiting. A soot-covered lieutenant had offered him tea, which he respectfully declined. Aside from that, no one had come to inform him of when a senior officer would join him.

After checking his watch, Schulz shifted in his seat again, causing an ache to lance through his wounded left arm. He adjusted the sling and winced. With his good hand, he fumbled in his pocket for his packet of cigarettes. He selected one, placed it in his mouth, and flicked his lighter on. Taking a long drag, he tried to relax back into his chair.

When he couldn't get comfortable, he leaned forward and patted the satchel he had placed on the desk in front of him. His heart pounded at the thought of the task that lay ahead. He and some of his officers had drafted what he considered to be a fair and responsible list of points to negotiate with the Allied commander. Some concessions remained inevitable, but he hoped to maintain the Wehrmacht's honour with anything short of an unconditional surrender.

Schulz's thoughts raced towards the days to come. An Allied victory seemed guaranteed given the betrayal of the SS. Cut off from resupply and reinforcements, the

Allies would need his Wehrmacht to keep the peace on the streets, especially if the SS refused to maintain order in the colonies. Like his predecessor, he suspected Reichsführer Wagner of having ulterior motives for stabbing the Wehrmacht in the back. Scenarios abounded through his mind at Reichsführer Wagner's overall plan, but Schulz doubted the Allies would ever do business with him. Once the Jewish slaves stepped up and demanded justice for the crimes of the SS, the Allies would have no choice but to arrest them all. Then the SS, realising the error of their ways, would fight back.

Taking another drag on his cigarette, Schulz tried to see things from the Allied perspective. He raked his brain in the hopes of anticipating anything they could throw at him. They would want to extract as much as possible from him, but they needed his Wehrmacht, of that he was sure. His soldiers, who had fought with such honour, bravery, and distinction, remained the glue that could hold the colonies together or the hammer that could smash them apart.

Schulz dropped his cigarette to the floor and reached for another one when the door to the back room swung open. He rose to his feet and examined the officer in British army attire. To his surprise, he recognised the rank markings of a major. His gaze darted to the ranks of the other two officers accompanying the British officer. His heart sank when he noted a French lieutenant and an American captain. Were the Allies trying to insult him, or was this a sign of how little interest they had in a negotiated settlement?

The three Allied officers filed in towards the opposite side of the desk. Their solemn faces betrayed no hint of emotion when they took their seats and placed several pieces of paper in front of them. Schulz took his seat wordlessly as a filthy-looking corporal filled glasses of water for them. When the corporal exited, a man with slicked-back hair in a plain black suit and tie entered.

Schulz did a double take, surprised at seeing a civilian looking so well—in the middle of a warzone. The stranger stepped into the room without a word and took a seat at the side of the desk between him and the Allied officers. Schulz noticed a slight quiver of unease cut across the opposing officer's faces, but they ignored the civilian's presence.

The British officer cleared his throat and spoke first. "General Schulz, my name is Major Jack Wellesley. May I also present Lieutenant Pierre Deschamps and Captain Roland Miller. Also present is Mr. John D. Myers. On behalf of the acting Supreme Commander of the Mars Expeditionary Force, Major General Alexander Hamilton, I have been instructed to begin discussions with a view to ending all hostilities within the New Berlin military district. If I may ask, sir, are you here at the behest of your government?"

Schulz looked over the officers in turn before his eyes focused on the stranger, who appeared disinterested in what was happening around him. The civilian fidgeted with his hand as his thumb probed a hangnail. Returning his focus to Major Wellesley, Schulz chose his words with care. "I speak for the German people and the Armed Forces, Herr Major. That should be sufficient." He reached into his satchel and removed a paper file. He flipped the pages open with his good hand, and turning the file around, he pushed it towards the Allied officers.

"After consultations with my officers, there are some points of interest I'd like to discuss before we bring up any talk of extending the current ceasefire—"

Major Wellesley shoved the file back towards him. "Pardon me, General, but there seems to be a misunderstanding here. Sir, I have been authorised to accept nothing less than a full, immediate, and unconditional surrender. Hostilities will resume without anything less than that."

The words struck Schulz in the gut. He had expected the Allies to play hardball, but the resolve leaking from Major Wellesley's eyes told him this man wasn't playing any games. The Allies wished for the unthinkable. He returned his own cool gaze back to Major Wellesley as he conjured the words needed to safeguard German honour.

"Need I remind you, Major, that there are several thousand of my soldiers within this colony and outside it,"

Schulz responded, trying to add steel to his voice. "They would rather die than face the disgrace of an unconditional surrender. Many times that number of your own soldiers will join them in the process. The journey to this world must have taken you a year. Can you really hold out that long for reinforcements?"

Major Wellesley leaned forward in his chair. His eyes were unblinking. "Need I remind *you*, General, that we have full aerial superiority. We have obliterated your soldiers outside the colonies. Should we wish it, we could annihilate your colonies outright. We will reduce New Berlin to rubble if we must, General Schulz. Even if we fail in our mission, more soldiers will come from Earth, as many as it takes, until we have hunted down every single one of you. Do not test our resolve, General. We are here to stay."

Schulz curled his hand into a fist. He remembered Generalfeldmarschall Seidel's outbursts and found himself at the precipice of launching into a tirade himself. He had no other option than to surrender in order to preserve the civilian population, but his pride stung at him.

Major Wellesley picked up one of the papers in front of him. His brow furrowed as he checked the contents of the paper, and nodding to himself, he placed it on the desk. With a slow push of his hand, he slid the paper towards Schulz.

"We know the SS are in the process of staging a coup," the major said, softening his tone. "We know they are quite happy to sit back as you and your men get slaughtered. We also know that a large portion of your civilian population are sheltered in the area between our forces and the government district. Your casualties are mounting, General. You have thrown everything you have at us and haven't been able to slow us down, let alone stop us."

Major Wellesley extended his hand and tapped his index finger on the document in front of him. "Sign, General Schulz, and you have my word that your soldiers will be treated within the parameters of the Geneva Convention. Surrender now before any more of your men or civilians pay the consequences of your pride."

Schulz picked up his cigarettes. With a shaking hand, he selected one. At the last moment, he held out the pack to the gathered Allied officers. The major and the French lieutenant shook their heads, but Captain Miller accepted one. Schulz leaned across the table and lit the captain's cigarette before sitting back and lighting his own. He inhaled the tobacco as his gaze ran over the Instrument of Surrender document in front of him.

"Your countrymen signed something similar a decade ago," Lieutenant Deschamps said, and a small smile crept across his face. "Your war is over. Surrender now or we will butcher you to the last man."

Schulz fought to control his temper as he read the text of the document. The fate of the civilians kept his anger in check. The weight of the world pressed down on his shoulders, threatening to crush him into the dust.

"Come on, General," Mr. Myers said with a smarmy look plastered across his face. "These gentlemen are right, and you know it. There's a reason why the SS didn't tell you a thing. It's the same reason they're content to let you slug this one out with us. They don't care about you, General. You and the Wehrmacht are a means to an end, and they don't need you anymore. Why do you think we are here on this godforsaken rock?"

Schulz met Mr. Myers's gaze, but he couldn't force any words out.

"Because your precious Führer wants us here," Mr. Myers continued. "He's found something in this hellhole, and he wants to do a deal. He knows what Majestic-12 want more than we know it ourselves. Everything you're seeing here is a pantomime, nothing more than a show to grab MJ-12's attention."

The three officers facing him shifted in their seats to glare at the civilian. Mr. Myers shrugged off their angered looks and kept his gaze on Schulz. He slid his hand into his jacket, and producing a pen, he held it aloft.

"Sign, General Schulz. Have your forces lay down their arms and comply with all orders given by the leadership of the Mars Expeditionary Force. Once you've been thoroughly de-Nazified, I'm sure we can find a place for you and your men in the new world order."

"Mr. Myers!" Major Wellesley jumped to his feet. "This goes way beyond your remit. You cannot—"

Mr. Myers banged his fist down on the desk, cutting the major off. He stood slowly, and the smile evaporated from his face. His nostrils flared as he stared with laser-like precision at the British officer. "Sit down, Major, or I promise you, before this day is through, I'll have you scrubbing latrines with a toothbrush."

Major Wellesley's jaw dropped at the sudden venom in the civilian's voice. His face flushed red, and his hands tightened into fists. Nevertheless, the major slowly lowered himself back into his seat. He glared at Mr. Myers, causing a wicked grin to cut across the civilian's face.

"You three," Mr. Myers said with a dismissive wave of his hand. "Get out. Dismissed."

The three Allied officers' jaws dropped at the same time. They exchanged glances, their eyes wide in surprise. Major Wellesley was the first to rise to his feet, with the lieutenant and the captain following close at his heels. They launched one last fury-filled look at Mr. Myers as they exited.

"Much better." Mr. Myers stood and unbuttoned his jacket. "Now, where were we?"

"You will spare my men and the civilians?" Schulz asked as he picked up the pen on the table.

Mr. Myers smiled. "I promise you. And your people will be treated a hell of a lot better than you ever treated the Jews. Now sign. I'm starting to lose patience, and I need your men out of the way so I can get closer to the government district."

Schulz blinked at the words on the paper. He imagined his heart turning into a lump of ice. Many of his fellow officers and countrymen would despise him for his actions. Even though he wished to serve his people and spare them from further suffering, he knew he was signing away his honour. With a sad shake of his head, he placed pen to paper and signed his name.

"Excellent!" Mr. Myers exclaimed and snatched back

the document. "Now, there's only one thing left to do."

He bounded to the door and gestured at someone standing just outside. The same grubby-looking corporal from earlier strolled into the room carrying a radio pack. His fingers worked the dials as he tuned in to the correct frequency.

Mr. Myers put his hand into his jacket, pulled out a piece of paper, and unfolded it. "Here." He handed the paper to Schulz. "I've taken the liberty of preparing a speech outlining the details of the surrender. Feel free to make any cosmetic changes as you see fit so it appears more natural, as long as the meat of it stays the same."

With his head spinning from the consequences of his actions, Schulz barely even noticed the paper in his hands. He looked down at the words, but no matter how many times he tried to read them, he couldn't make sense of it.

Mr. Myers took the handset linked to the radio and extended it towards him. "They're ready for you, General Schulz. New Berlin is listening."

NUREMBURG VICTORY ARCH AND MEMORIAL – NORTH OF THE CITY CENTRE
17.12 MST
DAY 2

"...effective immediately. All Wehrmacht, Volkssturm, Police, and auxiliary defence units are hereby ordered to lay down their arms and return to barracks or report to the nearest Allied position. Hostilities have ended and all military operations must be suspended..."

"Traitor!" Oberst Brandt screamed at the top of his lungs. "That degenerate, subhuman coward! How dare he betray the Reich and the Führer! Has he no honour left?"

Brandt bounced his fist off the side of his panzer, wishing it could be General Schulz's head. He imagined sinking his fingers into the general's chest, tearing out the man's black heart, and taking a bite from it as the general watched. Fury pumped through Brandt's veins, and he swung about to meet the glare of Captain Fischer. The two men stared at each other, reading the other's thoughts

180

without a word needing to be shared.

Brandt turned towards the other panzer commanders sitting aloft their battle-scarred behemoths. He sensed the fury of the infantrymen under his command as they focused on him. Aside from periodic bouts of gunfire rattling throughout the colony, General Schulz's words boomed through the air on a continuous loop. Enemy aerial craft hovered over the burning city, broadcasting the news of the Wehrmacht's surrender for all to hear.

Brandt studied the sky to ensure his battered units hadn't been seen and grabbed onto the side of his panzer. He hauled himself up and standing atop it, he looked at the gaunt and distraught faces of his men. They had fought bravely and deserved better than a stab in the back. He could see the glimmer of anger burning in their eyes. No defeatism had infected them. They stood proud, as true warriors of the Reich, determined to fulfil their oaths and give their lives for the Führer.

"General Schulz is a moron and a coward," he shouted and was pleased at the nods of agreement. "He is a deranged traitor, deserving a bullet to the head like the dog he is."

Claps rang out from officers and enlisted men alike. Many of them bobbed their heads in agreement, and some banged the butts of their rifles on the ground, adding to the growing din.

"I swore an oath to the Führer, as have each and every one of you. Perhaps, in his madness, the general may have forgotten the wording of this oath?"

Captain Fischer cleared his throat and pulled himself up onto the front of Brandt's panzer. "I swear to God this sacred oath," he called out.

Without delay, the voices of the soldiers of the Third Reich chanted as one.

"That I shall render unconditional obedience to the leader of the German Reich and people, Adolf Hitler, supreme commander of the armed forces, and that as a brave soldier I shall at all times be prepared to give my life for this oath."

A wave of pride and patriotism swept through Brandt.

His soldiers pulled their shoulders back, lifted their chins, and puffed their chests out. An unquenchable fire shone from their eyes as they stared at Brandt.

"Unconditional obedience," Brandt boomed and gazed at each of them. "Where was the general's unconditional obedience when he surrendered to the Allies? He has made a mockery of our oath. I say, if he will not give his life for his oath, then it is up to us to carry on the mantle of National Socialism. It is up to us to defend our Führer!"

A cheer rang out from the men of the Wehrmacht. They lifted their weapons above their heads, chanting in unison. An avalanche of energy crashed over Brandt, tearing away the exhaustion, and pain, and replacing it with ice-cold hatred.

He leapt from his panzer and extended his hands, clasping the shoulders of veterans and replacements alike. He patted faces and shook hands when his men moved closer to him. He listened and nodded as they demanded him to be the instrument of their burning thirst for vengeance. As the NCOs took charge, eager to strike back at the traitors and invaders alike, the surviving officers encircled Brandt.

"We await your orders, Herr Oberst," Captain Fischer said with a gleam in his eye.

Patting his subordinate on the arm, Brandt gave the captain a grateful nod of appreciation. He cast his gaze over the waiting officers, who stared at him, waiting for his word. Many of them had served in the last war. Some younger faces looked barely old enough to have fought in the Battle of Berlin, bleeding the Asiatic hordes for every inch of Reich territory stolen.

"Ready the men to move," Brandt ordered. "Get word to our brother officers, the men you trust with your lives. Find out who is with is us and who is prepared to betray the Reich. Have all who are loyal prepare to join us in one, decisive strike."

"How will we do it, Herr Oberst?" Captain Fischer asked as he ran a hand over his chin. "Many will follow the general's word, by virtue of his rank alone."

Brandt accepted a map from a lieutenant and took a

moment to examine it before glancing up at his second in command.

"The Allies have made it clear they wish to seize the government district, yet they stay careful not to strike it by missile or artillery shell. As our forces begin to surrender, I predict the invaders will move as many soldiers as possible into the city centre to mass for an attack. We will move along the perimeter of the government district for cover, under the pretext of surrendering to the advancing Allies. Once we are in place, we will strike using surprise and decisive force to push them back."

The surrounding officers nodded agreement and worked out how best to accomplish the task with their own units. A few took notes, jotting down names of fellow officers to contact.

"What of the SS, Herr Oberst?" one of the other lieutenants asked. "What if they *are* staging a coup against the Führer?"

Murmurs broke out from several of the officers standing beside the lieutenant. Although many had served with the SS in the last war, and even counted a few of its members as friends, the growing influence of the SS had not gone unnoticed. For years, Brandt had listened when senior officers grumbled at the increasing strength of the SS. Whispers abounded that the Führer sought to disband the Wehrmacht entirely. The possibility of an SS seizure of power had never been far from Brandt's mind but in these trying times, it remained easy to give in to fantastical rumours.

"If there is even a hint of truth in this, you have my word, they will be punished," he said with steel in his voice. "But first, we must deal with General Schulz and his new puppet masters."

"Heil Hitler!" Captain Fischer shouted, snapping his arm up in salutation.

"Heil Hitler!" the surrounding officers roared.

With a grin, Brandt returned the salute and prepared to drown the traitors and invaders in their own blood.

APPROACHING ALEXANDERPLATZ, MITTE DISTRICT,

CITY CENTRE
18.35 MST
DAY 2

Sitting on the back of one of the trucks stolen from the Wehrmacht, Private Jenkins examined the buildings of New Berlin as they sped past. While most of the outskirts of the colony looked to be warehouses, factories, and dilapidated apartment blocks, the city centre seemed like a world removed. Towers and more pristine apartments dominated the horizon, but the houses morphed from gaudy three-bedroom structures into what could only be described as manors. Expansive parks and public gardens broke up the urban landscape, mixing vibrant greens with polished white marble. Statues, pillars, and colossal monuments dotted the pristine streets, and swastika flags flapped gently in the artificial breeze.

This entire section of the city centre remained untouched by the fury of war. While the outer districts smouldered from the MEF's merciless artillery strikes, every one of the buildings Jenkins passed sparkled. To his surprise, he even glimpsed well-dressed civilians wandering the streets, oblivious to the invasion that had steam-rolled through the poorer sections of the colony. Those same civilians stopped and gaped as the convoy of trucks sporting British, French, American, and Soviet flags thundered past them.

Catcalls rang out from the truck when the men of the MEF spotted a group of women strolling up the street arm in arm. Another woman dressed in a brown uniform and armed with a baton ferried the women along, causing them to scurry down a laneway. Raising her baton, she screamed back in German at the MEF soldiers, her arms waving in frantic motions to display her anger. Her words disappeared beneath a tsunami of whistles, jeers, and graphic descriptions as the soldiers continued their antics. Red-faced, she stomped into a nearby building and banged the door shut to the laughs of the MEF.

As much as he wanted to, Jenkins couldn't give into the mood that had enveloped the advance units of their taskforce. Although the news of the German surrender swept the frontlines like wildfire, it felt dreamlike. The faces of those who had died beside him or at his hands haunted him. The idea of laughter at a moment like this struck him as a more alien concept than fighting a war on Mars.

The convoy of trucks halted at an intersection before chugging forward again. Even in their relaxed state, guns still pointed in every direction and gazes watched the rooftops and windows. In the darkening sky above, a transport tracked their every movement, ready to rain down death on anyone foolhardy enough to ambush them.

They swung around into another wide street lined with huge, imposing buildings. A roadblock manned by Wehrmacht and Volkssturm soldiers stood waiting for them. They stared at them from behind the thick lengths of barbed wire. The German soldiers held weapons in their hands or slung across their shoulders, but none raised them at the approaching MEF. When the trucks came to a stop, a series of commands rang out from up and down the line, repeated by Junior Sergeant Alexeev on their truck. The rear hatches banged down, and Jenkins and his comrades jumped off. They broke into all-round firing positions. The transport lingered high above them, ready to strike.

From the corner of his eye, Jenkins watched Major Wellesley approach the barbed wire barricades, flanked by his senior officers. Following a gruff exchange with the German commanding officer, the roadblock was lifted, and the German defenders moved sullenly to the right-hand side. As some of the trucks edged past the former Nazi defences, MEF soldiers moved in closer to the group of Germans. After several curt exchanges in English and German, the Nazis laid down their arms in a pile and formed into a single line. When the German soldiers were patted down to search for concealed weaponry, they were herded towards the outside of a boarded-up structure. With angry and distraught faces, they glared at the British and French soldiers, lit up cigarettes, or sat with their heads in their hands.

Following Junior Sergeant Alexeev's orders, Jenkins

and his platoon made their way up the street towards the towering Colosseum-like structure. To either side of him, groups of MEF soldiers streamed into the shops and businesses, searching for any holdouts trying to escape. Once cleared, snipers set up crow's nests, and soldiers moved heavier weapons and equipment into place. They tore down Nazi banners and flags, flung them to the streets below, and replaced them with flags from Britain, France, the U.S.S.R, and the United States.

At the top of the street, Jenkins spotted rows of barriers and trenches facing the SS lines across from them. From where he stood, he couldn't make out any SS positions, but a curious sensation of a thousand eyes watching him caused him to shudder. Taking a sip from his water flask, Jenkins looked on as a small group of Army of David fighters leapt from the back of a parked truck.

Before they departed, Major Wellesley had tried to forbid the Jewish freedom fighters from joining the advance task force. In a calm, concise tone, the major pointed out that the presence of Jewish fighters could dramatically fan tensions amongst the surrendering Nazis. He had pleaded with the Jewish leader Zofia to remain behind. It didn't go according to plan.

Jenkins had come across many tough women in his twenty years, but he had never witnessed a woman so fearless. Using a string of colourful expletives that could shock even battle-hardened veterans, Zofia screamed, roared, and cursed at the major. Several times, Major Wellesley tried to escape her foul-mouthed and furious tirade, but the Army of David leader refused to back down. In the end, she calmed down and agreed to a token group in the advance task force, as long as her fighters were prioritised in the second wave. Major Wellesley agreed before scarpering away like a dog with its tail between its legs.

When the Army of David fighters fanned out, they made a point of walking in the line of sight of the captured Wehrmacht soldiers. Jenkins couldn't help but smile while they strutted about, flashing their homemade Israeli flags around their arms and brandishing their weapons. Exactly as the major feared, several of the Nazi soldiers became incensed at the sight, and their angered shouts rumbled up and down the street. British and French bayonets kept the POWs in check as the Jewish fighters maintained their victorious march past their former masters.

After a few minutes, the orders came down for the Second Battalion to commence manning defences along the street closest to the government district. With Junior Sergeant Alexeev leading their platoon, Jenkins and the rest of his comrades plodded up the street. On either side, pockets of German soldiers threw down their weapons as they surrendered to the Allies. The faces of worried civilians glanced down at them from windows before quickly disappearing.

Jenkins and his platoon took over foxholes on the right flank. Several grimy, blood-stained Nazi soldiers stood at their arrival. They fired filthy looks at the MEF invaders but deferred to their officers, who snapped at them in quick bouts of German. Although Jenkins couldn't understand their words, from their harsh looks he guessed it wasn't complimentary. With the Wehrmacht soldiers disarmed under Junior Sergeant Alexeev's watchful gaze, he delegated a patrol to lead the POWs back towards the end of the street. Jenkins and his platoon seized their light machine guns and grenades and faced the barbed wire perimeter of the government district less than a hundred metres ahead.

In the street dividing their mutual positions, hundreds of bodies slumped on the concrete as far as the eye could see. Some of the victims wore the grey uniforms of the Wehrmacht, but others donned the grey, black, brown, and green jumble of the Volkssturm. Most of the victims wore civilian attire. Many of them lay face down on the cold concrete, with bullet wounds across their backs and heads. German or not, Jenkins couldn't fathom how terrifying their last moments must have been as bullets burst through them, cutting them to pieces. A pang of sadness engulfed his stomach, but it quickly faded when his mind replayed images of the Jewish civilians swinging from lampposts. Cold hatred replaced any form of sympathy. He eyed the SS lines again.

"Perhaps this is it," Private Moreau of the French contingent said from beside him. "The SS could surrender, and then we can spend the night drinking German piss water beer until we pass out."

Jenkins glanced at the Frenchman as the solider sank back into the foxhole and patted his uniform pockets for his cigarettes. Jenkins didn't know him well, but the French soldier held his own in a firefight.

"I doubt it, mate," Jenkins said and waved off the offer of a cigarette. "Seems too good to be true. We haven't even been here a full two days and nothing has gone according to plan. I doubt we'll start getting lucky now."

"You English always seem so serious about everything. You should be more optimistic. God has guided us here and God will grant us victory. You need to lighten up, my friend."

"You Frenchies don't seem to take anything serious at all," Jenkins retorted. "We've got hundreds of guns aimed at us and you're sitting there smoking. Get your arse back up here and pick up your weapon."

Moreau raised his hand in mock salute, and after tossing his cigarette away, he took up his rifle. Falling in beside Jenkins, he pointed his weapon towards the SS defences and let out a bored sigh. From the far side of the trenches, the sound of a commotion echoed as soldiers called out to each other. Searching for the sound, Jenkins lifted his head up ever so slightly to find the source of the noise. Several MEF soldiers peeked out of their foxholes, gazing at the street to the right past Jenkins's location.

Junior Sergeant Alexeev stood in full view of the SS guns, shouting into a radio mouthpiece.

Leaning out of his own foxhole, Jenkins looked towards the street on the right flank. His blood froze when he spotted a stream of panzers rolling towards the newly manned MEF defences. The lead vehicles sported white flags, but the sheer amount of Wehrmacht soldiers racing beside and behind them caused him to worry. None of them bore the gloomy looks of men preparing to surrender. They looked like men spoiling for a fight.

Jenkins turned his head to look back at Sergeant Alexeev. The Soviet NCO's face went from its normal stony demeanour to one of outright shock at what he heard on the radio. He looked up towards the panzers before diving back into his trench. Jenkins spun about in time to see Nazi soldiers cut the white flags from the panzers and the flags flapped back onto the blood-slicked street. The soldiers of the Wehrmacht hoisted swastikas in their place, and the tank turrets aimed at the MEF lines.

"All units! All units! Fire at will!"

The words cut across the comm channel before panzer shells smashed into MEF lines. Men disappeared in clouds of smoke and mounds of earth as bullets raged across the surviving fragments of the barricades. Jenkins wheeled his captured light machine gun about and pressed on the trigger in controlled bursts to blast at the approaching Wehrmacht.

German bullets pummelled the lines, knocking MEF soldiers into the dirt. Another volley from the panzers blew craters into the forward lines, and the enemy tanks raced to overrun them.

MEF reinforcements bounded into the nearby trenches and foxholes. The wounded tried to claw their way to safety, and medics dragged who they could to the doorways of vacant shops. Men filled every crater and foxhole they could find and threw what they had left of their dwindling ammunition at the approaching Wehrmacht forces. When pausing to reload, every one of them Jenkins could see slipped on their bayonets in preparation for the close quarters fighting.

"Lying kraut tossers!" someone shouted over the comm channel.

"Christ, contact on the left flank."

When the captured German light machine gun ran out of ammunition, Jenkins shoved it out of the way. Risking a glance to the left flank, he sighted several more swastika-sporting panzers racing towards them. As the Nazi formations bombarded the MEF lines, an image of a hammer and an anvil came to Jenkins's mind, with his comrades and him caught in the middle.

With bodies dropping from the Nazi onslaught, the MEF lines floundered. Their advance task force stood at a fraction of its total strength to engage in an offensive operation, let alone defend against heavily armoured panzers. Even with reinforcements being ferried towards the outskirts of the government district, it left a lot of unfriendly territory to their rear and flanks. If the Germans took advantage of their deceitful manoeuvre, they could easily cut their supply lines and leave them stranded.

When the first panzer swung out onto the main street in front of them, Jenkins aimed his rifle at the Wehrmacht soldiers jogging behind the armoured beast. While the turret swerved towards the men of the MEF, he tracked an exposed German soldier and squeezed the trigger. The round caught the Nazi in the chest, causing him to flail backwards. One of his colleagues leapt out, grabbed him, and tried to pull him into the protective shadow of the panzer. Jenkins fired again, blasting the second German in the side of the head. Blood splashed across his comrades, and they pointed their weapons in Jenkins's direction. With an unknown number of guns and a few panzers bearing down on him, Jenkins kept on firing. Activating his comm, he opened it up to the battalion channel and shouted as loud as he could.

"Kill them all! Kill every last one of them!"

Hundreds of voices thundered back in unison as the MEF prepared to exterminate every Nazi that came their way.

NEAR ALEXANDERPLATZ, MITTE DISTRICT, CITY CENTRE
19.14 MST
DAY 2

For hours, Sergeant McCabe and the MEF, their West German contingent allies, and the Black Visors had searched for a way to infiltrate the government district. Although the fighting hadn't spilled over to their area of the city centre, the presence of Nazi patrols and wandering civilians hampered their efforts. Even the West Germans disguised in Wehrmacht uniforms found it difficult to seek a way through without exposing themselves.

Eventually, they discovered that the areas facing the government district looked to be thinly guarded. From what they could uncover, the SS had turned on their former Wehrmacht colleagues and civilians alike and carved out a no-man's-land around their personal fife. With the bulk of their strength dispatched to slowing the advancing MEF, the Wehrmacht left under-strength units to protect their rear while they slugged it out with the Allied forces.

Then the news broke. Despite intermittent communications due to jamming, the broadcast came through as clear as day. A ceasefire had been declared when the Wehrmacht agreed to an unconditional surrender. The abandoned church they used as a temporary hiding place erupted in excitement at the prospects of the fighting drawing to a close. Even the Black Visors who sat protectively beside Lockhart let out a cheer.

As an uneasy stillness blanketed New Berlin, McCabe and the rest of the company moved through the colony. Darting across exposed streets in small groups, they stuck to the back alleys as much as possible and took turns carrying their wounded. The Black Visors assumed the lead, spurring them on at every slow-down. Their impatience to break into the government district intensified with every passing minute. In hushed whispers, McCabe overheard them mention Anna Bailey on multiple occasions. He couldn't be sure if she truly happened to be an MI6 agent, but he saw in their animated movements that her safety remained important to them.

Dodging a Nazi patrol, the combined group of soldiers pushed onwards, edging closer to where the MEF were setting up a staging area. McCabe hoped and prayed to see familiar faces. At least half of his original platoon lay dead so far. More than anything, he wished the ones who had stayed with Corporal Brown and Junior Sergeant Alexeev were alive and well.

As they surged several hundred metres behind the Wehrmacht's defensive lines, communications came through more clearly. McCabe tapped at his arm console, but he couldn't open a clear channel. Gritting his teeth, he spurred on the stragglers at the rear of the group, helping the wounded where he could. Minutes dragged on like hours. Finally, they rounded a corner. McCabe nearly cried out with joy when he saw his country's flag swaying in the light breeze, draped outside a massive building. Beneath that flag, he estimated hundreds of Mars Expeditionary Force soldiers stood occupying defences and stripping surrendering German soldiers of their weapons.

"We made it," he muttered to himself and leaned against the wall of the back alley. His gaze scanned up and down the street, checking for any sign of hostile enemy activity.

"Yes, we have," Colonel Henke said from beside him, "but we have much to do. We can at least have our wounded seen to and stock up on supplies."

"The job's not done yet, Sergeant," Dub grumbled and gave the all-clear sign. "We still have to break in there and—"

"Anna Bailey," McCabe grunted. "I get it."

Dub opened his mouth to speak when all hell broke loose. Tank guns boomed to life, heralding death and destruction. Buildings tore apart from direct hits from panzer rounds, and men disappeared in fogs of brick and dust. Machine guns banged to life, spewing death. From along the road, circling the government district, a dozen panzers swung headfirst into the street packed with the MEF.

Panic fire rang back in reply, pinging off the thick armour of the panzers. Wehrmacht soldiers sheltering behind the metal monstrosities sprinted towards nearby barricades and hurled themselves at the MEF soldiers. Screams and cries died as the Nazi forces continued their push, slamming shells into the MEF defences. German soldiers who had surrendered minutes before rushed the Allied guards, overpowering them. Other MEF units, seeing the chaos breaking out around them, trained their weapons on groups of disarmed POWs. They blasted on their Lee-Enfield's and Bren's, cutting down the Nazi soldiers before they had a chance to turn on them.

"We need to do something," McCabe shouted.

In the sky above, a transport swooped down like a falcon ready to grasp its prey in its talons. It unleashed a half a dozen missiles, catching the lead panzers head-on and leaving seared metal in their place. As Wehrmacht soldiers rushed from the side streets, the panzers focused their wrath on the Allied transport. Anti-aircraft rounds zipped through the sky, forcing the craft into a series of evasive manoeuvres to escape.

"You have your damned orders," Dub shouted back at McCabe. "Anna Bailey is the most important person on this rock. We need to get to her now."

McCabe envisioned ramming his fist through Dub's face. The chaos of the unfolding situation helped him to maintain his composure.

"We will render assistance here," Colonel Henke said, leaning in between the two men. "Then we will proceed with the rescue effort."

The Black Visors gently placed Lockhart amongst the wounded soldiers. They each leaned in and patted the unconscious boy, whispering soft words to him. Smack dipped her hand into her pocket, pulled something out, and rested a small device on his chest. She slipped two small buds into his ears and clicked a button on the device while whispering something about "Song 2." Strange music emanated from the two buds, causing a small smile to creep across the drowsy pilot's face.

"First Platoon, on me, double time," McCabe called out.

At his command, the two dozen MEF and West German soldiers of the makeshift First Platoon edged up. Pointing out the positions they needed to take, McCabe wasted no time and threw himself into the battle.

Bullets whistled through the air, gutting men on both sides when McCabe stormed up the left flank of the street. Seeing a small group of Wehrmacht soldiers sneak ahead, using doorways for shelter, he took aim as he ran. He pulled on his Lee-Enfield's trigger, dropping two soldiers. His platoon unleashed a wall of lead on the enemy, tearing them to shreds as the remaining West German and MEF soldiers spilled out of the back alley. The transport swung low again, turning another pair of panzers into a hellish inferno.

Having regained their composure, the MEF started to shove the Nazis back. Bolstered by reinforcements brought in by acquired trucks, they battered Wehrmacht and Volkssturm units with persistent fire. Their panzers in flames, McCabe noticed the German assault wane. Their soldiers flung themselves into the fight, but fewer and fewer enemy units seemed willing to brave the murderous onslaught. Screaming at the top of his lungs, McCabe kept up his pace. Working as one, the sections under his command took turns in laying down covering fire and pressing forward.

Bounding through the wreckage blanketing the street, McCabe sighted several civilians fighting alongside the MEF. Each of them carried German weaponry and wore homemade Israeli flags wrapped around their arms— Jewish insurgents. Given that Israel had been founded six years previously, he wondered how they could have learned of its existence while trapped here. Dodging a bullet, he filed that information away and watched them charge the Nazi forces with no regard for their own safety.

They braved the hail of enemy fire and fought to get close enough to shower their enemy with Molotov cocktails. Several Germans vaulted from their foxholes as the homemade explosives found their mark. MEF bullets pounded the burning Nazis when they tried to flee. On the right flank, regrouped Allied soldiers fired anti-tank rounds from their modified Lee-Enfield's, hitting the sides of several lumbering panzers.

Turning about, McCabe noticed Colonel Henke close behind. The colonel pushed through the wreckage and bodies that carpeted the street, directing light machine guns towards groups of defending Nazis.

In the sky above, the transport dodged anti-aircraft fire to slam another volley of missiles at approaching panzers. This time, though, the craft came too close. A German heavy machine gun pummelled the transport with high calibre rounds, denting the sides and punching through the cockpit. The entire ship shuddered before crashing to the ground like a meteorite. A column of Wehrmacht soldiers disappeared beneath its burning mass, squashed like bugs.

With more German soldiers streaming from the side streets, the now-rallied MEF charged the last of their defences in well-timed movements. Bren light machine guns punched endless streams of lead on the enemy, and rifles banged out at anything that moved. With bloodthirsty roars, the MEF and their Jewish allies leapt over their dead, keen to close the distance and crush the last scraps of Nazi resistance.

Urging on his platoon and the assortment of soldiers that gravitated to the left flank, McCabe rushed at the nearest barricade. Men fell to the ground when bullets cut them down mid-step. Grenades flew out from both sides, bursting men apart and splattering blood over the skeletons of panzers. Shrapnel whistled through the smog-filled air and sliced through flesh and bone, gutting entire sections. Howls from the wounded pierced the constant sound of gunfire as soldiers cried out for help that would never arrive.

With a furious roar, McCabe was the first one to dive over the Nazi barricades lining the top of the street. Surprised German soldiers swung their weapons about, but he reacted first. He emptied his rifle's ammo clip, sending Nazi soldiers crashing to the ground. Without even a moment to stop and reload, he lunged at the nearest Nazi and buried his bayonet deep into his stomach. He twisted and kicked the soldier to the floor and managed to raise his rifle in time to block a knife swipe from behind. A Volkssturm soldier with a bloody face moved to strike at him again when bullets tore through his chest. The German staggered and hit the ground seconds before MEF soldiers scrambled through the holes in the barricades, gunning down grey and brown uniforms in equal measure.

The German soldiers who could retreat ran towards the trickle of panzers flowing from the side roads for cover. Streams of lead continued to lash out at the oncoming MEF soldiers as they grappled with the few die-hard Nazis refusing to abandon their posts. Like crazed berserkers, the Jewish warriors mobbed what German machinegun nests continued to crack fire at them. They dodged around the ruins of the burning street and fired without remorse or hesitation, even as their brethren collapsed around them. Those who could throw themselves headfirst into the enemy foxholes did so. They piled onto the defending Nazis and lashed out with knives and axes.

The ground under McCabe rocked and thundered when another transport made its presence known. Wehrmacht soldiers firing from the adjoining side streets disappeared under a pillar of dirt and blackened smoke. McCabe struck the ground from the force of the explosion. He clawed himself back to his feet and rallied all who could hear him.

He slipped in a fresh magazine into his rifle and took aim. Three German soldiers raced around the corner and fired on the Jewish warriors who had overrun one of the nearby machinegun nests. He caught two of them in the chest while two of the insurgents dealt with the last Nazi. They pelted the German with Molotov cocktails, and, as he burned, they cleaved through his feet with axes. The burning soldier writhed in pain as the flames charred his flesh.

"Forward!" someone screamed from the rear. "Forward! Let's break the bastards now!"

Having seized the defensive line that faced the government district, the MEF dragged their wounded into cover and reloaded their weapons.

Columns of roaring Wehrmacht soldiers charged from both streets to the left and right, despite the near-continuous blasts from guns of all calibres. Several panzers disappeared under an avalanche of concrete and steel when the transport above bombed the apartment blocks and structures.

Screaming German soldiers tried to flee, but their bodies disappeared under a mass of bricks. The air turned thick, black, and heavy from the fires raging around the government district.

Surviving Wehrmacht soldiers flung down their arms and raised their hands in surrender. Unwilling to take any more risks, the MEF gunned them down where they stood. Cries of "Kill them all" rang through the air as they shot, hacked, and stabbed any Nazi who fell into their hands.

Just as McCabe and the MEF were about to push on towards the perimeter of the government district, a thunderstorm of noise erupted. Gun emplacements, snipers, and RPGs spewed death. Like a monster waking from a slumber, SS forces fired upon everyone who came into their sights. Green and grey uniforms collapsed together as snipers shot at anyone out in the open. Machine gun bullets chewed up the concrete streets. Bullets eviscerated soldiers without mercy.

While dashing for cover behind a burnt-out panzer, a piercing sensation ripped through McCabe's shoulder. He lost his footing from the shock and stumbled a few paces before glancing down. Blood trickled from a bullet hole. Seeing that intensified the pain that throbbed through him.

A hand grabbed him by the back of the neck and pushed him onwards. McCabe turned and saw Dub blasting his HK-17. "I'm getting sick of saving your ass, Sergeant," Dub said as he hauled him behind the metal carcass.

"The feeling's mutual," McCabe groaned.

He reached for the oozing wound as the Black Visors and some of the West German contingent fell in around him. Noid moved closer and methodically probed the gash with her gloved fingers.

"Looks like it went straight through," she said as she applied antiseptic and started bandaging it.

Looking across the Black Visors, McCabe saw blood splatters across their dark red and black uniforms. Each of them sported cuts across their arms, legs, and torsos. The West Germans and MEF soldiers looked no better. As SS bullets pinged down at them, he risked a quick glance towards the government district ahead. It didn't look good.

"Barbed wire and barricades across the whole perimeter." He fumbled for a cigarette. "Machine gun nests every twenty metres or so. Snipers on the apartment roofs. Heavier weapons spread out in interlocking arcs of fire. And that's only the first layer. They could have hundreds, even thousands of soldiers in those buildings."

McCabe flicked on his lighter and was raising the flame

to the tip of his cigarette when shots rang out from his left flank. Smack yelped and tumbled backwards onto the concrete.

"Smack!"

Dub jumped to his feet and searched for the location of the shots. McCabe spotted two Wehrmacht soldiers hunkering behind chunks of fallen concrete and scrambled to raise his rifle. Dub acted first and squeezed the trigger in two short bursts, killing the German soldiers. With their flanks and rear clear, he spun about and dove at his comrade.

Smack let out a howl and clutched at her wound. Dub and Noid grabbed at her. Fear leaked from their eyes. Smack clamped her jaws shut as Dub tore her hand away and checked her wounded side. He and Noid set to bandaging her wound as the MEF soldiers took pot-shots at any enemy that came into their sights. After a few minutes of furious work, they managed to patch Smack up and lifted her to her feet slowly. She winced from the effort and kept her hand protectively to her bandaged side, but she could move.

"Can you walk?" Dub asked, his tone surprisingly soft.

"Yeah," Smack said and gave a frantic nod of her head. But she bit her lip and closed her eyes when she tried to take an unaided step. Even with her face masked, the skin around her eyes tightened, and her lips curled tight to mask her pain.

McCabe turned to gain a better view of the SS forces in front of him. On their right flank, Colonel Henke and a collection of MEF soldiers had used the burnt-out panzers to advance closer to the SS lines. That left a large quantity of open ground, leaving the MEF as easy pickings for the hundreds of enemy guns trained on them.

"We'd need a tank regiment to break through there," McCabe said as his mind searched for a solution. "We could probe other points in their defensive ring for weak spots, but considering the amount of effort they've put in, I doubt we'll find any."

Just above them, another transport unleashed its payload against SS targets. The transport exploded in a massive fireball at the same time as its missiles struck two anti-aircraft batteries. Flaming wreckage and burning metal rained down on the streets around them in a savage hailstorm.

"I have an idea," Dub said to his Black Visors comrades. "I say, screw the damn timeline bullshit. I am sick of this crap! Playing it safe? Horseshit! Let's do what we do best and carve these sons of bitches a new one."

Wide-eyed, Noid crept towards Dub's side. "You thinking what I'm thinking?"

They maintained eye contact for a few seconds before a smile crossed their lips. They turned their vicious grins on Big Mo and Smack.

Big Mo shook his head. "This is never good." He rubbed a hand over his masked face. "When you two agree on anything, it tends to get messy."

"I think I know where you're going with this," Smack groaned. "Normally, I'd shoot it down in a heartbeat, but like the Sergeant said, we'd need a tank regiment to break through. Fine. Screw the timeline. Let's get stupid."

The four Black Visors nodded at one another before they took up firing stances. Using the panzer wreckage for cover, they spoke in hushed tones as they pointed out targets and enemy gun emplacements.

"Care to fill the rest of us in?" McCabe barked.

Dub turned his head to look at him.

McCabe repressed a shudder at the darkness burning in his eyes.

"We're going to carve a path through those Nazi dickheads. Keep your eyes peeled, Sergeant. You're not gonna want to miss this."

After nodding at each other, the Black Visors tapped at the side of their HK-17s. Even as bullets howled and whipped around them, McCabe heard a distinct, high-pitched hum emanate from their HKs. They placed a hand on top of their weapons and pulled back, like cocking a pump-action shotgun. They lowered their eyes behind their HKs sights. Collectively, they took deep breaths.

"Remember recharge intervals," Dub shouted. "Follow my lead, one at a time, and don't stop until everything in sight is a flaming wreckage."

McCabe leaned closer to Dub to follow his line of sight. "Fire!" Dub bellowed.

A bolt of green energy leapt from Dub's weapon, moving too fast to comprehend. One minute a Nazi machine gun emplacement chattered fire at the MEF. The next, a smouldering hole in the ground remained. McCabe flinched when similar volleys erupted from the other Black Visors' weapons, wiping out entire gun crews and leaving black ash in their wake. The Black Visors paused in between shots to re-cock the weapon at the top before taking aim again. SS guns fell silent as green energy blasts burst out, carving down men and metal like a hot knife through butter.

McCabe looked on in awe as the Black Visors reduced the SS defences to scorch marks. Machinegun emplacements vanished. Sniper nests were torn from roofs and windows. Barbed wire and steel defences melted into nothing. SS soldiers, who fell into the Black Visors' sights, disappeared or slumped to the ground after large parts of their bodies disintegrated. They fired again and again, refusing to stop until every SS position within sight was annihilated.

When they ceased firing, silence enveloped New Berlin. Never in his life had McCabe seen a weapon of such devastating power wielded by a soldier. With guns such as those, a platoon could lay waste to an entire city and destroy thousands with the squeeze of a trigger.

With this section of the government district demolished, Dub spun about to face him. A wolfish smile crossed his lips as he made eye contact.

"That, Sergeant McCabe, is a particle weapon."

McCabe couldn't think of anything to say as his gaze ran over the HK-17. A million questions floated through his mind about where such a weapon could have come from. Before words could form on his lips, Noid jumped to her feet.

"Enough talk," she said and motioned at the MEF behind her to rise. "Let's get the job done and go home."

"Agreed," Big Mo said as he, too, stood.

"I could really use a glass of wine," Smack groaned.

"Kill them all," Dub said and motioned at McCabe and the MEF to follow.

With their HK-17s raised, the Black Visors stepped out from behind the gutted panzer and started towards the government district. In awe of their destructive capabilities, McCabe followed close behind.

WE HAVE ALWAYS BEEN HERE

COMMAND AND CONTROL BUILDING, GOVERNMENT DISTRICT
19.38 MST
DAY 2

Reichsführer Wagner tapped his fingers on the console as he stared at the blank screen in front of him. To his right, a stack of messages had started to build over the last few minutes. Iron-faced runners entered his lab, saluted, and left updates from the deteriorating situation outside. Tearing his gaze from the blank screen for seconds at a time, Wagner skimmed the reports as they came in. Up until a half hour ago, only progress updates came on the Wehrmacht's suicidal assaults on the far superior Allied forces. Then everything changed.

Accounts of strange energy-based weapons eliminating the outer defences had piqued his interest. He had researched the designs of such weapons in ancient texts belonging to the ancestors of the Native Martians. At one point several years ago, he even assigned a team to try and develop them, but they lacked the technical knowledge to get the project off the ground. Since he ordered the executions of the scientists involved in that project for incompetence, that meant one other faction had them. The

Core Cadre had chosen this place and this time to make their stand against the future he envisioned so clearly. He wondered if these time-travellers even knew the extent of what they were involved in and the repercussions for humanity should they succeed.

Still, the news didn't bother Wagner. Intervention had always been anticipated. There remained little he could do to oppose them. At this stage in the game, he had practically won. Nothing could dampen his spirits. Even the constant stream of SS casualty lists barely registered.

The two things that mattered in his universe were Anna Bailey and the signal he so eagerly awaited on his screen. Resisting the urge to bash his fist on the console, he spun around to glance at Anna. An instant rush of positivity flowed through his body at the sight of her sitting as docile as a lamb on the edge of the trolley. Only her breathing betrayed her as more than a mannequin in a window display. Her eyes burned with rage, but he ignored that. He considered moving closer to her, knowing how her unique scent cleared his mood, but the lab door swung open and a black uniformed guard entered.

Just like the others, he saluted, approached Wagner, placed his report on the pile, saluted again, and turned to leave. After seeing the message underlined so heavily, Wagner ordered the messenger to halt. He examined the report. "How long until the Allies reach the Command and Control building?"

The SS soldier straightened his posture and tilted his chin up. "Minutes, Herr Reichsführer. We will fight them to the last man and the last bullet, but the Allies have strange energy weapons. They reduce men to ashes and can penetrate armour and concrete without effort."

"Very good," Wagner said with a dismissive wave.

The soldier flinched, as if he had been slapped. His mouth gaped open like a fish while his tongue and lips tried to form words. He cleared his throat. "Herr Reichsführer, it is not my place to question orders, but the safety of the Führer..."

The rest of the soldier's words died in his mouth under Wagner's glare. He looked the young solider up and down before taking a step towards him. The soldier visibly trembled.

"The safety of the Führer is not your concern," Wagner said with a brutal smile. "Now go. Fight the enemy. You do not have my permission to die until you have killed a hundred British soldiers. Is that clear?"

"Yes, Herr Reichsführer!" After giving another salute, he did an about-turn. He swung his rifle from his shoulder into his hands and marched out of the room.

Wondering if the soldier would last even five minutes against the Core Cadre, Wagner refocused his attention to the blank screen in front of him. A dozen scenarios danced through his mind as to why he hadn't received the transmission yet. He had his equipment checked three times a day, but had his engineers missed something? Could the data package have been intercepted by the Allies or blocked by the jamming? What if the data had become corrupted during the transmission?

He had pulled open a nearby drawer and was fumbling around for tools when he saw it. A single green light flashed on and off, heralding an incoming signal. Wagner stared at the screen facing him. He picked up his headset, adjusted the microphone, and cleared his throat. With a hand shaking from excitement, he flicked up a nearby switch and opened a channel.

"This is London Installation Two-Zero-One-Eight. Confirm." The voice sounded harsh, yet vaguely familiar.

Wagner pressed down on a button and spoke. "This is New Berlin colony One-Nine-Five-Four. Confirmed."

"Data package received, New Berlin," the voice continued. "Any irregularities?"

"Negative, London. Infiltrators detected but have not interfered with any stage of the tests."

"Core Cadre?"

"Possible, London."

The line went dead, causing Wagner to fear he'd lost the connection. He moved his hands across the dials in front of him in the hopes of boosting power to the signal. When the voice spoke again, he relaxed.

"Understood, New Berlin. No adverse conditions

detected. Primary timeline engaged and confirmed. Prepare for immediate extraction with the asset. London out."

Raising his hands in triumph to the heavens, Wagner rose from his chair. He slipped off his headset and tossed it carelessly onto the console. Wheeling about, he extended a hand towards Anna. Without delay, she obeyed and offered her hand to him. He pulled her up from her seat, and after sliding his arm around her waist, he proceeded to waltz around the room with her. Her feet moved in time with his, and her body pressed close to his, but her eyes blazed with the fires of hell.

Laughing aloud, he spun her around before releasing his grip on her. She came to an abrupt halt. Her murderous gaze tore into him, but her rigid body awaited instructions. He ran his fingertips from the base of her spine to her shoulder blades and moved his face closer to hers. Anna refused to even blink as she looked through him.

"You may relax now, Miss Bailey," Wagner said with a wink and stepped away.

Anna's posture fell loose. She flexed her joints and muscles. She ran a hand through her hair and fired a glare of pure loathing at Wagner. She flashed her teeth like a wild animal and stalked around him.

"We must prepare to leave this place," Wagner said and turned to disable his console. "The future awaits us. One where hundreds of thousands of our children stand ready to blaze a trail across the stars. A future where the might of Terran Supremacy holds entire star systems in its grip."

He reached into a container beside one of the trolleys and produced headbands for the Compression Matrix. He slipped one over his own head, nestling it beneath his hat, before placing the second one across Anna's forehead, resting it like a tiara.

"A crown fit for a queen," he said with a smile.

Running the back of his gloved hand across her cheek, Wagner started to speak again when the sound of gunfire reverberated through the corridors outside. He spun around in surprise. He listened as he tried to measure how far away danger lay. Surprised at the speed of the Allied advance, he dashed over to his console again. He worked his hands across the levers and control panels, before turning to inspect the Compression Matrix as it hummed to life. After beginning the activation procedures, he walked back to Anna's side.

Wagner drew his pistol, and cocking it, he returned it to its holster. Minutes separated him from a future filled with glory and power. He needed to hold out until the Compression Matrix was ready, and then all of humanity would rest within his palms. Not just the races of Earth or Mars, but all humankind spread across the galaxy, forgotten and lost to the ages.

Soon, they would know his name as he brought order to chaos and light to darkness. He, and his Hollow army.

CENTRE OF THE GOVERNMENT DISTRICT
20.01 MST
DAY 2

The SS blasted their weapons at the MEF soldiers, but nothing could stop the merciless Allied assault. With the Black Visors spearheading their relentless push into the centre of the government district, Sergeant McCabe continued to soak in every detail of their devastating weapons with awe and terror. Within minutes, the energy bolts from their HK-17s had not only reduced SS defences to rubble but allowed several battalion's worth of MEF soldiers to punch their way into the centre of the government district. The SS fought to the bitter end, refusing to surrender, but no amount of daring or courage could turn the tide against the Black Visor juggernaut.

With the West German company close at hand, McCabe stuck to the rear of the Black Visors, directing supporting fire. They paused at a courtyard flanked by buildings on all sides. The Command and Control building stood directly ahead. The Black Visors crept forward, firing quick glances up at the windows.

Smack turned to Dub and shook her head as the rest of the group waited for the signal to proceed. Noid tapped Big Mo on the shoulder and turned him around to ruffle through his backpack. She produced a small, hand-held rectangular device and pressed a button on it. Moving to the front, she extended her hand and waved it about. After repeating the motion several times, she stepped back to her colleagues and showed them something on the screen.

McCabe nodded towards the device. "What is that thing?"

"It's none of your business," Dub snapped.

Noid rammed her shoulder into Dub and ignoring his mumbled curses, faced McCabe.

"It's a type of scanner," she said quietly. "It allows us to see things we normally can't see, if that makes sense."

"Oh," McCabe said, trying his best to not sound like an idiot. "I don't suppose you have any spare ones you could share? It's come in handy next time I'm invading an alien planet."

Noid's lips curled tight as she tried to repress a smile. She returned her attention to Dub and pointed at a series of symbols on the screen. Flashing a glare at McCabe, Dub nodded and gestured at Big Mo.

They took the lead again and stepped a half pace forward. The barrels of their HKs waved from side to side, lingering momentarily on various windows as they divvied up targets. They cocked back on their weapons and unleashed flashes of flaming green energy before switching over to standard fire. They repeated the exercise again and again, pounding multiple targets with ferocious blasts of bullets and destructive energy.

Panic fire sprayed out at them from some of the other windows, but all died from the murderous rage of the HK-17s. In the end, at least twenty windows stood destroyed. The bricks surrounding them were vaporised, and the rooms they once sheltered stood as burnt-out ruins. With the courtyard cleared, the Black Visors pressed on with McCabe following close behind. They shot at the main entrance of the Command and Control building, blowing the reinforced doors clean off their hinges.

When they surged through the main entrance, several SS soldiers offered token resistance and fell to the HK-17s energy discharges. A dozen of them crumpled to the ground as ruins, with large sections of their torsos burned away. At least four disappeared entirely, leaving smoking boots and scraps of burnt uniforms. With the main lobby cleared, McCabe called what forces he had left and ordered them to cover the various doorways and corridors.

"Home, sweet, home," Big Mo said as they waited for Noid's findings on her scanner.

Dub eased Smack to her knee and checked on her wound attentively.

Noid moved her hand around, scanning the walls and the roof above them. At the same time, Colonel Henke issued instructions to his officers and NCOs, ordering the adjoining rooms to be cleared and secured. The sound of gunfire increased in tempo around them as the MEF steamrolled through the government district. In the sky above, transports smashed SS defences with missile fire to exterminate the resistance outright.

For all intents and purposes, the battle was over, but with thousands of SS fanatics left alive, McCabe and the MEF knew they had no choice but to keep the pressure on the enemy.

"I have them," Noid said. "Target one is located on the other side of the building. Target two is a few floors above us."

"Should we split up?" Big Mo asked.

Dub shook his head in answer.

"No. We need to stick together. Target one is priority. Everything rests on getting Anna to safety."

"Who's the second target?" McCabe queried.

"The ghost of Christmas past," Dub said with a grimace and gazed at the mass of MEF soldiers. "Colonel Henke, the main corridor leads directly to the primary command and control centre. It'll be heavily guarded, but if you take it out, you'll disrupt SS communications, jamming equipment and automated defences."

"I will organise the assault now," the colonel said with a slight nod of appreciation. "Sergeant McCabe, take some men and continue to support our...colleagues with their operation."

"Yes, sir."

McCabe selected two MEF soldiers and two of the West

Germans who stood closest to him and took a swig of water from his flask. While loading a fresh magazine into his Lee-Enfield, he gestured at the four soldiers under his command to follow. Then he fell in behind the Black Visors. Noid slung Smack's arm over her shoulder, and Dub and Big Mo took point.

With a nod from Dub, McCabe and the small group walked towards one of the corridors. They pushed the double doors open and moved with speed, scanning every nook and cranny for enemy soldiers waiting to spring an ambush. The lights in the corridor blinked every few seconds in time with the continuous volley of shells. Muffled sounds of gunfire leaked through the walls as the SS threw everything they had at the MEF.

As they reached the end of the corridor, a small band of SS soldiers came close to running headfirst into them. Big Mo shot first, carving a fiery-green swathe through the enemy group. Smoking arms hit the floor as Dub lunged towards them, smacking one of the survivors with the butt of his weapon. Noid fired her HK-17 and tore two more soldiers apart when Dub jabbed his bayonet into the chest of his fallen adversary.

McCabe and his MEF soldiers swung around into the connecting corridor. Bullets cracked out at them, and he flung himself onto the ground for cover. He pulled on his Lee-Enfield's trigger, dropping two more of the stunned Nazis before Smack stumbled into the fray. With a shaking, blood-stained hand, she fired the energy blast from her HK, incinerating the head off the last SS soldier.

Cocking their assault rifles again, the Black Visors pushed onwards.

Using her scanner, Noid directed them with hand signals. Two more panicked SS soldiers nearly crashed into their small group, but Big Mo dispatched them with lethal swipes of his HK-17's bayonet. The Nazis hit the floor, clutching at their bloodied necks while their mouths flapped open and gasped for air. The Black Visors walked past them, leaving the fatally wounded men to choke on their own blood.

After rounding another corner, Noid signalled to stop.

They froze as she waved her scanner from side to side. She moved farther down the corridor before stopping in front of a set of double doors. Lifting the device up and down, she turned to face her colleagues and nodded her head. She slipped the gadget under her belt, and after forming up with her fellow Black Visors, she started a silent three-count. On three, they threw themselves through the double doors.

The first room they entered was devoid of activity, but when McCabe and the Black Visors carried on, they all spotted something through a long glass window. An SS officer and a woman dressed in a body suit stood near a set of consoles and screens. The officer and woman spun around. They fixed their gazes on McCabe and the rest of the team but made no movements to draw weapons. McCabe ordered the soldiers under his command to hold the outer room and the door leading back into the corridor as the Black Visors made to enter. They smashed through the doors of the lab and scanned every part of the room for hidden SS soldiers. Neither the SS officer nor the woman so much as flinched at their presence.

Trailing close behind, McCabe looked on while the Black Visors lowered their HK-17s. For a moment, they appeared to forget the presence of an armed SS officer as they stared in awe at who he guessed to be Anna Bailey. The former MI6 operative wore no shackles or restraints of any kind and made no effort to join her supposed liberators. Suspicious, McCabe kept his Lee-Enfield trained on the SS officer as the Black Visors took small steps towards the woman they were sent to free.

"It's you," Dub said in a soft, reassuring voice.

Anna cocked her head. Her gaze scanned the masked band in front of her, but she said nothing.

"We're here to get you out of this place, Anna," Dub continued. "We're here to set you free."

In a slow, deliberate motion, as if to not spook a wild animal, he reached for the balaclava on his head. To McCabe's surprise, he slipped the piece of fabric off, revealing a round face with stubble across his chin and cheeks and a shaved head. McCabe was astonished to see how young he looked and placed him in his twenties, but something about him felt far older.

Dropping the balaclava to the floor, Dub motioned for the rest of his colleagues to do the same. They complied, removing the covering from their heads and dumping them onto the ground. McCabe looked them over one at a time, confused by their youthful appearance. Smack, lightly tanned, had her blonde hair tied back in a ponytail. Noid with her sharp features, porcelain white skin and jet-black hair shaved at the sides. Big Mo had a neatly trimmed black beard, olive brown skin and a nose that looked like it had been broken more than once.

"Anna Bailey," Big Mo said, beaming a friendly smile. "You need to come with us. We don't mean you any harm."

The SS officer laughed at that, causing the Black Visors to glare at him. The Nazi raised his gloved hands while glancing at McCabe's Lee-Enfield. Keeping himself behind the motionless Anna Bailey, he grinned at the intruders.

"I'm afraid you're too late," the SS officer said in perfect English. "You have the honour of standing in the presence of the first Hollow. Your Core Cadre cannot stop us now. We have already won."

McCabe didn't know what the Nazi officer meant by "Hollow" or "Core Cadre" but from the corner of his eye, he saw the Black Visors' body language change. McCabe glanced over at them and caught them shooting wary looks at one another before resting their gaze on the still unmoving Anna Bailey. The tension in the room ratcheted up as the MJ-12 operatives reached for something in their belts. They produced small cylindrical devices that looked like miniature syringes.

"You haven't won yet, you piece of shit," Smack snapped and limped from under Noid's arm to stand under her own power. "Last chance, asshole. Let her go or we do this the hard way."

The SS officer folded his arms and cocked his chin up in defiance. With a nod of his head, he drew their attention towards a countdown timer on one of the screens beside him. "You have a little over three minutes until myself and my dear, sweet Miss Bailey must journey out of here. You cannot fight the future. You will fail."

The Black Visors unslung their HKs and unholstered their sidearms. They placed their HK-17's in neat rows behind them and faced Anna with the mysterious syringe devices as their only weapons.

"Hard way it is," Smack retorted.

"Sergeant McCabe," Dub called out, without taking his gaze from the woman in front of him. "Regardless of what happens, under no circumstances are you to either point your weapon at or try to shoot Anna Bailey. But if the SS scumbag so much as sneezes in your direction, feel free to fill him with lead. Understood?"

Unsure of what he was witnessing or about to witness, McCabe nodded. "Understood."

Raising the syringe devices up, but keeping the palms of their free hand exposed, the Black Visors inched towards Anna. Her gaze flitted across each of them, but her hands rested by her sides.

"Anna." Dub stepped closer to her. "I know you hear a voice in your head. The Voice of God. You need to get it to activate the Salient Protocol. Do you understand? You can free yourself, but you need to initiate the Salient Protocol."

Anna remained rigid.

The Black Visors spread out amongst themselves as if to approach from every direction.

Big Mo moved in from Anna's left. "She's not responding to voice commands. Take it nice and slow, everyone. We know what she's capable of."

"Protect Terra," the SS officer said.

"Protect Terra," Anna responded.

Dub was the first to act, lunging towards Anna from her right, aiming the syringe at her neck. With savage ferocity and inhuman speed, Anna swung her right fist around with enough force to knock Dub from his feet and send him crashing back into a nearby trolley. Big Mo leapt at her from Anna's left. His hands nearly made contact, but Anna reacted with lightning speed. She spun about and swept her right leg across his feet while delivering a missile strike of a punch to his chest. Big Mo hurtled to the ground with sickening force, and the sound of the impact reverberated around the room. Anna raised her fist as if to deliver a deathblow when Smack and Noid fell upon her.

Noid wrapped her arm around Anna's neck, and Smack tried to jab at her from the front. Grabbing Noid by the head, Anna flipped her over, body slamming her onto the hard floor. She fended off Smack's weakened attacks before striking hard at Smack's bandaged side. Smack howled like a wounded animal and stumbled to her knees. Anna raised her hand to punch her in the face when Noid grasped her legs in an attempt to intervene. Anna lifted her foot and slammed it hard onto Noid's head, causing her skull to bounce off the floor with a thud.

At seeing Noid in danger, McCabe considered rushing to her aid. Dub's words kept him from acting, unsure if he'd make things worse by intervening. He glanced at the SS officer still with his hands in the air and a savage smile etched across his face as he watched the fight.

Dub and Big Mo, brandishing their syringes, tried to rush Anna, but she turned to face them with her trademark speed. She easily blocked Big Mo's swipe. He shifted his body with the strength of her defence, exposing his back. She drove her fist right into his kidney, causing Big Mo to stumble forward. Without pausing, she turned about again and executed a round house kick, catching Dub across the side of the face and sending him flailing to the ground again.

Without even having broken a sweat, Anna looked over her fallen opponents. Dub, Smack, and Noid lay slumped on the ground, groaning in pain but conscious. Big Mo remained on his knees facing her. He visibly struggled to pull his heaving body to his feet.

Anna peered over at McCabe. Her ice-cold gaze sent a chill down his spine. Her gaze focused on the Lee-Enfield in his hands aimed at the SS officer, and then back to him. Resisting the urge to act, McCabe obeyed Dub's instructions and kept the barrel aimed at the SS officer.

Having surveyed the carnage around her, Anna turned about to face the SS officer. He looked positively gleeful and, ignoring McCabe's presence, pointed at the monitor beside him.

"A minute and thirty seconds left, Miss Bailey. You may terminate them. They are enemies of Terra. Protect Terra."

"Yes, Herr Reichsführer," Anna said with a slight nod. "Protect Terra."

Anna snapped around to face the wobbly-legged Big Mo first. He raised his hand to try and jab her with his syringe, but she anticipated it. She blocked with her left hand, and fired a vicious blow to his face, bursting his nose. She grabbed his left hand and drove an uppercut to his upper arm. He screamed from the agony, and tried to headbutt her, but Anna side-stepped him, throwing him off balance. She gripped the back of his neck, and driving his head downwards, she snapped up her right knee. His face connected with her kneecap with a sickening crunch before he flopped back onto the hard floor.

Dub dove at Anna from her flank, making contact and spearing her to the ground. She landed on her back with Dub on top of her. He desperately tried to jab the point of the syringe into her neck, but Anna struck him across the face with her iron fist. Dub's hand fell away, and she smashed the palm of her hand into his jaw before driving her fist into his solar plexus. Bucking to get out from under him, she drove another lethal fist into his face and knocked him backwards. Anna jumped up and closed the distance between them. She wrapped her wiry arms around his neck as if to snap it.

Noid and Smack threw themselves at Anna. Noid clawed at Anna's face, and Smack tried to kick the feet out from under her. Anna grabbed Noid by the throat, lifted her from her feet, and threw her into Smack.

For a heart-stopping moment, McCabe thought that the fight was over, with all four Black Visors down, but then a weakened Dub acted.

With her back turned to him, Dub lifted his right leg and lashed it towards the back of her left knee. The force of the blow brought her to her knees, but undeterred, she turned to unleash her wrath on him. With her back exposed, Big Mo crashed into her and used his stocky frame to smash her face onto the ground. Despite her wriggling beneath him, Big Mo managed to wrap his arms under hers, stopping her from launching any more of her brutal attacks. After swinging himself to his back so that Anna's front lay exposed, the Black Visors converged on her. Noid hurled herself onto Anna's legs to keep them pinned down, and Dub leaned a knee on her left forearm. Anna's right arm and head frantically tried to inflict pain on Big Mo, but he remained unfazed. Smack leaned over Anna and jabbed the syringe into her neck. A second later, Dub pulled the headband from her forehead.

Anna's body fell still, and her wide eyes became unblinking as they stared at the ceiling above. A shudder crept through her muscles until her entire body shook. Finally, she opened her mouth and released a piercing shriek. She screamed until all the air left her lungs. Then she took a breath and roared again. A moment later, her shuddering stopped. McCabe eyed the SS officer. He stood rooted to the spot, his mouth gaping open with his gaze fixed on the subdued Anna Bailey.

The Black Visors glanced at one another before releasing her. She lay motionless on the lab floor as they dragged themselves to their feet. They sported bloodied faces and nursed ribs or damaged limbs, but they had prevailed. They nodded at one another and then faced the reichsführer.

The SS officer backed against the wall and checked the countdown timer. As it changed to twenty seconds, Dub charged towards him. Pulling his knife from his belt, Dub closed the distance and reached his target while the SS officer fumbled for his sidearm. Using his left forearm to pin him against the wall, Dub drew back his blade and stabbed it into the Nazi's chest. The reichsführer screamed as Dub twisted the blade. With a savage grin, he withdrew the knife and buried it again.

"You lose," Dub said.

The reichsführer's body trembled, but he managed to shake his head. "I have seen the future." He gasped. "I have witnessed the armies of Terra stretch across the galaxy..."

Dub gripped his left hand around the reichsführer's throat and jabbed with his knife again. The SS officer's face turned deathly pale, and yet, his eyes sparkled as he gazed into the face of the man who drained the life from him.

The countdown timer neared zero.

"Time's up," Dub said. He released the reichsführer and allowed his fatally wounded body to slump to the floor.

The SS officer shook his head as he tried to place his hand over the waterfalls of blood that stained his uniform. "I see you." He smiled faintly. "You are a Hollow. You all are. Don't you see? I've already won." The reichsführer raised a bloodied hand to his hat and pulled it off. A metallic headband covered his forehead.

Dub lunged for the SS officer again.

"I'll see you in the future, my children..."

Before Dub could reach him, the reichsführer's body convulsed, as if jolts of energy pulsed through him. His smile faded, leaving a lifeless corpse in its wake.

Noid limped forward and tapped at the console, but she shook her head at her findings. "It must have been programmed to erase the location as soon as the compression signal was finished transmitting. He's gone, Dub. He could be anywhere and anytime that has a Compression Matrix."

Dub let out a long, exasperated sigh. McCabe caught his gaze.

McCabe glanced at the lifeless body of the reichsführer and at the subdued Anna Bailey. He shook his head in confusion.

"There'll be time for explanations later," Dub said with a shrug of his shoulders. "But right now, we gotta—"

"We have company," Noid interrupted. She waved the scanner towards the corridor outside and shook her head.

"The guts of two platoons."

"Friend or foe?" Smack said, leaning in to gain a closer look.

Shots rang out from the corridor outside when the MEF soldiers guarding it started firing. A wall of return gunfire blasted back in response.

"I'd say foe," Noid said as she picked up her HK-17.

"It'll take a few minutes to recalibrate the Compression Matrix," Smack called out as she started working on the console.

"Get Anna back first, she's the only one who counts. We'll hold them off."

Without another word, McCabe and the Black Visors ran to face the Nazi onslaught.

ALEXANDERPLATZ, MITTE DISTRICT, CITY CENTRE
20.22 MST
DAY 2

General Schulz stood atop the ruins of what had once been the Nazi party central bank and stared at the government district. Large sections of the Colosseum lay in ruins from the barrage of missile and artillery strikes. Two of the towers that acted as offices for government and Nazi officials stood as nothing more than giant heaps of scorched concrete. Flames licked from the windows of the still-standing towers, in some cases engulfing entire floors. Muzzle flashes dotted from every corner of the government district. Overhead, two hovering transports fired tracer rounds.

With a heavy heart, he tore his gaze from the scene and surveyed what remained of his beloved New Berlin. To the east, columns of black smoke marked the advance of the Mars Expeditionary Force. Countless buildings and homes sat as little more than piles of rubble, smashed without mercy in the Allies' ferocious advance.

To the north, fires raged across the outskirts of the Jewish ghetto. Flames danced from building to building, tearing through the former slaves' shabby hovels. Gunfire flickered in the neighbouring areas.

What remained of the Wehrmacht fought to defend the German citizenry of the savage reprisals that awaited them. The MEF had moved swiftly into the vicinity to pacify it and protect the inhabitants, but in his bones, Schulz knew blood would be spilled for a long time to come.

Sighing, he removed his hat and wiped the sweat from his brow. In the streets below, the MEF soldiers continued to flow into the government district in a final bid to topple the Nazi regime. Rows of defeated Wehrmacht soldiers marched in the opposite direction under armed guard.

Thankfully, Oberst Brandt's treason hadn't spread to all the units under his command, but a sizeable portion of the traitors remained at large. The latest updates he had overheard mentioned the MEF having pushed the rebelling Wehrmacht forces to the sector north-west of the government district. Whether this was true and how many survived, he didn't know.

"Penny for your thoughts," Mr. Myers said.

Schulz turned about and saw the Majestic-12 agent extend a glass of brandy towards him. With a sombre nod, he accepted the glass and drained its contents in a single swallow. Grinning that cocky trademark smile, Mr. Myers rose from his seat. He grabbed his own glass and the decanter of brandy from the wobbly table beside him and refilled both glasses. Looking satisfied, Mr. Myers scanned his own eyes across the burning background of the once proud colony.

"If you're worried about your fate after all this, you shouldn't be," Mr. Myers said and paused to take a swig of brandy. "I'm a man of my word. You, and some of your officers and men, will have a place in the new order. Once you've been thoroughly de-Nazified, of course. But don't worry too much about that. It's mainly to keep the politicians back home happy."

Such thoughts of the future stood far from his mind as Schulz swirled his brandy. Below and around him, his men were dying. The home he had known and loved for a decade sat blazing on a funeral pyre.

Oblivious to his darkening mood, Mr. Myers refilled their glasses again.

After taking a large gulp from his, Schulz turned his vision towards the battle raging across the government district.

Mr. Myers swirled his half-empty glass. "He really does like putting on a show. Your Führer, I mean. I can't say I ever agreed with his politics, but he knows how to grab a person's attention."

"I don't follow," Schulz said, staring gloomily into his own drink.

"This!" Mr. Myers sang out and extended his arms towards the fighting in front of them. "He's showing us the sacrifices he's willing to make to secure humanity's future. He wants us to make a blood sacrifice of our own, and I think we've proven ourselves with that."

The sorrow welling inside Schulz evaporated. Anger rushed through his veins like poisonous lead. For a moment, he considered reaching out with his good hand and choking the life from Mr. Myers's smug face. Fighting to maintain control, he clamped down on his jaws to keep from launching into a furious tirade.

Mr. Myers finished his brandy and chucked the empty glass onto the street below. "All of this is a pantomime," he exclaimed. "Nothing more than a spectacle for the masses. Our peoples will suffer by the same design, but that suffering will ready us for the battles and wars to come. The Great War awaits us, Herr General. It may be decades away, but as sure as the Earth revolves around the sun, it is coming for us. Thanks to our actions today, we will be ready for it."

Schulz didn't know how to react. He studied Mr. Myers's face, wondering if this was an elaborate American joke. Despite his near-constant grinning, darkness cloaked Mr. Myer's eyes. He didn't seem to look directly at anything or anyone, but rather through them, as if he could see beyond what was perceptible to the human eye.

"Look at them," Mr. Myers continued with a shake of his head as he glanced again at the streets below. "They look like ants. Hundreds and thousands of worker ants. They live, they breed, but only in death will their lives have any true purpose. Their broken bodies and bullet-riddled corpses will be the foundation of our future."

Aghast at Mr. Myers's statements, Schulz found himself unable to speak. He opened his mouth, but words refused to form on his lips.

Smiling, Mr. Myers faced him. His dark eyes pierced through Schulz, sending a cold shiver of ice up his spine. "Well, I've burnt the ears off you for long enough, General. Time to get you into custody. Don't worry, this will all be over soon."

Still unable to form a single syllable, Schulz spun about and spotted two goons in black suits standing behind him. They gestured at him to walk towards the stairwell, but something about the way they looked at him made him guess they would love nothing more than for him to resist. He placed his hat back on his head and complied with the order. With his head held as high as he could manage given the circumstances, he marched off the roof, flanked by the two lackeys.

"Oh," Mr. Myers called out, causing his guards to stop Schulz. "Deactivate the planetary jamming signal and send a message to Wolf One. Tell him it's time for the final act. This war is over."

One of the goons grunted and nodded in answer. He shoved Schulz forward again, and slipping a hand into his pocket, he pulled out an unusual communications device. Before reaching the stairwell, Schulz caught a final glimpse of the mysterious Mr. Myers, who stood with his arms outstretched, as if re-enacting the crucifixion. Behind him the fires chewed through New Berlin colony.

COMMAND AND CONTROL BUILDING, GOVERNMENT DISTRICT
20.46 MST
DAY 2

McCabe aimed his Lee-Enfield and fired while bullets smashed around the doorway. A green energy bolt spit from Dub's HK-17 and sliced through SS soldiers. Noid sprayed fire at another enemy column, charging headfirst at them. Heaps of bleeding, eviscerated SS die-hards lay stacked around their feet, but still, wave after wave, they kept attacking.

Two of them managed to close the distance as Dub slapped in a fresh clip. Stumbling over the remains of their dead comrades, the SS soldiers pounced on him, trying to skewer him with their bayonets. Dub swung his HK-17 up to block the thrusts and shoved at them. He managed to level his weapon at one and squeezed the trigger, riddling his opponent's chest with bullet holes.

The second SS soldier lunged again, burying his bayonet deep into Dub's leg. He roared and slashed wildly with his HK. The bayonet attached to the barrel cleaved through the SS soldier's face, ripping his nose apart and knocking him to the ground. Unable to stand, Dub tumbled to the floor beside the SS soldier. McCabe tried to dart from his position to assist him, but a shower of SS bullets kept him pinned down. Dub reached for his knife, and rammed it into the chest of his attacker, stabbing repeatedly until his adversary no longer drew breath.

Shrieking like a mad woman, Noid alternated between energy blasts and semi-automatic fire as she targeted anything that moved in the corridor. Then she threw herself into the line of fire, grabbed Dub by the straps of his backpack, and hauled him back into the corridor of the lab, where she leaned him against the two wounded West German soldiers. She returned to her firing position at the doorway, joining McCabe and the two remaining MEF soldiers.

"Bail out, Dub," Noid screamed as she reloaded her weapon. "Anna, Mo, and Smack are clear. You're up."

"Bullshit," Dub retorted and dragged himself to his feet.

Dub wrapped a bandage around his leg and pulled it tight. After checking it held, he limped back to the door frame. With pain engraved on his swollen and bruised face, he forced himself into a sitting position. He cocked his weapon and unleashed another energy bolt. The blast ripped the head of an approaching SS soldier clean off, knocking his body into his comrades.

"You bail," Dub shouted over the din. "It'll be a cold day in Hell when I'm not the last one out."

"Stop being a dick for once in your life," Noid snapped.

"How about you stop being dick? Now get your skinny ass to the Compression Matrix."

Bullets snapped around them like hail stones on a tin roof. A bullet ricochet struck one of the MEF soldiers in the arm. He cursed aloud but raised up his Lee-Enfield again and fired back until he emptied his clip.

"Fine, shithead," Noid roared back. "You win. But you better not be far behind me."

"Understood, prick-face."

While McCabe slipped in a fresh magazine, Noid kneeled and passed Dub the scanning device. Their gazes met, but despite their animosity, McCabe noted a grudging respect when they nodded at one another. Noid extended a hand and gave him a hearty slap on the shoulder before standing up again.

"Sergeant," she called out.

McCabe removed his empty ammo clip and surveyed the situation. The SS assault ground to a halt. Dozens upon dozens of carcasses carpeted the corridor. The wounded tried to claw their way over the mountain of dead, desperate to reach their colleagues at the far end of the corridor. Exhausted, McCabe stepped back into the lab corridor to reload and found Noid still standing there.

"Safe journey," he mumbled as he reloaded.

"You know something, Sergeant?"

He made eye contact with her while clicking the fresh clip into his Lee-Enfield. She stood in front of him, gazing up at him. Blood splattered her face.

"You're kinda cute for an old guy." Then she pounced on him. She pressed her warm lips against his and rammed her body hard into his with enough force to knock him back into the wall. Confusion gave way to primal instinct as he melted into her. His hands grabbed at her waist as their tongues touched and probed.

As quickly as it had started, Noid pulled away, but not before biting his bottom lip. Dazed, he watched her blush and take a step back. She brushed a strand of loose dark hair behind her ear. Her eyes seemed to glow as her gaze lingered upon him.

"In another lifetime, Sergeant," she said and winked. Without another word, she turned about and disappeared into the lab.

Rubbing a trickle of blood from his lip and feeling rejuvenated, McCabe spun about. He caught Dub's eye. The Irishman flashed a smile at him but said nothing.

"I'm not that old," McCabe muttered, unable to mask his own smile.

Dub chuckled. "I wouldn't take it personally. Technically

speaking, she's a seventy-year-old woman trapped in a twenty-six-year old's body, if that helps."

"You people," McCabe said with a shake of his head. "Dare I ask what that even means?"

"You can ask," Dub said with a shrug and moved his eye to his HKs sight.

In the corridor, the only movements came from the wounded trying to crawl to safety. The two MEF privates took pot-shots at them.

Dub waved his handheld device from side to side, scanning for any other signs of activity. "It looks like they're regrouping for another assault."

"That's suicide," McCabe said. "Charging headfirst into a prepared position down a corridor with no cover makes no sense."

"They know the end is nigh," Dub said. "A lot of them are going to blow their brains out when the Old Man surrenders. They think they'll die with honour this way, the stupid wankers."

Dub checked his watch and clawed at the doorframe as he tried to pull himself up. Losing his grip, he fell back down, wincing from the pain.

McCabe extended a hand to help him up. "Leg at you?"

Dub took McCabe's hand and shook his head as he steadied himself on his feet. He lifted the shirt of his black and red uniform, revealing a wound to the stomach. Blood oozed from the gash, and he looked paler.

McCabe slung Dub's arm over his shoulder. "That's not good."

"I've had worse," he grunted.

Dub directed him towards the lab, dripping blood with every step. McCabe eased them into the room. He paused at the sight of Anna, Smack, Big Mo, and Noid stretched unconscious on the floor in the corner of the room. They lay with those metallic headbands resting on their foreheads. The Black Visors had their HK-17s draped across their torsos, and the rectangular explosives he had witnessed them use before rested in their hands.

"Over there," Dub said, nodding at the panels and screens.

McCabe guided the Black Visor over to the console. Dub ran his fingertips over several buttons and looked over the displays in front of him. After entering a command, the nearby Compression Matrix hummed to life again. A countdown timer appeared on one of the screens. Dub grabbed at one of the headbands and fixed it on his forehead. He then motioned at McCabe to set him down beside his friends. Trying to be as careful as possible, McCabe eased him onto the floor after slipping off his backpack. Dub squirmed to get comfortable. He, too, rested an explosive on his chest. In one of his hands he held a grenade.

McCabe stood over him. "So that's that?"

"That's that," Dub replied. "You should get your men out of here. When these charges go off, they're going to take the adjoining rooms above and below with them."

"You promised me answers."

Dub leaned forward. A trickle of blood oozed from his mouth. He glanced up at the screen on the console and settled back onto the floor. "You've got about two minutes to get far enough away from here to seek cover, so ask, Sergeant. I can't promise you'll like the answers, but I won't lie to you."

Every question, every single thing that had bothered McCabe slipped from his mind. Gaping like a fish out of water, he wracked his brain, searching for a question, any question while the timer continued counting down.

"That thing," he blurted out, pointing at the Compression Matrix. "What is it?"

"A device that allows near-instantaneous transmission of compressed data across time and space without any type of degradation. Primarily used for communications, until some genius figured out how to copy and send brain patterns. It can't transmit physical matter yet, but they'll figure that out in time."

McCabe nodded at the answer.

"And you? What are you?"

"They call us Hollows. My brain pattern was transmitted from Earth to Asaph Hall Research Station on Phobos where I awoke in a replicated version of my own body. It included a code dubbed the Voice of God that was originally used to manipulate me into fighting and killing the natives of this world by seeing them as giant insect-like creatures. I know. It sounds far-fetched even to me and I lived through it for a year."

"They?"

"The Mars Occupation Force. Also known as the MOF."

McCabe rubbed his forehead, unsure of the incredible claims and uncertain about what it all meant. He didn't know Dub well and could barely stand him, but he appeared genuine in his assertions. "Where are you all going now?"

Dub forced a smile across his face, but it was weak. "I'm going back to the future, Sergeant. Well, technically, it's your future and my past... Even though I won't be born yet. So, wait... Does that make it my future, too? It's all subjective, Sergeant McCabe. Even I can't wrap my head around this whole time-travel thing."

"Time travel?"

"Yeah." Dub checked the countdown timer again. "Like I said, the signal from the Compression Matrix cuts through time and space. I was forcibly enlisted into the Mars Occupation Force in 2018. They sent me to 1975, where I served for a year before I got locked up for two decades. I don't look a day over thirty, but from my perspective, I'm seventy years old and spent over forty years on Big Red. From my family's point of view, I've been missing for about three days. It's all relative."

"Do you really work for MJ-12?"

"In a way," Dub said with a shrug. "The future's complicated. I did something that I thought would free a lot of people, but then I discovered we were pawns in a much bigger game. We aligned with the lesser of two evils, a group called the Core Cadre, to buy Earth and Mars as much time as possible before the Great War kicks off."

McCabe scratched his chin while trying to process Dub's words. He patted at his pockets for a cigarette and tried to form a new question, but Dub reached up a bloodied, shaking hand, stopping him.

"We're almost out of time, Sergeant, but I have a confession to make before you and your men go." Dub's face crinkled in pain when he rested his hand on his chest, allowing the blood to ooze from his stomach wound. "I lied when I said your name wasn't on my list, Sergeant. I know exactly who you are. Over twenty years from now, my friends and I will do something stupid. You're the reason I spent twenty years behind bars rather than being dissected or lined up against the nearest wall and shot. You're also the reason I'm here in the first place. You're the reason I am the way I am now. I'd be lying if I said I wasn't bitter towards you, but I apologise for giving you a hard time."

"I don't understand," McCabe said, shaking of his head.

"You will."

Dub lifted his HK-17 from his chest and extended the weapon towards him.

"Here," Dub said as another small stream of blood leaked from the corner of his mouth.

McCabe accepted the assault rifle, curious of Dub's intentions.

"Give this to Mad Jack. You'll get a promotion out of it."

McCabe started to speak again, but Dub waved him off. He placed the pin of the grenade into his mouth. Keeping the clip pressed down, he pulled the pin out and spat it away. With an exhausted sigh, he lifted his hand and rested the grenade against his forehead.

Seeing the countdown timer pass the thirty second marker, McCabe jogged towards the doors of the lab. He turned about for a fleeting moment and looked over the unconscious Black Visors and their dying leader.

"Really," he blurted, "who *are* you people?"

Dub flashed a smile at that. "We're the good guys, asshole."

McCabe turned his back on the Black Visor leader. He sprinted out to where his MEF soldiers guarded the door. After hauling the wounded to their feet, he peaked around the doorframe.

The Nazi soldiers lingered in covering positions at the far end of the corridor. McCabe gestured at his soldiers to prepare to move and tossed a smoke grenade amongst the dead outside. A cloud of white smoke pumped into the corridor, giving the MEF soldiers and the West Germans a chance to escape.

Bullets pinged as the SS soldiers fired blindly into the smoke. They shouted to each other and charged towards the lab, tripping over their fallen as they advanced.

McCabe reached the opposite end of the corridor and started pushing his soldiers around the corner to safety. He had shoved the last of the wounded West Germans ahead when a deafening roar filled his ears. While his brain processed the ferocious sound, he hurtled towards the corridor wall. His already-wounded left shoulder bore the brunt of the impact, sending shards of agony throughout his limb and into his back and torso. He blinked his watery eyes clear as a piercing siren rang through his skull. The smell of burning flesh filled his nostrils when he leaned to the side for a better view.

The corridor outside the lab was burnt black with large portions of the floor missing. The doors had been torn from the hinges, as had several metres of the wall. Several smoking bodies lay in pieces across the corridor. A cold wind whipped in from the exposed outer wall and fanned smaller flames, causing them to dance across the chunks of wood and brick covering the splintered marble floor.

A warm trickle of blood dripped across McCabe's face. He raised a filthy hand to his forehead and wiped it away. His finger touched a shard of glass embedded in his skin. With a single, sharp motion, he pulled the shard out. Clenching his teeth to stop a groan escaping, he tossed it away. He turned to his soldiers, noted they were moving and trying to pull themselves to their feet. A wave of relief washed through him at seeing them alive, but that feeling died when he looked farther up the dark corridor.

Through blurry eyes, he spied a dozen figures charging towards him.

COMMAND AND CONTROL BUILDING, GOVERNMENT DISTRICT
21.01 MST
DAY 2

The intensity of the explosion threw Private Jenkins and what remained of his platoon against the corridor walls. A series of crashes followed, as if entire floors within the Command and Control building were collapsing in on one another. For a moment, the sound of gunfire died off.

Within seconds, it returned, albeit far quieter than earlier. After dusting himself off, Jenkins extended a hand down and pulled Junior Sergeant Alexeev to his feet. The Soviet NCO nodded his thanks before checking on the soldiers under his command. Taking point again, Jenkins raised his Lee-Enfield and continued his quick pace ahead.

After rounding the corner of the corridor, Jenkins saw several figures rolling and crawling around on the ground. He tightened his finger on his rifle trigger as he worked his way around the crashed ceiling tiles and lumps of concrete. His finger loosened when he noted the familiar design and colourings of British battledress. He swung his rifle behind him, dashed ahead, and helped Sergeant McCabe to his feet.

"Jenkins, is that you lad?"

Sergeant McCabe had certainly seen better days. A bandage covered his shoulder, and the rest of his battledress was stained with blood, dirt, and scorch marks. A stream of crimson flowed down his grimy face from gashes dotting his forehead.

Jenkins helped the senior NCO lean against the nearby wall. "It is, Sarge."

"Where's Corporal Brown?"

"Wounded, Sarge. Damn near got his leg blown off. Medics reckon he'll make it, though."

Sergeant McCabe winced as his fingers probed his ribcage. After he coughed into his hand, he reached for his pocket and pulled out a crushed packet of cigarettes. With trembling hands, he struck a match and took a few rapid puffs.

McCabe struggled to stay upright. "Who's in charge?"

"I am, Sergeant," Junior Sergeant Alexeev said from behind Jenkins. He stepped into view and helped Sergeant McCabe to straighten his posture.

"Thank you for looking out for my men," McCabe

grunted.

"They fight well for imperialist capitalists."

"It must've been the fear of that harsh Soviet discipline."

They flashed a rare smile at each another and Sergeant McCabe pushed himself off the wall. Around them, British, French, and West German soldiers tended to each other's wounds and shared flasks of water and cigarettes.

McCabe finished his own cigarette and tossed the butt to the ground He grimaced as he straightened his spine. "What are our orders, Junior Sergeant?"

Junior Sergeant Alexeev pressed on his left arm console and brought up a grainy image of the Command and Control structure. He pointed at it to indicate their position. Then he moved his finger to the far side of the building, a few levels above them.

"Colonel Henke and Major Wellesley have reported a secondary command outpost here. They believe there could be several companies' worth of SS inside preparing to make a last stand. Maybe even a battalion. Every available unit in the area has been ordered to converge there."

"Then let's not waste any more time, Junior Sergeant. Get the men moving."

Junior Sergeant Alexeev let out a series of bellows, which jolted the platoon into action. Jenkins moved forward with his platoon at a quick pace, searching for any signs of the enemy. He led them into the first stairwell they came across and scurried five levels up without incident. As he pushed ahead, signs of brutal fighting came into view. Shell casings covered the ground, and bullet holes marked every wall. The bodies of MEF and SS soldiers littered the corridors, sporting knife and bayonet wounds that gaped across their bodies. Some of their allies had died with their hands wrapped around their enemy's throat.

Jenkins continued to lead the way as his barrel covered every possible place an enemy could conceal himself. Several times he had to slow the platoon to check that mangled lumps of steel and concrete didn't conceal mines or explosives. As he surveyed the carnage, the MEF soldiers checked their fallen in the hopes of finding someone alive but discovered none. At times, they came across wounded

SS men, who still breathed despite their wounds. They finished each of them off with their bayonets, murmuring "Kill them all" as they went.

At the end of the corridor, Jenkins spotted a pair of MEF sentries and made his presence known. The sentries waved the platoon on and pointed them towards a hallway on the left. As they turned, Jenkins saw countless wounded MEF soldiers waiting along the sides of the corridors. Each of them looked as stained and as bloodied as the next, but fire raged in their eyes. As they sharpened bayonets and loaded ammo clips, they appeared determined to finish SS resistance in one final battle.

Sergeant McCabe took the lead and pushed his way through the crowds of wounded filing away from the upcoming battle zone. Jenkins sauntered close behind, glad to have his sergeant back, and even more so to be a part of the last thrust against the fanatical SS. Whatever those die-hard Nazis had in store for their final stand, it would be brutal. Although Jenkins had no wish to die, the idea of someone taking his place at the front bothered him.

Major Wellesley stood just out of reach of a gaping hole in the corridor on the right. Sergeant McCabe signalled them to stop and wait for his return. As he walked on, Jenkins and the platoon scrambled for what free space they could find on the floors. They shared cigarettes, guzzled water, or scoffed food if they had any. From somewhere beyond Jenkins's line of sight, a shot rang out. Although the faint sounds of the battle raging outside continued to leak through the walls, this shot sounded much sharper, but distorted.

Glancing around at the MEF soldiers already gathered in the corridor, Jenkins noted two leaning up against the wall, peering through a gap. He strolled up behind them and tried to see what they were focusing on. Unable to gain a view, he cleared his throat to make his presence known.

"Evening, lads. What's all the commotion about?"

One of the soldiers flashed a look back at him. He blinked a few times before stepping away from his spot and gesturing at Jenkins to see for himself. Jenkins accepted the invitation, took the soldier's place, and peered through the hole in the wall. A part of him expected to see an enemy position or SS soldiers scurrying about, readying themselves for the battle to come. Instead, his eyes drank in the sight of a lush green forest.

Huge trees dominated his vision. Their sturdy branches spread out and mixed with others. Dark green grass carpeted the floor of the area, and wildflowers dotted the landscape. A cool breeze kissed Jenkins's face, carrying with it primal scents that relaxed him and sharpened his senses. Although he couldn't spot them, birds chittered from the branches above.

Surprised by the surreal sight in the heart of the Nazi compound, Jenkins moved away and looked at the MEF private beside him.

"Beautiful, innit?" the private said as he retook his place.

Jenkins murmured his thanks and re-joined his platoon just as Sergeant McCabe returned. After a quick chat with Junior Sergeant Alexeev, Sergeant McCabe called the entire platoon together and pulled out a roughly drawn sketch of the forest area. The target looked to be a three-story housing complex at the far end of the forest. Already, the surviving members of the West German company had cleared the area ahead and posted themselves on the left flank. A jumble of soldiers from various gutted companies and battalions manned the centre and right flank. Under Major Wellesley's control, Sergeant McCabe and his platoon were to bolster the centre and search for a way to breach the enemy compound.

Jenkins grabbed what spare ammunition he could beg, borrow, or steal before Sergeant McCabe ordered the platoon to the hole in the wall. He passed bullets around to his platoon mates who were running low as they waited for Major Wellesley.

The major ordered them to enter. Fanning out, the platoon stepped into another world. A sharp, cold breeze cut through Jenkins, sending a welcome shiver through his body. While searching for any signs of a hidden enemy, he marvelled at the huge, ancient trees that reached towards the artificial sky above. Twigs crunched beneath his worn boots, and woodland creatures scarpered away.

The platoon moved as quietly as they could, wary of an unexpected ambush. When they approached the MEF positions, Sergeant McCabe stopped them. Ducking low, he crept ahead to scout out the area. After a minute or two, he called them forward and directed them into firing lines. They ducked behind thick trees and natural dips in the ground for cover.

Jenkins manoeuvred into one of the forward positions and hunkered behind a tall oak tree. Fifty metres ahead, sitting in a clearing, the massive three-story manor waited for them to seize it.

Outside the manor, sandbags protected six enemy machine gun emplacements. A solitary sniper perched from the roof above, but aside from that, no other SS units were visible. Although the building looked big enough, Jenkins couldn't imagine an entire battalion squeezing into the structure.

Major Wellesley ordered units to scout the area to the flanks and the rear of the building, but they too noted no other signs of enemy activity. The major called some of the officers and senior NCOs to form a plan when Jenkins spotted movement.

The front door of the manor swung open and an SS officer stepped out. With a white handkerchief in his hand, he held it above his head and moved towards the forest filled with MEF soldiers. He paced several metres away from the building and stopped to look about. Jenkins and his platoon focused their guns on him.

"I am Oberst-Gruppenführer Fuchs," he called out. "Who is in command here?"

Images of children strapped with bombs rushed through Jenkins's mind. He saw them running towards his lines and detonating themselves. He heard the screams of the wounded, the splatters of blood, and saw their broken, tiny limbs around him. A moment later, the white flags of truce slipped from the panzers roaring towards the MEF lines, replaced by menacing swastika flags. He blinked again, and the faces of Jewish civilians stared back at him as they hung from lampposts. He witnessed their bloated and battered faces. Blood dripped from the swastikas cut into their flesh. Their vacant eyes demanded vengeance.

"Drop your weapon, you stupid kraut bastard!" Jenkins barely recognised his own voice as the words escaped his lips.

Without any thought, he jumped from his position and dashed forward, aiming his Lee-Enfield square at the SS officer. The oberst-gruppenführer waved his handkerchief again, as if seeking some divine protection from the bullets eager to burst from Jenkins's weapon.

"Are you in command?" Oberst-Gruppenführer Fuchs said in a shaky tone as he studied Jenkins for any sign of rank markings.

"Jenkins, stand down!" Sergeant McCabe shouted.

The sights of murdered Jewish men, women, and children—tortured and tormented before being hung—stayed at the forefront of his thoughts. Jenkins closed the distance until he stood directly in front of the oberst-gruppenführer. The SS officer looked from Jenkins back towards the forest, unsure of what was happening under a flag of truce.

"I said drop your weapon, you lying kraut tosspot," Jenkins roared again, jabbing his bayonet in the direction of the SS officer's sidearm.

"Jenkins," Sergeant McCabe called out again. "Get your arse back here before I have you up in front of a firing squad."

The anger that bubbled under Jenkins's surface spilled over. The constant death, the loss of so many friends and colleagues, the sheer level of pain inflicted on helpless civilians; it all overwhelmed him. Even the fear of the repercussions was nothing compared to the suffering Jenkins had witnessed over the last two days.

The oberst-gruppenführer stood frozen, his face blanketed in terror as he glanced down the barrel of the Lee-Enfield. Seeing that he was too terrified to move, Jenkins stretched out a hand and spun the SS officer about. He snatched the officer's pistol from its holster and tossed it to the ground. Keeping the bayonet pressed into his back, Jenkins nudged at him.

"Order your men to surrender now, or I swear to God, I'll kill every last one of them." Rage dripped from Jenkins's words, but he meant every syllable.

The oberst-gruppenführer turned his head to speak, but Jenkins pressed the tip of his bayonet into his back in warning. "I...I'm ordered to open discussions with a senior officer—"

"I've seen what you scum do under a white flag," Jenkins hissed. "Order your men to stand down now. Last warning."

In his peripheral vision, Jenkins noted movement from the MEF lines. Sergeant McCabe kept roaring at him, demanding he stand down with immediate effect. He glanced from side to side and then up at the roof. On both flanks, the SS defenders lowered their gazes to the sights on their weapons. Laying on the roof, the lone sniper turned his weapon towards the small group of MEF soldiers flocking behind Sergeant McCabe for support.

"Stand down," Oberst-Gruppenführer Fuchs shouted.

His words disappeared beneath the sounds of the SS machine guns exploding to life. Bullets blazed into the forest and were answered in kind. Jenkins lifted his Lee-Enfield to the back of the oberst-gruppenführer's skull and fired. A thick mist of red blasted from a crater in his face as the SS officer's lifeless carcass crashed to the ground.

Bullets snapped around him, but time ground to a snail's pace. Jenkins raised his rifle and aimed at the sniper on the roof. For a moment, the soldiers made eye contact. Jenkins acted first. The bullet from his rifle burst free and struck the sniper square in the forehead. The SS soldier hurtled off the roof to the ground.

Surging ahead, Jenkins made straight for the opened front door of the manor. He levelled his Lee-Enfield at the nearest machine gun nest on the right and squeezed the trigger. The SS soldiers flailed as bullets tore through their chests, sending them flopping to the ground. He grabbed a grenade, pulled the pin out with his teeth, and flung it at the machine gun position to his left. By the time he reached the door frame of the manor, the machine gun nest exploded, throwing wounded soldiers onto the ground around it.

Pausing at the doorway, Jenkins slipped in a fresh clip. MEF units had overwhelmed the remaining machine gun nests, striking them from the flanks and showering them with grenades until they fell silent. He spied a furious Sergeant McCabe storming towards him, but Jenkins didn't care about the repercussions. The enemy had broken the white flag of truce already. They deserved no mercy.

Alone, Jenkins pushed into the main hallway of the manor. A winding, elaborate staircase led to the second and third floors. To his left and right were high-ceilinged walls adorned with huge oil-paintings of heroic images.

A soldier in SS garb burst from the room to the right. A look of surprise filled his face. He was unarmed, but Jenkins contained no sympathy in his heart for people who utilised children as weapons of war and strung up the innocent.

He fired once, catching the soldier in the chest, and drove forward. He buried the tip of his bayonet into the Nazi's stomach and twisted. Leaving the SS soldier to bleed to death, Jenkins ran into the room on the right, knocking over a table with an ornamental vase as he did. Two men dressed like butlers emerged from a hallway on the other side of the room and froze at the sight of him. Seeing nothing more than SS soldiers in disguise, Jenkins fired twice, dropping them to the floor.

"Jenkins!" someone shouted.

Sergeant McCabe reached to grab Jenkins's Lee-Enfield, but he pulled it away.

"Jesus Christ, lad, what are you doing? What's gotten into you?"

The rage, the hatred, the vicious ugliness of it all exploded from Jenkins like a volcano.

"Kill them all!" he screamed as loud as he could. "Kill them all! Kill them all! Kill them all! All of them, Sergeant. Every last one. They all need to die!"

Raising his hands as if in surrender, the sergeant took a careful step towards him. Frustration and anger continued to pump through Jenkins's veins, but his outburst eased the corrosive hatred that sloshed about in his gut.

Sergeant McCabe rested a hand on Jenkin's shoulder. He side-stepped him and extended it to his far shoulder. It wasn't an embrace or any form of affection, but a protective movement to show him that he didn't stand alone. "Easy, lad, easy," he said, in an unusually soft voice. "It's been a long couple of days. Just breathe."

The sound of gunfire erupted from one of the upper levels. Major Wellesley burst through the opened front door and glared at them. His eyes burned with fury, although Jenkins sensed none of it directed at him, which surprised him.

"Is your man okay, Sergeant?" the major asked, and then his eyes sparkled with recognition. "Ah, young Jenkins. Fancy that drink?"

"Not while I'm on duty, sir."

"Good, good. Sergeant?"

"He's fine, sir. Just got a bit rambunctious. Didn't hear me over the shooting."

Major Wellesley turned his gaze to the SS soldier at his feet and the two fallen civilians on the far side of the room. Gesturing with his pistol, he signalled for them and some nearby soldiers to move up the stairs while Junior Sergeant Alexeev cleared the bottom floor.

Leading the way, the major raced up the winding stairwell, and the soldiers scanned for any signs of SS defenders. A series of shots rang out from the corridor to their right, halting Major Wellesley's advance. He peeked his head around the corner but sprang back.

A bullet smashed into the wall near him.

"One that I can see," the major said to Sergeant McCabe.

"I have this," Jenkins said and, without waiting for orders, threw himself into the open corridor.

Bullets belched out at him, but they all missed as he hit the carpeted ground and rolled. In a firing position, he spotted a single silhouette standing against the bright light of a window. The figure aimed his weapon again, but Jenkins pulled on the trigger until his clip emptied. At least three of the bullets hit their mark, sending the SS soldier stumbling towards the window. Glass shattered, and he tumbled backwards onto the grounds below.

Jenkins picked himself up and reloaded. He jogged towards the SS soldier's former position while his colleagues cleared the rooms to their left and right. More artwork adorned the walls, showing ancient knights and large-chested SS soldiers looking heroic and virtuous. Jenkins spit on the ground in contempt and reached the large double doors where the soldier had stood. He peered through the broken window to see the lifeless body of the SS soldier smashed on the ground below.

Swinging his gaze to the double doors in front of him, Jenkins kept his finger on his Lee-Enfield's trigger. He extended his left hand. Without touching the wooden handles, the doors snapped open, causing him to jump back in surprise. A tall SS officer with a scarred face stood in the centre of the doorway and fired a scowl at Jenkins.

Jenkins fired once, catching the SS officer in the face and knocking him straight to the ground. When Jenkins lifted his eyes to view the room, his blood froze.

Two rows of SS officers flanked a large wooden table. At the head of the table, a chair with its back turned rested in front of a blazing fire. Dominating the room, a massive portrait of Adolf Hitler glared down at him. None of the SS officers flinched at the sight of Jenkins and their fallen comrade. With hands folded in front of them in a uniform manner, they continued gazing at him as he stood there taking in the strange sight.

The chair at the head of the table wobbled slightly as it turned, causing Jenkins to aim his weapon at it. The chair rotated slowly until its occupant faced the doorway. Jenkins's jaw dropped when he saw the withered face and drooping eyelids. His gaze flashed to the portrait above and back down to the occupant of the seat. He looked aged, saggy, and sickly, but the same dominating gaze blazed from both portrait and person alike—Adolf Hitler, leader of the defeated Third Reich and war criminal.

"That'll be enough," an American accent said from behind the door.

To Jenkins's surprise, a man in a black suit and slicked-back hair stepped directly in front of him, blocking his view of the Nazi Führer.

Major Wellesley, Sergeant McCabe, and a dozen MEF soldiers reached Jenkins's location and looked past the civilian. They drank in the shocking scene.

"Who's in charge here?" the American snapped.

Major Wellesley stepped forward. His face dropped, as if he recognised the stranger. "Mr. Myers. What a surprise," Major Wellesley hissed.

The American slid a hand into his pocket. He pulled out a set of papers and handed them to the major.

"On the authority of Majestic-12, I order you and your men to stand down. Contact Major General Hamilton and order him to report here immediately. The National Socialist government and the SS have agreed to an unconditional surrender."

Major Wellesley's face glowed red from the tone of the civilian's voice, but he followed his words to the letter. He ordered everyone to stand down but instructed them to remain directly outside the room. Jenkins, Sergeant McCabe, and dozens of MEF soldiers stood there, gaping at the assorted collection of Nazis and their mysterious MJ-12 guest.

After fifteen minutes, Major General Hamilton arrived with his cadre of senior officers. He strolled through the corridor towards the conference room in a pristine, immaculate uniform. Likewise, his senior officers didn't seem to have a spec of dirt between them. Jenkins and the MEF soldiers outside stood to attention as Major Wellesley delivered a salute. The major general snapped his hand to his head and returned the gesture before marching into the room. He hesitated in the doorway of the room while inspecting the assembled crowd of SS officers. He stepped in and circled the right side of the room, coming to a halt a few paces to Hitler's left.

Hitler reached for a hand-carved wooden box resting on his lap and placed it on the table. He opened the lid. A golden light emanated from the box, shining far brighter than the fire that burned behind him.

Major General Hamilton ground to a halt at the sight.

His eyes opened wide in shock as he peered down at the contents. Without a word, an unseen guard closed the double doors on Jenkins and Sergeant McCabe, giving the MEF and Nazi leadership privacy.

Rather than have them stand around outside, Sergeant McCabe assigned everyone duties. Jenkins found himself posted at the top of the stairs, pacing back and forth in a monotonous loop to keep his tired limbs from seizing up. His thoughts moved to the strange light in the box, but his weary mind was unable to process what it could have been. After fifteen minutes of guarding the steps, the double doors to the conference room swung open again. Jenkins took aim with his rifle, half-expecting the SS officers to storm out of the room shooting.

He lowered his weapon after Sergeant McCabe signalled at him to stand down and watched in bewildered silence as Major General Hamilton strolled out with a huge smile on his face. He paused briefly to speak with Major Wellesley before he and his staff officers made to exit the manor. Jenkins stood to attention as they passed by him, noting that one of the officers carried the mysterious wooden box in his hand.

"All right, lads," Sergeant McCabe called out to anyone in earshot. "Spread the word. The surrender has been signed, but we need to evacuate this building now. Everybody out!"

Dumbfounded by the sergeant's words, Jenkins watched the SS officers stroll out of the room. Each looked more content than the last. Like a procession, they tore off their swastika armbands and Nazi party pins and dumped them at Major Wellesley's feet. A few of the junior officers drew their pistols and dropped them carelessly to the ground. Then the SS officers formed themselves into two lines and stood at attention.

"C'mon, Jenkins lad," Sergeant McCabe said, falling in beside him. "Outside. Looks like this is done and dusted."

"But Sarge," Jenkins said, trying to mask the explosive fury building within him again. "We're letting those SS sacks of shit go?"

The decrepit figure of the "defeated" Führer joined the

assembled SS officers. Flanked on both sides, he started walking. His withered hands twitched with every step.

"That's above our pay grade," Sergeant McCabe said as he eyed the procession. "Now, outside with everyone else."

Without making eye contact, the small group of Nazi murderers marched towards the stairs. They were wheeling about to descend the staircase to the lower level when a short, sharp command halted them where they stood, directly in front of Jenkins and the sergeant. Out of instinct, Jenkins went to raise his Lee-Enfield, but Sergeant McCabe's iron grip fell onto the barrel of his weapon, freezing it in place.

Hitler lifted his withered face and eyed the British soldiers. The flesh under his eyes hung loose, giving his sinister features a more reptilian quality. He ran his gaze over the men before opening his mouth and mumbling something in German. After a few moments, he spoke again. Then he and the SS officers continued on their way.

"What was that about?" Jenkins asked as his gaze tracked them down the stairs.

Sergeant McCabe shook his head. "Forget it."

"C'mon, Sarge. What did he say?"

Sergeant McCabe took a step onto the stairs but came to a halt. He looked back at Jenkins and sighed. "He said something I've heard too many times since reaching this God-awful place."

Jenkins's curiosity piqued. "Which is?"

"We have always been here."

NORTH OF THE CITY CENTRE
21.32 MST
DAY 2

Oberst Brandt aimed his pistol and fired again, emptying the clip at the approaching Allied soldiers. The street ahead of him lay ablaze. Dozens of his panzers were engulfed in flames. Mortars pounded the buildings around him, sending avalanches of concrete spilling onto the street, washing his men away forever. Overhead, a single enemy aerial craft twisted about, avoiding the anti-aircraft fire from his surviving panzers and preparing to launch another barrage of missiles.

Dodging a flurry of enemy bullets, Brandt leapt towards Captain Fischer's panzer. He clicked another clip into his Luger, took careful aim and fired. Two of the oncoming British soldiers hit the ground while the other three dove for cover. To his right and left, another volley of enemy shells obliterated groups of his infantry. Particles of concrete sprayed high into the air, showering everything and everyone in reach.

"We need to fall back," Captain Fischer called out after he swung open his panzer's hatch. "We've lost too many panzers. We need to regroup."

"We've fallen back far enough," Brandt snarled and pointed his weapon at the enemy again. "We draw the line here. Here, and no farther."

As if bolstering his words, the panzers opened fire in unison. Shells smashed into the ranks of oncoming invaders and blasted large craters into the ravaged street. The Allied line waivered as many sought shelter. Less than a heartbeat later and the enemy advanced again.

The Allied aircraft rolled about in the sky above them. Like a bird of prey swooping, it dove straight at the German columns. With machine guns blazing, it ripped Brandt's soldiers to shreds, tearing men apart where they stood or cowered. Cries died as another thunderstorm of shells blasted the empty husks of what had once been homes.

"Oberst!" Captain Fischer yelled over the ever-increasing din of battle. "Oberst!"

Brandt ignored his subordinate's calls as he raised his reloaded Luger. He tracked a British soldier trying to help an injured colleague and squeezed the trigger. The first two shots went wide, but the third struck him in the side. The soldier hit the ground, and his face contorted in agony. A cascade of return fire forced Brandt to hunker on top of the panzer.

"Oberst!" Captain Fischer called out again.

"What, damn you?" Brandt shouted back in answer.

Braving the storm of lead and shrapnel, Captain Fischer slid out of the hatch and rolled to Brandt's side. He aimed his own pistol and fired. With his free hand, he drew out the earpiece connected to his panzer's communications system and shoved it into Brandt's ear.

The Allied push faltered as German firepower broke their most recent assault.

Brandt kept shooting his weapon as he listened to the words in his ear. It took a few moments for him to register the meaning of those words and the voice of the speaker. The noise of the raging battle faded into nothingness. Only the mesmerising words of the Führer existed for him, drawing his full attention and sucking him in. But as he listened, patriotic duty and fierce national pride didn't sweep through him. He sensed the undercurrent of rage and defiance, but the Führer's words spoke of something unthinkable.

Surrender.

"No," Brandt screamed and bashed his hand off the scratched panzer armour in frustration. "No, no, no, no, no!"

The Allied aerial craft circled about the dimming New Berlin sky. It dodged between anti-aircraft flak explosions. Missiles crashed into the panzer up ahead, killing the entire crew and reducing the machine of war into a pile of burning scrap metal. Brandt saw it all, but he found himself unable to react. Even as bullets pinged around him, the idea of another defeat tore through him.

"Herr Oberst," Captain Fischer pleaded. "We must withdraw now. There are other units within the colony and outside it that we can link up with. We can serve the Führer and our people, but we must go now."

"No," Brandt spat and lifted his pistol.

He tapped on the trigger, shooting at any enemy soldier in sight. Even after the clip emptied, he kept squeezing the trigger, willing his hatred to morph into an endless stream of rounds to cut down the invaders. With fire and flame ravaging the structures around him, Brandt jumped to his feet. He snapped in a fresh clip and continued blasting his pistol, daring any and all to give him a glorious hero's death in the name of the fatherland.

A devastating wallop gutted an apartment block to his

left. The violence of the blast caused him to stumble, and a piece of shrapnel belted him across the skull. He collapsed onto the roof of the panzer as if a thousand tonnes of concrete had struck him. Pain cut though his skull and jaw and carved deep into his flesh. With blurry vision, he tried to look up, but the world refused to remain steady. Hands grabbed at his limbs and dragged him towards the panzer hatch while the sounds of fighting faded from his ears.

"Retreat!" Captain Fischer's voice called out from somewhere far away. "Fall back to the northern entrance. Retreat!"

Brandt's head hung heavy, as if filled with lead, causing his vision to blur in and out. He tried to compel his lips to move as he found himself dragged into the heart of the panzer.

"No," he tried to shout. "Stay and fight." But his words disappeared into nothingness amidst the growl of the panzer's engines. He tried to summon the last of his reserves to speak, but the energy leaked from him and spilled onto the floor of the panzer.

"All units," Captain Fischer roared again. "Fall back to the northern entrance. Repeat, fall back to the northern entrance."

Brandt shook his head as his chance for vengeance slipped from his grasp.

"Do not worry, Herr Oberst," Captain Fischer shouted. "They may have won the battle, but they will not win the war. We will have our revenge for Führer and for fatherland, this I swear."

Darkness closed around Brandt, and a single word floated to the forefront of his mind—revenge. If he survived this night, he vowed to never rest until he had humiliated and vanquished his opponents.

Whether it took a day, a month, a year, or a lifetime, Brandt would have his revenge.

GOVERNMENT DISTRICT
04.23 MST
DAY 3

243

McCabe groaned as he slipped his backpack off and allowed it to drop to the floor. In the hours that followed the news of the German surrender, chaos reigned across New Berlin. Although virtually every SS member who didn't blow his brains out surrendered with immediate effect, a few Wehrmacht units continued to hold out.

To add to the chaos, the Army of David resumed their attacks on the Nazis, determined to reap vengeance upon their oppressors. Mobs ransacked and looted homes and businesses owned by the Germans, causing the citizenry to pick up the weapons of their fallen soldiers and fight back. Fires spread throughout the housing districts, leaving thousands homeless. Through all this, the MEF fought to establish some semblance of order.

Officially, the ceasefire came into effect as of one o'clock in the morning, which led to a lull in the madness, but MEF units still found themselves ferried to all parts of the colony to disperse mobs and demobilise surrendering German soldiers. Exhausted from the two days of fighting, McCabe nearly collapsed where he stood when Major Wellesley dismissed him and his platoon and ordered them to snatch a few hours of sleep. He handed over the HK-17 Dub had given him and wasted no time in finding shelter for his men.

McCabe and his platoon trudged through the wasteland that was the government district of New Berlin and seized an abandoned police station. They piled inside, eager to find a corner of floor to curl up on. Despite his tiredness, McCabe ordered his platoon to strip and clean their weapons, which they did in record time. Once finished, several collapsed where they sat, not even bothering to remove their equipment. McCabe on the other hand found a carpeted office in the back of the police station. After delegating a picket to stand guard, he stumbled into the back office and stripped off his equipment.

Corporal Brown, who had checked himself out of the field hospital, shared one side of the office. His long-time colleague had braved the ongoing street fighting with a wounded leg to search for his section and found Jenkins the only one left alive.

On the other side of the room, Junior Sergeant Alexeev lay sprawled out, his AK-47 resting in his arms. He snored quietly. The Red Army NCO remained a man of few words, but McCabe admired his abilities. He appeared fearless under fire and inspired respect and fear from the men under his command.

McCabe slipped off his helmet and belt and sank to the floor. He rested his head against his bag as a pillow and sighed. His shoulder and arm screamed in pain when he fidgeted to get comfy, but his tired limbs thanked him when he discovered the perfect spot. Darkness was creeping over his vision, as his mind drifted towards slumber, when the static from a radio jolted him awake. Sitting bolt upright, he saw Corporal Brown lying on the floor with a portable radio to his ear, adjusting the volume of a broadcast.

"Sounds like the other colonies have surrendered, too," he said, oblivious to the frustrated stare burning from McCabe's eyes. "The outposts and research stations as well. We have the planet. It's over!"

"Great," McCabe grunted. He lowered his head back onto his backpack, rolled onto his side, and closed his eyes. Again, he started drifting off when the screech of static cut through him. With his temper flaring, he bit the inside of his lip to stop from screaming. Clearing his throat, he sat back up and tried to burn a hole through Corporal Brown's face using the power of his mind. "Jim, turn that damn radio off or I'll ram it so far up your arse, it'll come out of your throat."

"Jesus," Corporal Brown exclaimed, pressing the radio closer to his ear. "You hearing this?"

"Hearing what?" McCabe snapped.

A few seconds passed as the corporal listened to the transmission. He tilted his head from side to side, as if adjusting it by a few degrees would allow him to hear it better. With a shake of his head, he switched the radio off and leaned himself back against the wall. "They're advising all units to be on the lookout for werewolves."

"Werewolves?"

"Yep, werewolves."

"Christ," McCabe said as he rubbed the bridge of his nose, "not this again, Jim. We heard this shit in the last war. The so-called Nazi *werewolf* plan to lead an insurgency against the Allies was bullshit then, and it's bullshit now. Sure, there's bound to be some form of resistance, but it's just Nazi propaganda. It'll fade once the hype blows over."

Corporal Brown shrugged his shoulders. "I'm not so sure. Things are different here. It's not like we can fly in reinforcements from Britain or the US. We're totally cut off, surrounded by a hostile population with nowhere to retreat to but two heavily damaged floating wrecks in orbit. We're a good year away from rescue at best. I'd say an insurgency would stand a good chance."

"Jim."

"Yeah, Sarge."

"Go to sleep."

"Okay, Sarge."

McCabe stared at Corporal Brown until he rolled over and fell quiet. With a heavy sigh, McCabe returned his head to his backpack and glanced up at the cracked ceiling above. Although the MEF had declared victory over the Nazis, it left a bitter taste in his mouth. Good men had given their lives to rid the universe of the last fragments of the Third Reich. MJ-12's intervention and the way the Nazis surrendered towards the end made him wonder what was really going on.

His mind ran over events surrounding the Black Visors. Everything about their presence seemed bizarre. He replayed Dub's words again, trying to piece the titbits of information together, but his mind screamed for sleep. He closed his eyes once more and felt himself drift off.

"Excuse me, Sergeant, messenger here for you."

McCabe snapped upright and focused his worn eyes on the figure at the door. He blinked until he recognised Private Jones, one of the soldiers he had assigned to guard duty.

"How long have I been out?" he asked, squinting to check the time on his watch.

"About five minutes, Sarge. Messenger here from Major Wellesley."

"Send him in."

Jones stood aside and allowed another private to enter the office. The private stood to attention and held out the message in his hand. McCabe snatched the paper off him and dismissed him with a growl as he checked the contents of the message. It took him three attempts to fully process the words before he crumpled up the paper and tossed it away.

"Jim, Boris. Wake up."

The NCOs rolled over and gazed at him with tired eyes.

"Come on, time to get up, lads. There's been an incident. A Wehrmacht barracks has been raided and some weapons stolen. Looks like we've been assigned to werewolf hunting duty."

"Told you," Corporal Brown groaned. He sat up and started dragging on his gear.

McCabe reached for his backpack, belt, and Lee-Enfield. With a shake of his head, he eyed his colleague and let out another exhausted sigh. "You know what, Jim? I think we're in for a very long year."

"Kill them all," Junior Sergeant Alexeev grunted and swung his AK-47 into his hands.

With a silent nod to one another, the three NCOs rallied their men to go hunt werewolves on Mars.

The End

About the Author

Damien Larkin is an Irish science fiction author and co-founder of the British and Irish Writing Community. His debut novel Big Red was published by Dancing Lemur Press and went on to be longlisted for the BSFA award for Best Novel. He currently lives in Dublin, Ireland.

Website:
www.damienlarkinbooks.com
Facebook:
www.facebook.com/DamienLarkinAuthor
Twitter:
www.twitter.com/Damo_Dangerman

Other great science fiction titles!

Big Red
By Damien Larkin

"There is drama and heartache here, insights in the light and darkness of humanity's soul. This book makes you think." – Phil Parker, author

We have always been here...

Print ISBN 9781939844606
eBook ISBN 9781939844613

CassaStar
By Alex J. Cavanaugh

"...calls to mind the youthful focus of Robert Heinlein's early military sf..."
- Library Journey

To pilot the fleet's finest ship...

Print ISBN 9780981621067
eBook ISBN 9780982713938

Lost Helix
By Scott Coon

Lost Helix is the key...

Print ISBN 9781939844682
eBook ISBN 9781939844699

CPSIA information can be obtained
at www.ICGtesting.com
Printed in the USA
LVHW032312150821
695378LV00001B/137

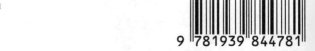